Plain Kate

ERIN BOW

SCHOLASTIC INC.

To the memory of my sister Wendy —
artist, friend, and fierce good soul

ISBN 978-0-545-16665-2

Arthur A. Levine Books hardcover edition designed by Lillie Howard, published by Arthur A. Levine Books, an imprint of Scholastic Inc., September 2010.

12 11 10 9 8 7 6 5 4 3 2 1   12 13 14 15 16 17/0

Printed in the U.S.A. 40

First paperback printing, August 2012

ONTARIO ARTS COUNCIL
CONSEIL DES ARTS DE L'ONTARIO

The author gratefully acknowledges the support of the Ontario Arts Council.

contents

one

THE *SKARA ROK*

A long time ago, in a market town by a looping river, there lived an orphan girl called Plain Kate.

She was called this because her father had introduced her to the new butcher, saying: "This is my beloved Katerina Svetlana, after her mother who died birthing her and God rest her soul, but I call her just plain Kate." And the butcher, swinging a cleaver, answered: "That's right enough, Plain Kate she is, plain as a stick." A man who treasured humor, especially his own, the butcher repeated this to everyone. After that, she was called Plain Kate. But her father called her Kate, My Star.

Plain Kate's father, Piotr, was a wood-carver. He gave Kate a carving knife before most children might be given a spoon. She could whittle before she could walk. When she was still a child, she could carve a rose that strangers would stop to smell, a dragonfly that trout would rise to strike.

In Kate's little town of Samilae, people thought that there was magic in a knife. A person who could wield a knife well was, in their eyes, halfway to a witch. So Plain Kate was very small the first time someone spat at her and crooked their fingers.

Her father sat her down and spoke to her with great seriousness. "You are not a witch, Katerina. There is magic in the world, and some of it is wholesome, and some of it is not, but it is a thing that is in the blood, and it is not in yours.

"The foolish will always treat you badly, because they think you are not beautiful," he said, and she knew this was true. Plain Kate: She *was* plain as a stick, and thin as a stick, and flat as a stick. She had one eye the color of river mud and one eye the color of the river. Her nose was too long and her brows were too strong. Her father kissed her twice, once above each eyebrow. "We cannot help what fools think. But understand, it is your skill with a blade that draws this talk. If you want to give up your carving, you have my blessing."

"I will never give it up," she answered.

And he laughed and called her his Brave Star, and taught her to carve even better.

They were busy. Everyone in that country, no matter how poor, wore a talisman called an objarka. Those who could, hung larger objarka on horse stalls and doorposts and above their marriage beds. No lintel was uncarved in that place; walls bore saints in niches; and roads were marked with little shrines on posts, which housed sometimes saints, and sometimes older, stranger things. Plain Kate's father was even given the honor of replacing Samilae's weizi, the great column at the center of the market that showed the town's angels and coats of arms, and at the top, supported the carved wooden roof that sheltered the carved wooden gods. The new weizi was such a good work that the guild masters sent a man from Lov to see it. The man made Kate's father a full master on the spot.

"My daughter did some of the angels," he told the man, gathering Kate up and pulling her forward.

The man looked at the faces that were so beautiful they seemed sad, the wings that looked both soft and strong, like the wings of swans that could kill a man with one blow. "Apprentice her," he said.

"If she likes," Piotr answered. "And when she is of age."

When the guild man went away, Plain Kate chided her father. "You know I will be your apprentice!"

"You are the star of my heart," he said. "But it is two years yet before you are of prenticing age. Anything might happen."

She laughed at him. "What will happen is that I will be a full master by the time I am twenty."

But what happened was that her father died.

It happened like this: The spring swung round into summer, full of heat and flies. The wheat crop withered. The first frosts came and found food already short. And then a sickness called witch's fever ate through the town.

At first Plain Kate and her father were too busy to worry. People wanted new objarka — some wore so many of the carved charms that they clacked softly when they moved. They carved all day, and into the night by the bad light of tallow lamps. They carved faster than they could cure the wood. And then they grew even busier, because there were grave markers to make.

Witch's fever was an ugly thing. The sick tossed in their beds, burning up, sobbing about the devils that were pulling their joints apart. They raved of horrors and pointed into shadows, crying, "Witch, witch." And then they died, all but a few. It seemed to Plain Kate that even those who were not sick were looking into shadows. The cressets in the market square — the iron nests of fire where people gathered to trade news and roast fish — became a place of hisses and silences. More fingers crooked at her than ever before.

But in the end it was not her the town pointed to. One day, when Plain Kate and her father were in the market square selling new objarka from their sturdy stall, a woman was dragged in screaming. Kate looked up from her whittling, and saw — suddenly — that there was wood for a bonfire piled around the weizi.

The screaming woman was named Vera, and Plain Kate knew her: a charcoal burner, a poor woman with no family, with a lisp from a twisted lip. The crowd dragged Vera to the woodpile, and Piotr picked Plain Kate up and swept her away, though she was too big for it. From their shop they could still hear the screaming. The next day the square was muted and scattered with ash.

And still the sickness ate through the crooked lanes and wooden archways. Plain Kate and her father stopped selling in the square. Their money grew short. The plague burned on and the town shut its gates. Carters stopped bringing food from the countryside; the barges stopped coming down the looping Narwe. Kate had her first taste of hunger.

But slowly the dewy frost gave way to brilliant, hard mornings, and the fever, as fevers do, began to loosen its grip for the winter. Plain Kate went down to the market to see what food could be had, and found little knots of people around stalls heaped with the last of the fresh harvest: winter-fat leeks and frost-tattered cabbages. The frowning shops that fronted the square seemed to sigh and spread their shoulders.

Plain Kate came home with her basket piled with apples, and found her father slumped at his workbench. He'd left the lathe whirling: a long hiss, winding down in the clotting silence of the shop. She could hear the shudder in his breath.

Somehow she got him up on her shoulder. It made her feel tiny, smaller than she had in years; he was so heavy and she could hardly hold him up. She took him to his bed.

Not everyone who got witch's fever died. She kept telling herself that. She tried to give him water, she tried to make him eat. She was not sure if he should be kept warm or cold. She tucked his red quilt over him and put a cold cloth on his forehead. Like the others, he sobbed and he saw things. She talked to him day and night until she grew so hoarse that her mouth tasted of blood. "You are here, you are here, I am with you, stay where you belong." She stayed awake, day and night, saying it.

After two days and three nights, somewhere in the gray hour before dawn, she fell asleep. She woke still sitting on the chair by the bedside, her forehead resting on her father's hand.

"Katerina," he rasped.

"You're here," she stuttered, lifting her head. "I am here, Father, right here."

"Not you," he said, breaking her heart. "Your mother." There was a screen in the shape of climbing roses between their room and the front of the shop. Light was piercing through it, the long slanting yellow of dawn. Her father was staring into it, his eyes runny and blind. "Look."

Plain Kate turned for a moment to look, then turned back, afraid of what she might see if she let herself. "Father," she said. "Papa."

"Katerina," he said again. "She is in the light. She's here. Katerina, you're here!"

"Don't go," said Plain Kate, and clutched his hand to her cheek. "Papa!"

He looked at her. "Katerina, Star of My Heart." He breathed in. He breathed out. And he stopped breathing.

"I'm right here," she said. "Papa, I'm right here." She kept saying it for a long time.

The year of the hot summer, sickness, and starvation came to be called the *skara rok*, the bad time. It had emptied their purse. Plain Kate took what money they had left and bought Piotr Carver a decent burial. Then she went back to the shop and spent a month carving a grave marker for him. She would make one and cast it into the fire, make another and still not find peace.

"People think we are witches because we show them the truth." She could see her father's face, feel his hands on hers. A carving had just snapped apart when her knife found some hidden flaw in the wood. "You will learn to know where the knots are and how the grain flows, even deep inside the wood where no one can see it. You will show people that truth: the truth in the wood. But sometimes, in your carving, people will see another truth. A truth about you. About themselves." His hands were warm on hers, sturdy as his smile. "And that is magic," he said. "You will know it when you feel it."

She wanted the grave marker to show the truth: that Piotr Carver had been a wonderful carver, and she had loved him. But the only thing it said was that her father was dead.

At last she could not leave the grave unmarked anymore. So she finished the marker, and placed it.

And when that was done she had nothing more to do. She stood by his lathe like a girl under a spell. Her hands hung empty at her sides.

And then the wood guild sent another carver to take the shop.

His name was Chuny and he wasn't half the carver she was, but he had a warrant from the guild. Plain Kate had nowhere to go. She'd been born in that shop. She'd been a baby watching the light shift through the rose screen. She'd been a chubby-fisted toddler putting wood shavings in the pottage. But now the guild warrant gave Chuny claim over the shop and its fittings, its tools, even the wood Kate and her father had cured but not carved.

Master Chuny stood watching her pack. There was very little she was allowed to take. A bit of food: apples and oats, a jar of oil. Her own three dresses. Her father's smocks and leggings. His leather carpenter's apron. There were two bowls, with porridge dried like parched earth at the bottom of the one that had been her father's. Two spoons. The red marriage quilt from the big carved bed, which smelled like her father and like sickness. Her own small hand tools: knives and chisels and awls and gouges.

"The carving things stay with the shop," said Chuny, still watching.

Plain Kate was slotting the tools into the pockets of her own leather apron. "He gave them to me," she whispered. She did not look up; the hair around her face hid her strange eyes and the tears in them from the man watching her. She raised her voice: "These are mine. My father gave them to me."

"An apprentice's tools —" Chuny began. The rule was that an apprentice's tools belonged to his master, and through the master to the guild.

"I was not his apprentice." She looked up and she was not crying anymore. "I am going. Do you want to search my bags?"

"I —" Chuny began, then shook his head. His fingers were twined in the rose screen; it hurt her to see his hands there. Kate and her father had had an old joke where they would smell the carved roses, but even outside of the joke Piotr would never have closed his hands round a blossom, as Chuny was doing now.

She tore her eyes away. "I am going to the market," she said. "I am going to live in our stall."

"*Live* in it?" he echoed, shocked.

"The bottom drawer will be big enough."

The stall too belonged to the guild. Plain Kate raised her witch's eyes, daring Chuny to make that claim. He looked back, then looked at his shoes, and didn't. Kate picked up her bags.

"They, uh," he said, "tell me you can carve a little. I would — when you are of age, that is, if I still need an apprentice —"

She was insulted by the awkward half kindness. "You have nothing to teach me," she said. "And I don't have the fee."

"Go, then," he said, angry.

So she did, with her head held high.

In the market, she put down her bags and looked at the square with new eyes. The tall and narrow shops seemed leering to her, the streets crooked. Underfoot, cobble-backs rose like islands from the packed and dirty snow. Above it all the weizi towered, sending a long sunset shadow across the gray roofs of Samilae and toward the black wall of the hills beyond.

Her father's stall was sitting in that shadow: a big box cabinet with many drawers, large and deep on the bottom and little on top. The front was carved to show a deer hunt: a stag leaping into a patch of wood, hounds and riders at its heels. Plain Kate had always thought before that it looked as if the stag was going to get away. Tonight it looked different; one of the riders had nocked an arrow, his aim true. The poor beast was dead and just didn't know it.

The cold grew bitter as the sun fell; her breath swirled around her. She pulled open the big bottom drawer. She put the quilt in it, and pushed it as much closed as she could and still get in. Then she rolled in through the gap and lay down.

The wood was hard despite the quilt; the air was stale. She couldn't see, but the drawer walls pressed her shoulders, and the sense of the wood above pressed her from inches away. *A coffin*, she thought, and pushed the thought away. It came back. *This is my coffin.*

With no standing in the wood guild, she could carve but she couldn't sell, not without telling all who asked that there was a guild shop not a hundred steps away. An apprentice's fee was the price of a matched team of horses, a fortune she couldn't imagine earning. A dowry was beside the point for a skinny girl with witch's eyes. She was going to starve. It was just a matter of time.

But she wasn't hungry yet. She lay still and listened. The drawer grew brighter as her eyes grew used to darkness, then darker as the world darkened. Finally she couldn't see anything. As the night grew still each sound got sharper, and each sounded like it was coming for her. Boots. The bark of a dog. Like a knife through the darkness, the bell of a watchman, calling the hour.

The night grew quieter and quieter. Her eyes ached from seeing nothing. Her ears strained after little sounds. She heard the river singing to itself. She heard the wind snuffling at the gap where she'd entered the drawer. And finally, littler than any of those things, she heard something crying.

The small cry came from somewhere close. Plain Kate's first thought was that it was a ghost, that its next whisper would be "Katerina, Star of My Heart." But she was not the sort for ghosts, so she lay listening, afraid but brave. She moved her head from side to side to track the sound, and decided that the crying was coming from one of the drawers above.

So she climbed out of the drawer and looked.

In the smallest drawer of her father's stall, among the lace-fine carvings packed in straw, she found them: kittens. They were mouse-little, with their eyes still sealed closed and their ears tucked flat. There was no cat. It was almost dawn and frost furred everything. The market square was as still as the inside of a bell after the ringing has stopped. The straw nest was getting cold.

Plain Kate stood for a while and watched the kittens stagger about. Then she scooped them up and squeezed herself back into the drawer.

And that was the beginning of her new life.

There were three kittens: a white cat, a black cat, and a gangly gray tom. Their mother never came back. The next morning Plain Kate traded the cowherd girl the mending of a milk stool for a squirt of milk, and the promise of more each morning. She watered the milk and let the kittens suck on the twisted end of a rag. She kept them in the felt-lined pockets of her leather apron, under her coat during the day, and beside her at night in the warm, closed darkness of the drawer. Day by day, their dark eyes opened and their ears untucked and their voices grew louder.

She was patient with them, and took care of them every moment, and against all odds all three lived. The black cat grew wild and fearless and went to live on one of the pole barges that plied the shallow, twisting Narwe River. The white cat grew crafty and fat, and went to live on mice and milk with the cowherd girl. The gray tom grew long and narrow, and stayed with Plain Kate.

He was a dandy with one ear cocked, a gleam on his claw and a glint in his eye. He sauntered through the market square elegant and tattered, admired and cursed: a highwayman, a gentleman thief. His name was Taggle, for the three kittens had been Raggle, Taggle, and Bone.

Plain Kate grew too: skinnier and stronger, but not much taller. The years were thin. But against all odds, and with the cat by her side, she too lived.

The guild man kept the shop, but Kate was the better carver. He took most of the work, because no one could afford to defy the guilds for small matters. Kate made most of the objarka, the carved charms that drew luck. Luck in that place was a matter of life and death, and that made the guilds worth defying.

Plain Kate's own objarka was a cat curled up asleep. She had made it herself, from a burl of walnut that her father had given her. Burl wood, with its tight whorls, was the hardest sort of wood to carve, but she had carved it. Slowly and patiently she followed its flowing lines, looking for the wood's truth. When she was finished, the curling wood grain suggested lanky strength at rest.

"Kate, My Star," her father had said, "this could be a masterpiece." He meant the piece an apprentice makes when the apprenticeship is finished, to gain admission to the guild. The little objarka was not big enough for a master-piece, but, her father said, it was good enough. "Look at it," he said. "It is telling you about yourself."

But he would not tell her what it said.

Plain Kate gave the cat objarka to her father, and he wore it always, around his neck on a leather thong. It was almost black now, shiny with the oil of his skin. She wore it inside her own shirt, over her heart. But if it was telling her some-thing, she could not hear it.

After a while she stopped listening and simply tried to live. She made a hinged front for her drawer, so that she could lock herself in. She put ragged hems in her father's striped smocks when her dresses wore out. She carved when there was light. When there was no light she fished, and caught trout with her wooden dragonflies. Taggle brought her mice and rats, birds and bats. She learned to suck the meat from the smallest bone. She got by.

The kinder folk of the market square gave her what they could not sell: bruised apples, carrots with strange legs. The crueler gave her curses; they spat and whispered. She was lonely, though she didn't know it. Folk said she had a long shadow.

But every night Taggle came to wrap himself around her as she slept in the lowest drawer.

And so it went for cold days and hot, wet days and dusty, and long, hungry winters.

Then one summer day, change and magic came loping and waltzing into her life, wearing white, and in that moment nothing seemed dark.

two

THE STRANGER

The stranger was white. His hair was white-gray like bleached wood, his eyes white-silver like tin, his skin was white as if he were a day dead.

Albino was the scholar's word for it — but witch-white was what they said in Plain Kate's country. It was unlucky, and perhaps, Plain Kate thought, it was what kept him wandering. She felt a surge of sympathy for the man: It was far too easy to lose your place in a town or farmhold, to be forced onto the roads. A chance turn of skin color was more than enough.

But the man was no starveling beggar, she could see that. He was thin but strong, and he moved through the market like a lord. Across the square from Plain Kate's stall, he flipped open a blanket and spread out an array of tin trinkets. He sat down on the blanket edge with a tambourine on his knee.

Kate was working just then on an objarka for Niki the Baker — a mask in the form of the Wheat Maiden, to hang on the stall door of the new horse he was planning to buy. It was a good-sized piece, and it would earn her a few weeks without hunger. As she carved, she listened. The stranger played the tambourine as she'd never heard it played: not just bangs and jiggles, but music, lively as a quick stream, bright as birdsong, the sort of music that made you tap a toe. The music drew people to his blanket. He tipped his chin up and smiled at one and all, chattering like a baby bird — but he listened like an empty well.

The stranger puzzled Plain Kate. The trinkets he was selling wouldn't keep him fed. There must be more than that. As evening gathered, Niki the Baker came by to check on his carving. Niki was a big man, soft as bread dough and as kind, and one of the few people in the town of whom Kate might ask an unguarded question. She jerked her chin toward the stranger. "Who's that one? What's he selling?"

"That one?" Niki snorted. "Useless frippery. Useless." The baker hated things that were useless, from lapdogs to wedding cakes. "You watch him, Plain Kate. That one might steal everything that's not nailed down, and some things that are nailed only loosely." Without comment he set down a pair of rolls that were too stale to sell, and without comment Plain Kate took them and bit into one. It was a regular thing between them.

The roll was hard as an uncooked turnip. "Easy on that," Niki said, watching her eat. "It might be the last for a bit — flour's low."

She nodded and wrapped the other roll up to tuck away. Niki looked at the bundle with his sad-dog eyes. "It's bad, bad," he sighed. "The wheat barges are overdue at least a week. No grain and no news. Something's amiss upriver." He crooked his two middle fingers into the sign against witchcraft.

A hungry time. Plain Kate felt cold in the warm evening. The *skara rok* had begun this way.

Plain Kate listened to Niki and watched the stranger. He wasn't selling much: a few toys and tin charms Kate could have made better in wood. Three days of music put three lonely kopeks into his begging bowl. What he seemed to be selling mostly was talk. When Plain Kate came back from fishing, his blanket was still spread, white in the thickening twilight, alone in the evening-empty market.

Plain Kate was thinking of witches. How in bad times people were more eager to buy her objarka, but also more inclined to take a step back, to crook their fingers at her when they thought she wasn't looking, or when they were sure she was. How they wanted the witchcraft to protect them, but how they looked too for a witch to blame. It didn't matter that there was no magic in her blade; people saw it there. They saw witchcraft in her skill, witch marks in her mismatched eyes, her bad luck, her long shadow.

The stranger was selling things in the shadows. All sorts came: from the ragged charcoal man to the wife of the lord justice, men and women, young and old. They came in ones and twos, shying from the others, looking around them. He sold them glass vials that twisted the firelight from the market's cressets, sold them herbs and feathers knotted with string.

Charms, Kate thought. Charms against empty wombs, indifferent loves. Against hunger, sickness. Against the rumor of something worse that came off the river. The stranger was selling the witchcraft that people craved to protect them. But he would likely be gone when they began to look for someone to blame.

Plain Kate watched for four days and thought. On the fourth day a sudden silence made her look up, startled as if the river had stopped running. The stranger had set down his tambourine. He stood and stretched and sauntered over toward her.

She watched him come. He moved like a jumping jack that was strung too loosely, so that he seemed about to turn a flip or clatter into a pile of bones and string. His zupan's loose skirts swirled around his knees and its undone sleeves swung as he walked. Every man in Kate's country wore such a coat, but on this man it hung like a costume. Kate wondered if he was foreign. His strange, witch-pale skin and hair made it hard to tell. The white coat bleached him further, made him look like a painting that had half washed away.

"Lovely lass," he drawled, leaning sharp elbows on her counter, "I hear you work wonders in wood."

Now, Plain Kate had caught no fish for two days. Niki's bread was gone and she was hungry. But she was required to turn down work, and she did: "There's a wood guild shop —" she began.

He laughed elegantly. "Master Chuny? Boxwood for brains, dead twigs for fingers. No, no, Little Knife. I want someone with some feeling. You see" — he widened his eyes at her — "I've suffered a loss." And he drew from his back, where it was slung like a sword, a length of wood. He set it down in front of her.

The thing was the size of a small branch, polished and curved. The back of the curve was splintery and broken, like a bone. A snapped string curled around it. Plain Kate picked it up. "What is it?"

"A courtier to the queen of all wooden things," he said.

Plain Kate raised an eyebrow and waited for a more sensible answer.

"It's a bow," he said. "A bow for my fiddle." And he half sang: "A walker, a wanderer, a trader in tin — a roamer with a violin. My name is Linay, and I grant wishes."

Just then, Taggle sprang from nowhere and landed neatly in front of her. He stuck his long nose into Linay's pack. Plain Kate picked him up. The cat squirmed, then relaxed into her arm and started to purr. She eased him onto one shoulder and he slunk around her neck, where he draped bonelessly, like a fur collar with glittering eyes.

"Why," said Linay, "no silver mink could match that." He reached out to chuckle the cat's chin.

Taggle bit him.

Linay pulled his hand back and smiled with many teeth. "Sweet-tempered little beast."

Plain Kate had recovered from the strangeness of Linay's singing, and his eyes that shone like new tin. She ran a finger down the broken bow. "Yes, I think I could make you another. What can you pay me?"

"Mmmm." Linay leaned close. "I could write a song about your eyes."

Kate avoided snorting at a paying customer, but she answered shortly: "Something I can eat."

Linay smiled, slow as a fern uncurling, and sang: "What do you wish for, at night in your dark drawer — what do you wish for, Plain Kate?" As he sang he reached out and brushed the side of her face with bony fingers. His hands smelled of herbs, and something shot through her like ice on the neck. She leapt backward.

"Now that's a wish," he said, smiling at her distress. "But I wouldn't. To raise the dead, it's a tricky thing, goes wrong most often."

Plain Kate was panting. "I don't want you to raise my father!"

"Of course you do, orphan girl. All folk want their dead back, and I should know. I've spoken with the shadowless, and how they come shambling, how they come hungry, how they come wrong as a bird in water —"

"Stop it!"

Linay laughed, merry but not kind. "Well, what do you want, then? Beauty? Luck? I sell them all." He leaned in, smelling bitter as burnt spices. "Of course, the trinkets are nonsense, fodder for fools. But I have true power and a will to use it. It's more than the work is worth, but we might trade."

"What do you want?"

"Your shadow." His own shadow fell across the table between them, and it seemed thin to Kate, swirling as if cast by smoke, not solid flesh. "If you give me your shadow, I'll grant the secret wish of your heart."

"But why? Why do you want it?"

"Ah." He winked at her. "I know a lady who lacks one." She must have been gaping at him, because he crooked a finger under her chin to close her mouth. Taggle swiped at him lazily. Linay jerked clear, his smile folding up. "I've been listening to talk in this town. They say your shadow is long and that no one loves you. You are luckless and defenseless. Do not doubt that I can twist things until you are glad enough to give me anything I like."

Then suddenly his smile was back and the roiling edge of his shadow was gone. "But in the meantime, what about my bow? Would you like a beauty charm, perhaps, in payment, Plain Kate?" On his tongue her name suddenly sounded like the insult it had once been.

"I'll take turnips," she said sturdily. "Or fishhooks. Fine wood maybe. Coin on the off chance you have it. But I'll have no deals with witches."

"Won't you now?" He was merry again. "I have no turnips or fishhooks or oxcarts or sailcloth. Two silver."

"Five," she said.

"Three."

"Five," she said again.

He shrugged as if it didn't matter. "Five."

Plain Kate put the coin he gave her in advance in her pouch and pulled out her slate to sketch the bow. Taggle's fur was soft against her neck, and that was the only part of her that felt warm. Linay was eyeing the part of her hair. Finally, as she kept working, he turned away, whistling.

three

THE FISH, THE AXE,
AND THE BARGAIN

For the next three days Plain Kate sketched and carved in scrap wood, trying to learn how the bow worked. She kept her head down even though it was a lively time: There were Roamers in the market.

Roamers were wanderers; they lived in tents and traveled from town to town, trading, singing for supper, telling fortunes. Begging, sometimes. Stealing, people said. They were a people with their own language and their own ways. They had skin like polished walnut, eyes like chestnuts, clothes like a carnival. They lived on the edges of things, and tended to be thin.

Most Roamers were not much welcome in Kate's little town, which lived too close to hunger to take joy in jugglers, too close to fear to like fortune-tellers. This particular clan, though, came once a year and traded in horses, which was so sensible that even Niki the Baker did business with them. He bought a sturdy pony from the two young men, twins, who tended the little herd. "A dull life she'll have, driving my millstone," he said, "but she'll not be beaten."

Linay, as if driven out by the other strangers, had melted away. Plain Kate put his bow down and worked on Niki's objarka instead. She found her thoughts chasing one another. There had been a time, in that country, when the Maid of the Wheat was a real woman. When she was led into the last standing quarter of the ripe grain and tied there while the fields were set on fire. Her burning spirit kept the gods fed; her blood was plowed into the ground.

Now they had only one God, and the Wheat Maiden was just a talisman. But women still burned. Plain Kate worked to turn the ends of the objarka's hair into bearded barley, to turn crosshatch cuts into a woven wheat crown that sat against the smooth forehead. She wished Niki had asked for a horse's face — the horses in the market were full of life; their hooves clattered on the cobbles like good music. Better than Linay's tambourine, much better. Kate was sad as evening fell, and the dark-skinned men in their bright colors led the horses away.

When it got too dark to work, Plain Kate went down to the docks to catch dinner. Taggle went ahead of her, with his tail curled in anticipation of fish. The fishing boats were just coming in, the great beacon fire was being lit, and the dock was busy. Plain Kate fished as the stars came out, throwing her line into the darkening water.

Plain Kate caught only one bony bitterling in the first hour, but as the fishermen came by with their barrows, things changed. Where her line went in, the river suddenly swarmed with fish, thick as waves in a whirlpool. Taggle dug in claws and leaned down until his nose almost touched the water. His golden eyes were huge; his teeth clicked with excitement.

The fishermen stopped to look. "Would you look at that," said Big Jan. He loomed over her in the moonlight. "A body could stand on them." He nudged Taggle's twitching rear end with his boot.

The cat fell and twisted as he fell, sinking claws deep into the dock and kicking at the water. Plain Kate grabbed him by the scruff and dragged him out. Taggle dripped and yowled and hissed at Big Jan, who laughed. "Fierce beast you've got there, girl," he said. "Don't you want to see if he can walk on fish?"

"Leave be, Jan," said the oldest fisherman, whose name was Boyar. "What happens here, Plain Kate? How did you draw the fish?"

"I didn't!" she exclaimed. "They've just . . ." She had no explanation. "They've just come."

Big Jan sneered and even Old Boyar looked skeptical, but he said, "Fish, then. Don't turn your back on blessing." He eased the dripping cat from her arms so that she was free to fish. Taggle squirmed loose and bolted, swiping at Big Jan's ankle on the way by.

The fishermen stood a moment, watching as Kate cast her line into the swarm, pulling out fish after fish, big trout that flashed white in the moonlight. "It's an uncanny thing," said Old Boyar.

"A witchy thing," muttered Big Jan.

"Ah, leave off, Jan," said Old Boyar. "Let's get the catch in." He walked away and the other men followed.

A little way downstream, an unfamiliar little boat — a small punting barge — lay tied up at the bank. Moonlight caught at it, and Kate saw something move there, something white. Linay was standing on the deck like a ghost on a battlement. She saw him lift his hand in ironic salute, and remembered his threat: *Do not doubt that I can twist things . . .*

She believed him. But she was hungry, and she kept the fish.

In the end, Plain Kate caught twenty-seven trout. She traded the fixing of a cracked spar on Old Boyar's boat for a share of his space in the town smokehouse. One fat fish she stuffed with wild dill and onion and roasted over the market square fire. She ate as much of it as she could and was full for the first time in weeks. But she was uneasy. The lively chatter of the Roamers and the horse buyers was gone, and Linay was back, brooding in the corner of the market like a stork. With him he'd brought foul weather: The sky had slid shut under a lid of low clouds.

Plain Kate had not quite finished the Wheat Maiden objarka when Niki the Baker came to collect it for the new horse's stall door. She was shamed but he shrugged it off and paid her anyway, then stood, shifting, as if he wanted to say something. Plain Kate was not much good at such things; she didn't know how to help him find words. "Uncanny," said Niki at last, poking at the leftover fish that was wrapped up in oilcloth at Kate's elbow. "'Twas uncanny, those fish. You should take care, Plain Kate. People say . . ." He stopped.

Plain Kate crossed her arms in front of her, her fingers finding the bony knots of her shoulders. "What do they say?"

But Niki just looked away. "Take care, Plain Kate," he said again.

In the damp heat of the afternoon, as she worked on

Linay's bow, Plain Kate felt that warning like a hand on her neck. She knew she lived mostly by the town's thin kindness. She could feel just how thin it was, between her and the whispers of the market square. A strange smell, sour and stale, came from the smokehouse, roiling in the foggy heat. Linay's tambourine rattled and jangled in her head.

Taggle came and presented her with a half-dead bat. Plain Kate hit it with a hammer and hid it in a drawer to eat later. It would not do to eat such things in daylight, not now, with people talking. When she looked up she saw people watching her as if she were already eating it, as if she had the membranous black wings coming out of her mouth. She looked down.

Taggle made a bleat that sounded like "want, want," and butted at her hand.

"After dark. You can have some when I cook it." She pegged together the wood for the bow.

The cat flopped down on top of her work.

"You're in the way."

"Wrmmm," Taggle whirred. He rolled to show his belly, pink under his gray fur.

"Thanks for the bat, cat. But you're still in the way." She scratched him, then leaned her nose into his soft, warm fur. "Everyone's watching us, Tag," she whispered. "I —"

But Taggle flipped to his feet and hissed. Plain Kate looked up. Linay was lounging against the prop of her awning.

"I've heard your name in strange tales, Katie girl. They say you witched the fish." And he sang, "Witch, fish, flinch, kiss — won't you let me grant your wish?"

"No."

"Hmmm." He smiled. "I wonder how much it will take to make you change your mind." And he sang:

> *Plain Kate, Kate the Carver*
> *No one's friend and no one's daughter*
> *Little Kate might meet her fate*
> *Whittling sticks till it's too late*

Plain Kate stared. "You drew the fish."

"But you caught them. And it's about you they whisper." Linay's smile was long and narrow. "I tell you true, Plain Kate, I would not want to see you hurt. You know that, don't you, about us witches: We tell the truth."

She had heard the tale: that witches could not lie. People said that as the devil gave witches power, God bound their tongues to truth. It did not seem to her a likely story, and she did not trust Linay.

Linay's tin-gray eyes glittered as he said, "I want you well. But there are other things I want more. And a swarm of fish might be just a beginning. Think on it. Your shadow for a heart's wish. Is it such a bad bargain?"

"What I *wish*," she said, "is that you would go away."

And as if answering a command, Taggle slunk around the awning prop, sprang out, swarmed up Linay's shirt, and attacked his ear. Linay shouted and spun and flailed like a man who'd stepped on a beehive. All his dignity and all his menace gone in a whirl of squeaks and ungainly limbs. Plain Kate laughed. Finally the cat went flying out of the melee and bolted across the square. There was scattered applause.

Linay bowed. "Until tomorrow," he said to Kate, and sauntered off, bleeding.

When they opened the smokehouse the next day, the fish were bones and ashes. They fell to dust at a touch. Only Plain Kate's trout were still plump, smoke-yellow and pink, perfect.

The master of the smokehouse summoned her, and she had to go stand before him in the drizzle with her strong hands curled into silent fists. The master was a grand man, his hands fat and many-ringed, his white hair dressed in curls, yellowed with smoke, smelling of fish. His chair was grand too, with arms carved into the form of leaping salmon: her father's work. She remembered helping him with it, his big calloused hands over her small calloused ones as he taught her the way of wood grain — oh, her hands had been so small, and she had been happy.

"I have decided," the master said, leaning back in the beautiful chair, dry under his awning, "that your catch will be split among the men whose fish were in the batch. Since, after all, only luck has spared your fish alone."

Only luck. He was daring her to contradict. No one thought it was luck. She looked at the salmon, so strong she could almost sense the whip of their muscle. There was a little crowd gathered at her back. She thought the salmon were swimming hard against the current of their looks. "That's fair," she said at last. "But I didn't burn the fish."

"As I say, girl," he frowned. "Only luck."

"It's not luck, it's witchcraft," she said, and at her back the silence hardened. "The stranger, Linay. He drew the fish."

Big Jan, behind her, said what Linay had said: "But you caught them."

"The fish will be split," the master said. "And that's enough from you, Kate Carver."

Plain Kate could feel how it was going to be. Linay was

useful; he was powerful. Those that knew he was a witch wanted his protection; those that didn't would take an easier target. Stranger though he was, people knew that Linay was not someone to cross. He was powerful as a cornered dog. If the town was going to choose someone to blame for the hard times coming, it wouldn't be Linay.

Plain Kate turned on her heel, swam silently through the knot of people, and went back to her stall. The bow was lying on her countertop. She wanted to smash it, but it was beautiful. It was quiet and strong. She picked it up, and went back to work.

She was watching for Linay, but he still managed to sneak up on her. "Fair maid of the wood," he said, making her jump. "How goes the work?"

Plain Kate steadied herself and shrugged. "It will be a good bow," she said. "I am a good carver."

"Too good, they say." He tapped her nose. "They call you 'witch-child' already, Katie girl."

"If they do, it's because of you."

He caught her words and sang them back at her:

> If they do it's because of you
> What they see is because of me
> That may be, that may be,
> But I see what I say and I say what I see

He smiled at her. "Do you know what happens to witches, Plain Kate? Have you seen the fires?"

The sour smell from the smokehouse suddenly seemed stronger. "Over a few fish?" Plain Kate tried a laugh; it came out tight.

"Well," said Linay with a bow, "there might be more."

"Go away. Or I'll set my cat on you."

And he went away. But not very far.

The next day there was no catch — or no catch of fish. Old Boyar brought in three boots. Big Jan caught a dead dog. On the next day the nets were wholly empty. The whole week there was no catch, and the grain barges didn't come, and rain fell like a long fever.

Then Boyar took a punt upriver into the fog banks, and the next day the boat came back drifting. Boyar was lying on the deck like a king of old, not dead but sleeping — an unnatural sleep from which he could not be woken.

Talk in the market turned to muttering. Plain Kate saw Big Jan swat Taggle from his nest atop a coil of rope. The cat was kicked and cursed from every stall.

Kate herself kept to her work. The bow was nearly finished. The Wheat Maiden haunted her. The carved face was smooth and beautiful — but in its narrow sadness and quiz-zical brow, Kate saw her own reflection.

At night she locked herself in her drawer and lay awake in the hot darkness. Her thoughts chased themselves until Taggle came in through the little door she'd made him. He flopped on her face. Plain Kate cuddled him under her chin like a fiddle, and they both went to sleep.

And so it went, for a week. Then one night someone took an axe to her stall.

Lightning. She thought she'd been hit by lightning. It was that loud.

And cold. Night air got dumped over her as if from a bucket. Something smashed into the blanket by her head. Taggle's claws raked her throat as he bolted out of his hole.

She was awake now. There were daggers of wood everywhere. Her safe little drawer was a nest of splinters. And again something clapped past her ear. An axe. Kate screamed.

The axe yanked free and came again. Air and light and falling things hit her.

Plain Kate yanked the door lever. The drawer lurched and jammed.

Her stall was shattering. Smashing through a gap came that swinging axe.

She pounded her fists against the drawer above her. Something gave way to her hands. She shoved and scrambled and hit air.

Plain Kate lurched to her feet. The square was quiet, full of fog. Whoever had wielded the axe was gone. A few folk had clustered outside the inn door, drawn by the noise. Linay was sitting up on his white blanket, looking sleepy. Heads hung from windows. The town's watchmen came pounding through the river arch. And everyone was looking at her. She didn't feel anything. She didn't even feel frightened. She had gone so far beyond frightened that it would take a while for fear to catch up with her.

The running watchmen stopped when they saw it was only her. The drinkers from the inn had begun to talk again, and wandered inside. Windows closed. Plain Kate stood alone. Her muscles were so tight that they made her tremble, the way wood trembled when bent almost to breaking.

Her father's stall — her home — was a jagged, jumbled ruin. Tools and half-finished carvings were scattered across the wet cobbles. One pale deer, still whole, leapt toward the edge of a splintered piece of awning. She lifted it and looked at it for a while. *Where shall I put it?* she thought. *I don't have anywhere to put it.* She took four steps away from the wreck, and set the deer gently on bare stones.

Taggle came back and tangled around her feet, bleating. She stooped, stroked him between his ears, then picked up an awl that had spun out from the shattered heap, a little way. She set the tool down beside the deer. She edged back toward the wreck. She moved one broken drawer. Things tumbled out of it. It made a lot of noise, but Plain Kate said nothing. No one came. She worked without a word, sorting carvings and tools from junk and straw.

After a while, Linay came over from his white blanket and worked beside her, and he too was silent.

Plain Kate knew that the axe had come because of the rumors Linay had twisted into life. Perhaps he had even sent the axe wielder — a nudge, a seemingly innocent word in the right ear. But she took his help because some of the things she had to move were heavy, and because his strange, washed-away face was hollowed as if someone had died. He pulled her parents' marriage quilt from under the last of the rubble. She saw the axe holes in it, the way the fog moved through them like snakes.

Plain Kate folded the quilt into a mat; she hammered some broken planks into a rough workbench. Day came.

Summer thunder cleared the market square. Soaked and cold, Plain Kate worked alone to finish the bow, her hair dripping into her face, stinging her mismatched eyes.

When the bow at last was finished, it was as good as anything she'd ever made. It had no ornament, but its simple lines were beautiful, like one bird against the sky.

And now that it was finished, Kate had no more work to do.

She sat for a while, empty as the empty square, thinking. Then without a word she stood up. She picked up the bow like a sword and went off to find Linay.

The afternoon was damp and clammy. Plain Kate followed the faint sounds of the tambourine around the puddles and the horse droppings, through the riverward gate of the town. Down by the docks she found Linay sitting on the roof of the hold of a small boat. It was the punt she'd seen him on the night the fish had swarmed: a small, neatly made little barge, painted grassgreen. Linay was singing a sad song about river spirits, to entertain the men who were smearing pitch in the chinks. She walked toward him, ignoring the looks that beat on her like rain. Big Jan grabbed her arm. "You're not welcome here, witch-child."

Linay stopped singing and stood up. "Her business is with me." Big Jan was broad like a wild ox, but Linay was skinny like a rabid wolf, and Jan backed down. Linay swept by and caught Kate up in his wake. She trailed him down the dock, then down the road toward the forest.

The rain had stopped. The light was storm-green and the trees were stirring restlessly. The smell of the river was heavy in the air.

Plain Kate held out the bow. Linay took it as if it were a rose, and bowed over it. He looked at her silently. She looked back.

At last Linay moved. "Your four silver." He pulled coins out of her ear, like a merry juggler — but his eyes were piercing. "Does that finish our business?"

"I'm leaving," she said. "I need food, things."

"Hmmmm," he said, sinuously. "Did you have in mind a trade?"

"For my shadow," she said. "I want oilcloth. And a sleep roll, and a pack. A packet of fishhooks, a camp hatchet. Ten yards of rope."

He laughed. "Do you think you can live on the road? In the woods?"

"I'll get by."

"You'll get by, you'll get by," he sang. "I'd almost like to see you try." He drew himself up. "Done."

Faraway thunder clacked. It sounded like a latch closing. "Done," she said.

Linay wiped the rain off his face. "The docks. Meet me beside my punt, at the third bell past midnight." He turned back toward the town.

Plain Kate, empty-handed, went over to the ruins of her father's stall. She thought about what she could carry and what she must leave. Behind her she heard Linay's fiddle begin to play: Wild and powerful as a storm, it swept across the rainy twilight.

She took one of her silver coins to the cobbler and bought good boots: deerskin, double stitched and sturdy. She took a second coin and bought a haversack from the tanner, who took her money but spat on the doorstep as she left. She took the third to the butcher to buy jerky, but he would not trade with her at all. She took the last coin to Niki's bakery to buy hardtack, but by then the light was sinking and the bakery was dark and shut. She went back to where the splintered heap of the stall lay like a dead horse among the puddles of the market square.

Plain Kate packed her best tools in their felt pouches; she packed her one pan; she packed her two striped smocks and extra socks. She coiled her fishing line and twine. She came to her parents' marriage quilt. It had once smelled of her father, and though it now smelled of sawdust and cats, she remembered how that smell had wrapped her, her first night in the drawer. But she needed a coat, and the quilt was too big. She was practical. She sliced it in half. She cut a hole for her head, pulled it on over her wet hair, and belted it with a bit of rope. The other half lay on the cobbles, soaking up rainwater.

She picked up the piece of the wreckage with the carved stag on it. It was too heavy to take. It served no purpose. She set it back down. It seemed to blur and leap in the half light, and it took Kate a moment to realize that her eyes were tearing. She picked the stag back up. She put it back down.

Taggle was sitting on top of the heaped wood, watching her. "I'll leave it," she told him. "I don't need it." Her eyes stung as she said it. She dashed her hand across them, disgusted with herself. The cat chirruped inquiringly. "It's nothing," she told him, her throat angry and aching with the effort of not crying. Decisively, she took the carving knife her father had given her — the knife her hand had grown up knowing, the knife that had shaped her — and thrust it into the sheath in her new boot.

"Now we can travel," she told Taggle. She sat down on her makeshift workbench. "I couldn't go without my knife. Though I don't suppose I'll find much work, living wild." The wet evening was sinking into darkness. The cat hopped down and ambled over to sniff her ankles.

"What about you?" she asked, lifting him into her lap.

"A dog would come without question — but I suppose a cat must make his own choices." It was foolish to talk to no one, and she stopped. And so she left unspoken her deepest wish: that she did have someone to talk to, that she didn't have to go alone.

Deep in the night, Plain Kate went down to the river. She carried her haversack on one hip and Taggle in her arms. No cat would follow a wanderer; she realized that now. But she was not ready to give him up, to leave him as she had left the carved deer from her father's stall, propped up against her workbench in the abandoned square. Not yet; not quite yet. And maybe he would follow her, a little way.

Away from the cressets of the market, under the lid of clouds, it was very dark — and very quiet. She heard the throaty murmur of the river, the plop of a jumping fish. Behind her, someone pulled a shutter. Across the river, a fox barked.

Linay was sitting quietly, watching the black gleam of the river, dangling his legs off the dock like a child. A piercework tin lantern sat on the dock beside him, and in its feeble light he looked pale as a moth in the deep of the night. He was eating a meat pie. As Plain Kate came up he held a second pie out to her. She ignored it. He shrugged, licked the gravy from his dagger, and set the pie on the wet wood at her feet.

Taggle's nose started twitching.

Plain Kate stood over Linay. Taggle had begun twisting in her hands like a strong fish — a fish who wanted meat pie. She would have to put him down soon. "Now what?" she asked.

"Blood," Linay said. Kate drew back and he laughed. "Oh, mine, Little Knife, don't worry."

"Kind," she said, trying to mock, though her voice felt high and tight. Linay's dagger looked as if it could gut a deer.

"Blood draws things. And it would be foolish to draw your own shadow to you." He hesitated a bare second, then picked up his dagger, flipped it round, and drew it fearlessly across his wrist. His white face didn't flicker, but Plain Kate winced for him as blood welled. Taggle gave a strangled cough, as if she were squeezing him too hard.

Linay leaned over and opened the lantern's top. He let the blood dribble onto the flame. Plain Kate braced herself for darkness, but instead of dousing the flame, the blood caught fire, burning like oil, brightening the night.

"What —" she started to ask.

"Fire to set loose the spell," he said absently, watching his blood catch. "You'd be surprised, the things a witch can make burn."

His absentness and the way the blood ran with flame made the night suddenly eerie. Taggle hissed and Kate backed away.

"Where are you going?" said Linay.

Plain Kate began to babble something — but Linay had risen to his feet silently as a wave. His hand flashed, his wrist flicked. Blood flew and fell over Kate like a net. She leapt back shouting, and Taggle spilled from her arms and howled like a dying thing. Then the air turned to glass.

"Stay," said Linay, soft, coaxing, into the sudden silence.

Kate couldn't move. Couldn't breathe. Taggle lay belly-flat as if his back was broken.

Linay looked at her with his head tilted, smiling softly as a father smiles at a sleeping child.

Plain Kate thought she was dying and that when she died she would remain as a statue, held in place by the stiffness of the air. Linay reached out a hand for her. She was sure she would die when he touched her but she could only watch his hand coming.

And he touched her.

The air was air again. Kate staggered and crashed to the dock. The world spun and sparks shot through her vision. Linay loomed over her, dim and white as a pillar.

"Well," said the witch. "That's that."

"What —" Kate gasped. She coughed, blinked. Taggle shook his head hard.

"I have left your goods at the third big stone around the bend of the road."

"But —" Kate couldn't stop him, couldn't even see him. He was a sort of white shadow above her. She lay panting on the wet wood, her hair hanging over the dock edge, down toward the river.

He looked down at her, his face fuzzy — she thought he looked genuinely sad. "The loss of a shadow is a slow thing," he said. "You will have a little time before someone notices. Find a place to belong before that happens." Then he sang:

> *Go fast, Plain Kate, and travel light*
> *Learn to walk the shadowy night*
> *Without a shadow, flee from light*
> *Become a shadow, truly*

He crouched down beside her. "Will you come with me to the stone city?"

"No." She could hardly get the word out.

"No," he echoed. "But I will see you again, I think." He looked over at Taggle. "The pair of you." And he rose and went, leaving her lying helplessly in the dark, beside the water.

It was a long time before she could sit up, before Taggle could gather himself enough to resume sniffing around the meat pie. Plain Kate leaned forward and pressed the heels of her hands into her eyelids until she saw spots. Something had been taken from her, and though it was supposed to be her shadow, she felt as if it might have been her soul. "What did I do?" she muttered.

Over by the meat pie, Taggle gave a hiss and a hair-ball cough. Plain Kate opened her eyes. "Mussssssicians," the cat spat. "Do you know what fiddle strings are made of? Bah! I'm glad he's gone. Let's eat."

four

THE ROAMERS

Plain Kate scooched back and stared. "Taggle!"

Taggle was absorbed in the meat pie. "It's covered in *bread*," he huffed. "What fool has covered *meat* with *bread*?" He batted at the crust, then sprang back as it broke, and began licking gravy off his paw. "Ooooo," he purred. "Ooooo, good."

"Taggle," gulped Kate, again.

The cat looked up from his licking. "Oh. Well. I could share." He arched his whiskers forward and, like a lord, demonstrated his beneficence by giving away what he didn't want. "There is bread you might like."

"You're —" Kate closed her jaw with deliberation. "You can talk."

"It was . . . hrrmmmm . . . your wish." His yellow eyes seemed to look inside himself. "So that you would not have to go alone."

"Oh." *I will grant the secret wish of your heart,* Linay had said.

Taggle cocked his head at her. "There's meat too. Besides the bread. You may have some of that as well."

The night was cool and rustly with rain. Everything she had in the world was in a haversack crushed against her hip. She was wearing an old quilt belted with a bit of twine, and the damp night was wrapped around that. And now her cat could talk. Plain Kate felt ridiculous and relieved and terrified and — despite the cat — very alone indeed.

"It is beneath my dignity to coax you." Taggle butted at her hand. "Eat."

So she did.

Full of meat pie and trailed by a talking cat, Plain Kate turned her back on her town and walked into the mouth of the road. Her legs wobbled and her mind whirled. Her cat could talk. She had made a deal with a witch. She was leaving her only home. She was heading for the bend, the third big stone. What she would do if Linay had not left her gear there, she didn't know, and couldn't think about. She had only a little food in the haversack of tools and half-done carvings. If there was nothing behind the third big stone, she would simply and slowly die.

Taggle sauntered along, arching his whiskers and tasting the night. He was wordless, and Plain Kate could almost believe she had been dreaming. *So you wouldn't be alone,* he'd said. Whatever was going to happen next, she wouldn't be alone. She spotted the stone. Leaning against it was a basket.

It was the kind of basket farmers wore on their backs, to haul harvest to market: shaped like half a barrel, with leather straps to go over the shoulders. It was new and finely made: Plain Kate fingered the smooth paleness of the woven ash splints. Taggle reared up and put his front paws on the basket rim. He worked his head under the hinged lid. "Do you suppose he packed more meat pie?" His voice was muffled, but not a dream.

"Well," she said, feeling dazed, "let's look."

There were packets of hurry bread that made Taggle sniff in disgust. There was a bedroll of oilskin and fur. A hatchet. A sheepskin coat, too big for her. A hat and mittens of rabbit fur. A jumble of small things: a fire flint, a leather folder of fishhooks and another of needles, tall wool socks, a linen shift.

Linay had been generous. The thought made her uneasy.

Plain Kate took off her haversack and started tucking her tools and carvings into the basket. The last thing she pulled out was the Wheat Maiden objarka. She stopped and looked at it. The woman's carved face seemed to shiver in her hands, and Kate realized she was shaking.

The objarka was finished and paid for. Fear urged her down the road, but honor made her turn around and look at the dark bulk of the town behind her, the weizi rising like a ship's mast from a bank of fog.

Plain Kate set the basket on a rock and struggled into the straps. She had just managed to get herself upright when Taggle sprang up onto the basket lid and skidded to a stop by her ear. Kate yelped in surprise and wobbled as the cat shifted and turned, his side rubbing against her neck and his tail flipping around her head. "What are you doing?" she demanded.

"I'm coming with you," he drawled. "Please wake me when we are done fleeing."

"You couldn't follow?"

"*Dogs* follow," he said, in such a horrified tone that she didn't bother arguing. She felt him sway behind her as she walked, then settle into the movement. They went on in silence for a while, beside the river.

A thick fog slid off the water and over the road and the town. It was like moonlight hanging in the air: a little light everywhere, so that nothing could be seen. It wrapped sounds around her, changing her footfalls and the chuck-ling of the river into an underwater music. It lulled and rocked her, singing.

Plain Kate felt muddled and strange. She hadn't slept since the axe. The music seemed real; she could hear a fiddle in it, a voice singing in a language she didn't know. She thought the river itself was singing, or the moon, or all the ghosts in the world. She shook herself, and out of the night the town's wall suddenly loomed. Kate stopped with a bump.

"We have been fleeing," Taggle intoned, "in the wrong direction."

"Did you hear that?" There was still ghost music, somewhere.

"Yes," the cat said haughtily, "it's real. I can talk. You wished for it. And I was saying, this is the town where they were going to kill you."

"I have to give the objarka to Niki."

"Hrrmmmm," he said. "Well. No one is trying to kill *me*."

But just in case, he wormed his way under the basket lid. Plain Kate felt him settle against her shoulder blades. She squared them and set off into the dark streets.

At the bakery, Plain Kate stopped in the doorway. She had meant to leave the Wheat Maiden on the doorstep like a baby — but she had forgotten that bakers rise early.

The half-moon mouth of the oven glowed with the coals ready deep within it. The long-handled peel lay across a table like a pike. Niki the Baker was standing at the dough trough, punching down the dough for white bread — dead pale, sticky stuff. Plain Kate watched the muscles bunching in his big arms. He looked up. "Plain Kate!"

She stood on the doorstep with the night at her back. "I brought . . ." She held out the objarka. "It's finished."

"Come in, come in." Niki rubbed his sticky hands together, making worms of dough that dropped to the floor. "This has to rise for the morning baking. You needn't have come so early — too early for anybody but bakers! Set her down, let's have a look."

Plain Kate set the objarka down and took a step back. She needed to go, but she couldn't stop looking at the Wheat Maiden's face. *The truth*, she kept thinking. *The truth is —*

"Plain Kate. Katerina. You're running away."

She shrugged.

"Yes," he said. "Yes, you are. Ah, Plain Kate. Where will you go?"

She shrugged again, and Niki sighed. "But it's wise, little one. Wise. There's talk."

She stood, still looking at the objarka. Niki faltered and looked at it too. "It's very fine, you know, very fine work. You have a way with a knife, that's sure, a blessed blade. This will be lucky for me, sure. But I'll miss you." As if the admission embarrassed him, he started to bustle. "I can give you bread. Two-day-old millet, only a little stale. And I think" — he was rummaging — "there's some hurry bread, you know, for traveling. I —" He stopped as a thought took him. "You should go with the Roamers."

Unexpected hope rocked her. Going with other people — even a foreign and despised people — would give her a real chance to survive. "The Roamers?" she echoed.

"Yes, that's it, Roamers," said Niki.

They both looked at each other, not sure of how one went about being taken in by outcasts. "I've dealings with them, you know, over the horse," said Niki at last. "So they'll talk to me, I suppose. They're down by the sheep meadows."

He stopped, seeing her face. "No fear," he said, patting her hand. "Roamers are right enough."

But he had mistaken her: She was afraid not that the Roamers would take her in, but that they would turn her away.

So, at dawn in misty rain, Plain Kate found herself with Niki the Baker at the edge of the sheep meadows, just outside Samilae's lower gate. The Roamers were just stirring: an old man uncovering a banked fire, two young women chatting and gathering eggs from sleepy chickens. Their bright-painted wagons floated in the morning dew-fog. On the far side of the camp, two dozen horses wove like shadows in the mist, and a young man in blue moved among them.

"Wait a moment," murmured Niki, and left her standing by the low wall of stones and raspberry brambles that marked the edge of the meadow. She watched Niki go toward the horses and stood waiting. After a moment she shrugged off her basket. The lid lifted and Taggle poured himself over the side.

"Are we finished fleeing?" the cat asked, the last word swallowed by a huge yawn. He stretched forward, lengthening his back and spreading his toes, then sprang onto the wall beside her. His nose worked. "Horses," he said. "Dogs. Hrrmmmmm. Humans. Chickens. And — ah, another cat! I must go and establish my dominance." He leapt off the wall.

Plain Kate lunged after him. "Taggle! Wait!" She snatched him out of the air by the scruff of his neck.

"Yerrrrowww!" he shouted, hanging from her hand. "The insult! The indignity!"

Kate fell to her knees and bundled the spitting cat against her chest. "Taggle!" she hissed. "Stop!"

"I shall claw you in a moment, no matter how much I like you. Let me *go*!" He writhed against her chest.

"Tag, you can't talk."

"I *can* talk," came the muffled, outraged voice. "I can also claw and bite and scra —"

"No," she interrupted. "You *can't*, you mustn't talk. Listen to me. They'll kill you if they hear you talk."

The cat stopped twisting. "Who would? Who would dare?"

"The other people. Please, Taggle. They'll think it's magic. They'll kill us both."

"It *is* magic," he said, reproachful. "And it was *your* wish."

"I know — I'm sorry. But please."

"Well. I am not afraid. But to protect you, Katerina, I will be discreet." Plain Kate considered a cat's idea of discretion, and was frightened. But it was the best she could do.

"Now, let me go," said Taggle. "I have business to conduct in the language of fur and claw."

"Good luck," she said, and wished hard.

Plain Kate was still sitting with her back to the wall when Niki reappeared with the young man who'd been tending the horses. "Up, up," the baker fussed. Kate stood and kept herself from backing into the wall. "Meet someone. Meet Behjet, who sold me my horse. Best horseman among the Roamers, it's said."

The flattery made it obvious that Niki wanted something. Plain Kate wanted to wince, but the man just said, "And who have we here, Nikolai?" He was soft-voiced, slender, wearing a blue shirt with a green kerchief knotted round his neck: kingfisher colors.

"She is, this is," Niki sputtered, "Plain Kate. Orphan girl, orphan to Piotr Carver." He drew Plain Kate forward into the crook of his arm. "Behjet, she needs a place."

"Among the Roamers, you mean?" The man, Behjet, wiped his palms on his groom's apron. "That's no small thing to ask. Where is she going?"

Plain Kate pulled away from the soft, doughy warmth of Niki and answered for herself. "Away."

"Hmmm," said Behjet. "And why's that?"

From far off, Plain Kate heard Taggle's yowl of victory. The cat was establishing his dominance. Finding his place.

"Because." Kate swallowed. "Because they'll kill me if I stay here. They think I'm a witch."

"Which she's none of," Niki added.

"Ah," said the young man softly. Like all the Roamers, he had dark skin and wide, uptilted dark eyes. They were horse deep and horse soft; they made him look kindly. But still he didn't move.

Niki fluttered his hands. "And you were saying you were in need of a carpenter, that you had to fix your wagons in every other town and wished for a carpenter among you. Plain Kate is a woodworker."

"A good one," added Kate. Her voice came out level. She was proud of that.

Behjet blew through his lips, whuffling like one of his horses. "Taking in a *gadje* — it's not for me to decide. But let me take you to meet my mother." He started off across the close-cropped, drizzle-gray grass.

Plain Kate pulled on her pack-basket and hurried after him, with Niki trailing. "What does 'gage-eh' mean?"

"Gadje-eh," Behjet corrected, pulling her *g* toward *z*. "It means 'not one of the Roamers.' It's not the kindest word, and I'm sorry for it. But you must not think that because we have no walls, we have no ways. We are not wild men, for all that we are not welcome most places. Now then." They had come to the wagons. They were small, with high wheels, their beds wooden and heavily carved, bright with paint. Their decks were covered by canvas pulled across bows of wood. On the back steps of a red-painted wagon, an apple-faced old woman was plucking a rooster. She was bundled in green and yellow skirts and many scarves. Gray hair frizzed from under her turban and dripped into her dark face.

Niki did not bow, but he twisted his hands in front of him as if he thought maybe he should. "Mother Daj," he said.

"Daj," said Behjet, who did bow a little, and then added something in another language. It seemed to Plain Kate like a long speech, and she was frustrated. If her fate was being decided, she wanted to understand.

Behjet fell silent. Plain Kate found the woman looking at her, her eyes small and bright as a hawk's among her wrinkles. Copying Behjet, she bowed, but said nothing.

"A carver, eh?" the woman drawled. She used the rooster's beak to point at Kate's objarka. "Just fancywork?"

Plain Kate planted her feet as if about to fight. "Plain and fancy. Boxwork, wheelwork, turned wood. But mostly carving." She took off the objarka, which her father had called a masterpiece, and passed it to the woman.

She turned the dark wooden cat round and round in her dark hands, put its little nose to her big one. "She's a good blade, Mother," said Niki. But the old woman ignored the baker, intent on Kate's objarka and some internal question. At last she said, "Well, we could use a carver, and that's sure, child." Her head was still down, as if she were speaking to the carved cat. Then she looked up, her face soft with wrinkles. "And though you keep it from your face, I think you could use us. You have your own gear? Your own tools?"

Plain Kate nodded.

"I can't promise you a place. But come with us to Toila. A month on the road. We'll sniff each other out."

A test. Plain Kate understood tests. She nodded again. A lump was tightening in her throat, but she wasn't sure if it was hope or fear.

"Well, then," said the woman. "I'm Daj. Or Mother Daj if that sets better on a town tongue. And you're Kate."

"Plain Kate," she corrected.

Daj raised her eyebrows, but before she could say anything, Taggle sauntered up. There was a fresh scratch across one ear and a dead rat in his mouth. He dropped the pink-footed body at Daj's feet and stood there grinning. Plain Kate winced. "I also," she said, "have a cat."

"A fine beast, Mother Daj," put in Niki. "A famous mouser."

"Well," said Daj. "A useful pair, then. Welcome, cat."

And Taggle nodded.

Plain Kate, at Daj's gruff coaxing, swung her basket into the wagon bed, and Taggle, with no coaxing at all, sprang up beside it. "Did you see?" he said, arching his back into her hand, preening. "My gift has proven that we're useful."

"Taggle," Kate hissed. She looked round. No one had heard.

The cat sulked. "One would think praise was in order."

"*Please* be quiet," she said. "Look, here." She pulled her new coat out of the basket and spread it, woolly side up, for him to nestle in.

"Ah," he said, stepping onto the wool like a king deigning to enter a hovel. "Better." He high-stepped daintily in three circles, then curled up, tucking his tail over his nose.

"Sleep quietly," she urged him, rubbing a thumb between his ears. He gave her a bleary glare and closed his eyes.

Plain Kate rushed after Behjet and Niki the Baker. Their feet had knocked down the dew and left dark prints in the silver grass, which was short where the sheep had grazed. The trail of darkness made her think of her shadow. *The loss of a shadow is a slow thing*, Linay had said. *Find someplace to belong.* If the Roamers took her in, if she proved herself useful, then there would come a moment where she could explain, before someone saw.

Niki left her with Behjet, though not without fluttering about like a bird trying to get its nestling to fly. Behjet sighed after him, then went back to tending the horses.

Plain Kate watched him work. She was desperate to be of use, but didn't know what to do. Behjet was tending a dun mare, holding one of her hooves up clamped between his legs, and working a stone from the hoof's spongy bottom with a little hook. The other horses milled around. Plain Kate had never been so close to horses. They were big. She smelled horse sweat, leather, and dung each time one shifted. Behjet's dark head was bent; he murmured to the restless beast. The work looked dangerous. She didn't even dare ask how she could help.

Behjet finished with the mare and moved on to another horse. He spoke smoothly to the animals in his own language. Plain Kate liked his voice: calm but rich. It made her a little more comfortable, and she almost missed it when he began speaking to her. "It was the witchcraft that swayed her," he said.

"What?" said Kate.

"Daj. I told her your people took you for a witch. It is why she decided to take you in. You should know."

"Oh," said Kate.

"My brother's wife — she was burned for a witch. It happens to Roamers. More than our share." He stood up, wiping his hands on his leather apron and mopping the drizzle from his face with his green kerchief. "Stick to Daj, Plain Kate. Don't take her for softhearted — she's badger fierce. But if she decides to take your part, your place here will be sure."

Plain Kate didn't know what to say to that. A sure place — it was too big a thing even to think about. Behjet had read her heart's wishes as well as any witch. Not alone.

"Off you go then," said Behjet. "It's busy work to break camp; I'm sure your hands will find something."

Plain Kate found Mother Daj still sitting on the wagon steps. The rooster was mostly plucked, and Daj wore a spray of glossy tail feathers tucked into her turban. She was presiding over two younger women shaking out great rugs and another bent over a jumbled box of gear. At Daj's feet, a girl a little younger than Kate was scouring a pot. The girl looked up with eyes as bright and frank as a sparrow's.

"Mother Daj," Kate asked, feeling shy. "Can I help?"

"There's naught that needs carving this minute," Daj answered. Kate swallowed — it was such a quick dismissal. Daj seemed to see the twitch and guess the reason. Her face softened, and she said, "Drina, lass. Finished that, nearly?"

The girl with the pot replied, "I have to go for more sand." Her voice was a sparrow's too: clear and piping, hiding nothing. She had a narrow nose and a wide mouth, and big eyes that were uptilted, like a cat's. Though younger than Kate, she was taller, and softer: a girl who had never been hungry. Her long black hair was bound back with a scarf of green and yellow; her dark skirts were embroidered with poppies.

"Take this one," said Daj, pointing an elbow at Kate while she turned the chicken over. "This is Kate Carver, who will go our way a while."

"Plain Kate," corrected Plain Kate.

"Hmph, so you said." Daj eyed her. "As you'd have it, kit. But you're not so plain as it needs remarking on every moment." Kate blushed, and Daj smiled softly, and said, "Drina here will show you about. Keep you from being trampled." She lifted the limp, feathery head and pointed around with it. "What with the great bustle."

So Drina picked up an empty pail and led Plain Kate down toward the river. They climbed over the loose wall of stones at the edge of the sheep meadow and into the unkempt land where the river sometimes flooded. The grasses there were tall and bent with water. Sapling birch trees trembled and dripped in the misty rain. Plain Kate's leggings got soaked and heavy. Drina's long legs shone wet, and her skirts drooped around her knees. The two girls went silently, sneaking glances at each other.

"You wouldn't really get trampled," offered Drina after a while. "Daj was joking."

"Oh, it was funny," said Kate. She meant it but it came out dry, and Drina laughed.

"Anyway — you must be used to more people than this."

"Yes, but —" Plain Kate wasn't sure how to explain. "They don't usually talk to me."

"Well," said Drina, swinging her pail in a full loop, "if you go the Roamer way, we're not short on talk. Lots of other things, but not talk, is what Daj says."

"Is Daj your mother?"

"Oh, no!" Drina laughed. "She's too old! I just call her that. Everyone does. It's respect."

"Call her . . . ?" Kate was lost.

"Daj. Oh, you don't speak the tongue. You'll have to learn a little. *Daj* means 'mother.' But she's not, she just looks after me, because my mother is dead."

"So's mine." Plain Kate was glad of it, for the first time. It gave her something in common with this cheerful, well-loved girl.

"Oh!" Drina stopped swinging her pail and stood there, skirt-deep in the soaked grass. She looked legless, like a chess piece. "Do you miss her?"

"No. She died when I was born."

"Oh," said Drina, and started walking again.

"I miss my father, though." Plain Kate was trying to keep the flow of talk going. "He died four years ago, in the *skara rok*. He got the witch's fever."

And Drina — cheerful, smiling Drina — snapped at her, almost snarled: "Don't call it that!"

Plain Kate felt her shoulders tighten and come forward as if to protect her heart. "Don't call it — *skara rok*?"

"Don't call it 'witch's fever.' Witches don't make fevers or sicken cows or kill crops or any of that."

"I didn't say they did. But witch's — I mean, the sickness. Everyone calls it that."

"I know." Drina's voice was softer now. They had reached the river at the inner side of a broad curve where a slope of clay and pebbles eased into the water. Drina walked on the margin, placing her feet delicately as a heron and watching her prints fill with water. "But it's — with the *skara rok*, people look for someone to blame. Ugly people. Outsiders. Witch-whites. Roamers."

Carvers, thought Kate. She thought she knew more

about being hunted and blamed than Drina did, but she did not say so.

The winding river Narwe was turning again; there was a huge stone a pace or two into the channel, and jammed against it a wall of tangled trunks and limbs, remnants of some old flood, cut across their way. Drina blew through her lips in frustration. "Nothing here!"

"What are you looking for?"

"Sand. Clean sand, to scour the pots."

The anger that Drina had shown a moment ago had slid from her completely and easily, like water off of oiled wood. That sort of generosity was a new thing to Plain Kate; she didn't know how to take it. But she said, "There's sand just alee of this fall." She pointed past the snarl of bleached wood. "That's what I use."

"I guess even a town girl has to scrub pots," said Drina, swinging up over the timbers, staining her legs with moss.

Plain Kate climbed carefully up behind her. "I've only got one pot. I use the sand to smooth wood. For carving. That's who I am, a carver."

The drizzle had broken into patches as they walked. As Drina scooped up the pale sand, Kate found herself standing in the smudge of shadow cast by the deadfall. She had never before noticed the way shadows gave things weight, made them look heavy and real and connected to the ground. Without hers . . .

She edged into the light.

Her shadow looked strange and thinned. It seemed not cast against the ground, but floating above it, like a fog. What Linay had said was true: No one would notice this, at first. It was just an uneasy little change, like the half-felt movement of a boat that slowly induces a great sickness.

"Got it!" Drina's voice came from her elbow, suddenly. She scrambled up the bank toward the field, and Kate followed. At the meadow wall, Drina stopped. "If we go back now, we'll have to pluck chickens." She snuck Kate a sly, friendly look. "Let's go see if Behjet needs help."

"I asked him already," said Plain Kate, then regretted it as Drina's face fell.

Drina rubbed a bare foot against the other leg, smearing mud. "Well. Let's go see the horses, anyway. Just for a moment." She swung up onto the wall and walked along the loose, wobbly stones, easy and graceful. "Come on!" Plain Kate walked beside her, though Drina's feet were level with Kate's shoulders. Even if she could have walked the wall — and it looked like an acrobat's trick — Kate would not have dared. It could attract attention.

The horses were picketed on the far side of the camp.

There were about two dozen drays: big, powerful animals, the engines of farms and towns. Scattered among them were a handful of draft ponies, and some of the smaller, faster, feistier horses meant for riding.

Drina flipped off the wall, heels over head, landed neat-footed, and ran over to them. Kate came cautiously with her. Drina was stroking a cart horse's pink, freckled nose. The horse was nearly white, but dappled with dun patches, like butter floating in buttermilk. "This is Cream," said Drina. She stooped and pulled a handful of grass and held it out. The horse wrapped her tongue around Drina's hand. "She's mine." Drina glanced sideways at Plain Kate, then twitched a smile and amended: "I mean, she's my favorite. I helped her be born." Cream worked her jaw and whickered. Drina leaned her cheek into the hollow between Cream's huge collarbones. Her face looked like stained walnut against the horse's coat of pale new pine.

Drina looked at Plain Kate, eyes shining. "Do you want to ride her?"

Plain Kate looked up at the horse: way up. "I don't know how."

"I'll teach you. It's not hard, you just have to hold on."

"I . . . Shouldn't we get back?"

"We should." Drina wrapped her arms up toward Cream's shoulders and kissed her chin. The horse whuffled and lipped Drina's hair. "But I'll teach you to ride soon. You can't go the Roamer way without riding."

There were a hundred things to tend to, a thousand things to do, in the breaking of a camp, and Plain Kate didn't know how to do any of them.

She didn't know how to unhook a cooking tripod and bind the three legs together into a single iron staff, or where to tuck the tripod under the cart. She didn't know how to fold a wet rug so that it wouldn't mold. She didn't know how to oil horse tack or fix a harness.

There were eggs to gather and chickens to catch and stuff into wicker baskets, which were in turn piled into a rough iron cage. "A bear cage," said Drina, her arms full of squawking feathers. "We had a dancing bear for the markets. She died." Plain Kate didn't know how to catch chickens.

"I'll show you," offered Taggle, who was still drowsing on her coat.

"Tomorrow," she whispered, and hoped she could keep him quiet that long.

The Roamers hoisted the iron cage onto the top of one of the wagons with a block and tackle. Kate didn't know how to use a block and tackle. She didn't know why the one wagon was like a little house on wheels, built of solid wood, while the others were like tents. She couldn't even keep the three women straight: one was Daj's daughter, and the other two some sort of complicated cousins. She wasn't sure where the men were or whether she was allowed to talk to them, since the other women did not.

But she did know how to scrub a pot. It was not too different from smoothing a finished carving, and was done with a folded square of leather, dipped wet into sand. Plain Kate scoured pots until they gleamed black as the night reflected in the river, and by the time that was done, the Roamers were ready to go.

And when they went, Plain Kate went with them.

five

THE ROAD AND THE RAIN

Despite what Drina had said, it turned out you could go the Roamer way without riding. Mostly, you walked.

The caravan bunched and inched down the road. People on foot went first, where the road was merely sticky and rutted with water. Then came the loose horses, with the horsemen among them. And finally, churning up the mud and the new horse dung, came the wagons. And last of all came Plain Kate.

Walking at the back was Daj's idea, to keep Plain Kate out of sight until they were far from town. "Harder for some fool to turn you loose, then," she'd said. Plain Kate had been taken aback; she'd thought her place among the Roamers was Daj's to give. But, no, explained Drina. Big decisions like that were a matter for the men. "Never fear, kit," said Daj. "Trust Mother Daj. I know how to lead from the last wagon."

So Kate walked in the back. It was hard going. She'd lived her life on cobbles, and the mud of the road was new to her. It clutched at her heels like a dying thing. Her boots grew dark with water. Her tall socks got wet and her feet squelched and soon blistered. But she said nothing, and kept walking.

Her little town sank behind her. Samilae. She had never left it before, and had never had to think of its name. Her father when he was alive had been only Father. Dead he was Piotr Carver, and she had to say his name sometimes. And now her home was Samilae. She looked back and saw it become a huddle of roofs, with the tall spire of the weizi above them — her father's handiwork, casting its finger of shadow after her. She did not cry, and kept walking.

Drina spent the day walking beside Plain Kate and then dashing forward to be among the horses, then dashing back again. She turned cartwheels for no reason, and sang like a lark tossing up ribbons of tune into the air. Once she made Plain Kate's hair stand on end, singing the song Linay had been singing by the docks, long ago but only yesterday, a sad tune about ghosts in the river.

The rain drizzled down. Plain Kate got soaked and began to ache: She was strong, but walking was unfamiliar work. The straps of her pack basket rasped her thin shoulders. Taggle spent the day asleep inside the basket, just between her shoulder blades. His warmth made her hurt less.

Finally they stopped, deep in the summer evening.

Through the day the country had thinned into a strip of fields between the river and the heavy, wooded darkness of the hills. And now there was nothing but woods and water.

They stopped in a patch of meadow, sending deer leaping into the woods and rabbits scampering. There was a scrambling between Kate's shoulder blades, and, a moment later, a cat on her shoulder. "Rra —" he started, and Kate was sure he was going to say "rabbits," but he stopped, peered at Daj watching them, and said, "Meow."

"Now that," said the old woman, "is a soft way to travel. Hello, king of cats."

Taggle preened and leapt down, heading over to twine around Daj's ankles.

The Roamers set camp in two rings and built two big fires. Plain Kate and Drina were sent to fetch water, then again to find fallen branches for the fire. When they came back the horses were picketed and the chickens were loose, the rugs laid, the pots bubbling. Trestle benches had appeared. Plain Kate sank onto one of them and pulled off her damp socks. Her feet were wrinkled with wet and had a dozen dead white blisters big as thumbprints.

"Goose grease," said Daj. She was squatting by the fire, stirring a sliced onion around in a pan. "Tomorrow I'll get you some grease for your boots, to keep the water out. Silly not to think of it before." She gave the pot of goulash a poke and stood up, creaking. "Tonight we will go to the men's fire. Let me present you to Rye Baro."

Plain Kate was startled by *present*. People got presented to the mayor or the guild masters or the lord executioner. "Who is Rye Baro?" she said.

"*Baro* means big man, and Rye is our *Baro*: the leader of these *vardo* — wagons, that is. If you go our way, you're his to judge, his to keep or turn loose."

Kate stood up and squared her thin shoulders. "Will he turn me loose?"

"Oh, no," laughed Daj. "He'll not say no to me."

Kate thought she didn't sound entirely sure.

"Sit and let me see those feet, kit," rumbled Daj. Kate sat. Daj lifted her feet in her hands. "You can't go among the men bleeding," she said, and Kate saw that, indeed, her heel was blistered deep and seeping blood. It didn't hurt much more than any other part of her feet, and she hadn't noticed. But Daj was wrapping it with a scrap of green scarf.

Kate was embarrassed. "It's not bothering me."

Daj shook her head. "Among the Roamers blood is

powerful," she said. "A woman's blood specially. Some women can work great magics while in their blood — scares the menfolk down to their socks, knowing that. When we get our monthly blood, they make us sit where they can keep an eye on us."

"I'm not, though," said Kate. "I can't do magic. I'm not a witch."

"And I'm not a muskrat," said Daj. "But neither one of us will walk about bleeding. I'll explain our ways, town child, when I think of it, but whether you understand them or not, you must respect."

"I —" Plain Kate began, but Daj silenced her with a finger on her cheek. Kate found herself fixed on the texture of Daj's hands: so calloused and worn with work that they were glossy-smooth, like the inside of an ox yoke or the edge of an oarlock. Smooth as dry dust. Her father's hands had been a little like that. Such hands had not touched her in a long time. Daj tucked Kate's frizzing hair behind her ears. "Come with me now, *mira*. I'd say be brave, but that I can see you are."

Daj led the way from one fire to another, and Kate followed her, feeling the soaked, loamy earth give like soft bread beneath her feet, feeling the bandage on her heel grow loose with wet. She was trying to take in the labyrinth of rules Daj was telling her: Don't pass between a man and a fire. Don't walk between two men who are facing each other. Ask permission to speak. If you walk near a man, gather up your skirt so that it does not brush him.

"I don't have a skirt," said Kate. She was wearing, as always, the striped smock that had been her father's. It skimmed her knees, but it was no dress. Among the bright layered scarves of the Roamers, the russet and indigo stripes seemed drab.

"Ah, so you don't," said Daj. "Well, don't mind it, child. For here we are." And Kate followed Mother Daj into the circle of firelight as silently and solemnly as if into a church.

There were only a few men about; Plain Kate could hear them farther off, moving among the horses. But to her surprise, Behjet was sitting on a stone near the fire, whittling. He looked up at her, cold and blank, as if he didn't know her at all. Could this be courtesy? It was like a door slammed in the face.

Daj led her to where an old man sat on a carved and painted bench. His face was grooved like a winter road. A cane rested at each knee; his feet were almost in the fire. Daj curtsied to him, not elaborately, but the way a sandpiper might dip its beak, natural and fast, without reverence. "If a woman might pass among you and speak," said Daj. And then, without waiting for an answer, she said: "Rye Baro. I have brought a guest. This is Plain Kate Carver, of Samilae. She would go the Roamer way."

Rye Baro had eyebrows like caterpillars before a long winter. He raised one. "With these *vardo*?"

"Aye," said Daj. "She's orphan, I'm told, and has nowhere else."

Behind them, someone said, "Are we a pack of dogs, then, taking in strays?" Plain Kate turned. The man had Behjet's face, but the whole way he held himself was different. He sat hunched up like a drawn bow.

"Are we dogs, then, talking piss at the fire?" Daj clouted the man on the head affectionately. "Show manners, Stivo."

The man — Stivo — shrugged. Twins, Plain Kate realized. Behjet and Stivo were the twins she had seen selling horses in the Samilae market, a few weeks before.

"Well, it wouldn't be manners to set her loose in wild country, would it?" said Rye Baro. He had a voice like a fine rasp: rough but polishing. "Makes a man wonder how she got into wild country with the Roamers in the first place."

"Hmmm," said Daj with a wink in her voice. "That is a puzzle."

No one seemed puzzled or much surprised. "Behjet says her people want to burn her for a witch," said Stivo.

"Aye," said Daj. "He said that to me too."

The whole circle turned to Stivo, and waited. He poked at the fire, sending sparks spiraling up into the rainy darkness. The fire hissed. Stivo said nothing. A log snapped and crackled. And still Stivo said nothing.

At last Daj spoke again. "Plain Kate is a carver," she said. "We need one of those."

"We get by well enough, seems to me," Rye Baro mused.

"If the yellow *vardo* goes another week before the tongue snaps, it will be by the Black Lady's mercy," said Daj. "But I was thinking: She can make real coins to clink together."

"Do they carve those now?" Firelight played across Rye Baro's face. "I hadn't heard."

"She makes objarka." Daj wrapped an arm around Plain Kate like a wing around a chick. "Best I've seen. They'll sell, and for silver too, not copper."

"In the market of Toila?" said Rye Baro.

Daj nodded. "That was my mind."

"Come here, *gadje* child," said Rye Baro. Plain Kate stepped toward him, and — guided by Daj's hand on her shoulder — knelt. The old man pointed to her objarka, and Kate took it off and offered it up to him. He took it, and as Daj had done, studied it in silence. Kate stayed kneeling, her leggings wicking water up from the wet ground, her cheek and ear getting hot where they faced the fire. At last, Rye Baro looked down at her. "The matter of witch burning is not our affair," he said. "It is your trouble and you must not bring it upon us. But your work is fine. Stand up."

Plain Kate stood up.

"This is your duty, then, child," said Rye Baro. "To earn a place by your skill, and coins for your clan." Plain Kate took a step back, staggered by the weight of the words *your clan*. She almost didn't hear Rye Baro add: "Have your objarka ready for Toila. And make them burji. Times are bad."

Burji. While objarka drew good luck, objarka burji scared bad luck away. They had the faces of demons.

Plain Kate had no interest in ugly things, but she answered, "Yes, Rye Baro."

And back at her own fire she lifted her face into the kiss of the rain.

Only much later did she remember what Behjet had said: *My brother's wife was burned for a witch.* And she wondered what Stivo had been seeing in that fire.

The Roamer *vardo* went on through wild country. The road looped along the river, and where the banks grew too marshy, back into the woods. There were riders or carters, but only occasionally. In the woods, only fingers of chimney smoke going up into the gray sky told them of other people. On the river, sometimes they saw a boat or one of the small painted barges that made Plain Kate think of Linay, standing and watching her catch the enchanted fish. There was a green one that made her head turn sharply whenever she saw it — but it was always trailing them, and never came near.

Plain Kate greased her boots and bandaged her feet, and soon she could walk like a Roamer born. She helped Drina with the water and the wood, and in the long, wet evenings she carved the objarka burji.

Plain Kate carved fast and learned slowly. She learned to ride a horse, or at least hold on to a horse. She learned to cook goulash: a spicy stew of peppers and whatever meat could be scrounged. She learned to snag a chicken with the flick of a crook. She learned the Roamer language and the ways, which were many and complicated. She learned, for instance, how each camp must have a stream, and each stream must have four buckets, and each bucket was used for something different: the first for drinking and cooking, the second for washing, the third for the animals, the fourth for the latrine. But a woman bleeding must use the fourth bucket even to wash.

She was bewildered much of the time, but Daj called her *mira* again, and when she asked Drina what it meant, the girl replied, "It means she likes you. It means you're family."

Family. It could have kept her walking for a hundred miles. And she did walk far. The country grew rougher and quieter, with deer browsing in the middle of the road. The rain kept falling. The *vardo* wheels grew thick with mud, and at night socks were propped up on sticks at the fire like toasting sausages. It was miserable, but secretly Plain Kate was glad. She didn't have to look at her shadow.

Every once in a while, when the rain broke into gusts of drizzle and sun, she saw it: what was left of her shadow. It moved in ways she did not. It stood in the air where no shadow could stand. It was too long and too thin, and it pointed, sometimes, in the wrong direction. She was losing it, and she was not sure what would happen when it was gone.

Plain Kate lay next to Drina at night, with Taggle in the crook of one arm. She closed her eyes and the *vardo* seemed to spin. She set her back against Drina's warm back, and pulled Taggle closer to her, and listened to Daj snore. Often she dreamt she had two wings, and one was frightened, and one was happy.

All the time they drew closer to Toila, where the Roamers would decide whether to keep her or abandon her. It depended on her carving.

Plain Kate obeyed Rye Baro and made her objarka as burji as she could stand, ugly enough to scare off even a return of the *skara rok*. She made a man with a pig snout, a bat-faced thing with comically hinged ears, a face that was nothing but teeth. She made the screaming face of the woman she'd glimpsed burning in the witch fire. She made the impossible face she saw sometimes in dreams, a blankness with eyes of hair. They would sell, she thought. Surely they would sell.

Taggle, meanwhile, made himself popular, killing rats and bringing a rabbit into camp every evening, preening in the praise — silently, thank God, though at night he recounted choice bits to Kate: "Rye Baro says I am a princeling; he split the leg bone for me so that I could eat the marrow. They love me. And I'm sure they'll keep you too."

Mira, she thought, and treasured it each time she heard it. *They must keep me. Family.*

The *vardo* inched down the road, deep in the wild country. Plain Kate had always known that Samilae was a little town, a long way from anywhere. But she hadn't known what it would be like to walk for weeks and see no one, to follow a road through a wood that seemed as large as the story of the sea. Inside its dripping tunnel of branches, the road was sloppy, and her boots had to be greased every night against rot. She oiled her tools too, but rust still dappled them.

At night the fog was thick and full of lights, and sometimes voices.

One night the river fog came up so thick that the *vardo* seemed like islands in it, like boats. Plain Kate sat on the steps of the red *vardo* where she slept with Drina and Daj, carving with Taggle curled over her toes.

The fog was so thick that she couldn't see the ground. It billowed, and when Drina came walking up, it rippled in her wake. Drina swung up beside Kate and settled in. Taggle cracked an eye open, stood, stretched as if for a long journey, then took the two steps over to Drina's feet and flopped down over them instead.

"Faithless," Kate scolded, nudging him with her toe. He leaned his cheek on her foot and rubbed her toe with the corner of his mouth, purring.

Drina reached down and scratched Taggle between his ears. "I wish I had a cat. Before my mother died I had a raven."

As Drina said it, Kate suddenly remembered seeing it. She had been whittling a top at her father's feet. The wood she was working had been light birch; it had been that week in springtime when winged maple seeds stuck up between the cobbles; she had been watching Roamers put on a show for coin. How many years ago had that been? She had been careless and cat-less and happy. The show had lifted her spirits: a man playing a fiddle, another man juggling, and a girl — a little younger than Kate — who had a raven on her shoulder, and tumbled.

"I saw!" Plain Kate said to Drina. "You and the raven. And —" Yes, she remembered now: Her father had broken two fingers when a chisel slipped, and Kate had thought it was the end of the world. One of the Roamers was a young woman, who had sad eyes but a quick smile. She re-broke the fingers and set them, singing all the time, a strange, liquid tune.

"That's worth true silver," her father said, wincing and

holding his hand up, sweat beading on his face like resin coming out of pine when it is very hot. "You sang the pain right under."

The woman laughed. "And that's why you're more pale than me, I suppose." Kate remembered that she had been a witch-white, like Linay: her hair and skin the color of sunned linen. Before she began her work she'd plaited two rings for Piotr Carver, strange braided things of weeping willow and her own white hair. "I'll take copper," the woman said, "and thank you to spread no tales."

The woman called the girl to her and the raven came flying — and that was the end of Kate's memory.

"I saw you," Kate told Drina. "You came to Samilae before my father died, before the *skara rok*. You had a raven, and you tumbled for coin."

"I went everywhere." Drina leaned forward. Taggle half rolled over and allowed her to rub the wishbone hollow under his chin. "I went everywhere with my mother's clan. We tumbled, and sang, and told the bones and the stars." She leaned farther forward, touching noses with the cat. "When my mother died, my father took me and came here. This is his clan." Her hair swung around her and Kate couldn't see her face. "No one asked me."

"There was a woman," said Kate hesitantly, caught by the memory but cautious. "A healer woman, a witch-white . . ."

Drina's head flicked up, her loose hair flying. "That was my mother! You knew her?"

"I —" Kate began, but just then Taggle, who was no longer getting petted, rumbled, "Oh, please, don't stop."

six

SECRETS AND ROSES

Drina leapt to her feet. Her skirts swirled and tangled and she stumbled and tumbled to the ground. Fog billowed up around her. "Did he —" she gasped. "Did the cat — ?"

"Did he what?" the cat drawled.

"Talk," gulped Drina.

"Drina . . ." Plain Kate shivered and her skin burned. She was ready to beg but not sure what to beg for, or how to begin. "Drina, if you tell — if people find out —"

"They'll kill you." Drina looked white-eyed as a frightened rabbit, ready to bolt.

It was so quiet for a moment that Plain Kate could hear the flame in the lantern behind her beating its wings. "You know," said Taggle, "you were just reaching that itchy spot over the jaw."

"Taggle," hissed Kate. Then suddenly words came spilling out of her. "Drina, *mira* Drina, please, I'm not a witch, there was a man, and he was a witch, he made me give him my shadow — he's the one who made Taggle talk."

"You're under a curse," said Drina. "He cursed you."

Plain Kate hadn't thought of it that way, but she nodded. Her throat had almost closed and her skull felt as if it might break through her skin.

"I'll —" Drina's voice broke; she swallowed. "I'll help you break it."

Plain Kate stared at her. "You will?"

"My mother —" Drina looked down at her hands, rubbing her thumb against the place on the step corner where the red paint had worn away. "My mother was a witch. I have her power, I think, and I was learning when she — she was going to teach me. But they killed her."

"They —" said Kate.

"In this city, Lov. It was in the *skara rok*, the witch's fever. They were burning witches. They found out she had power and —"

Kate remembered thinking that she knew more about witch-hunting than Drina did. She had been wrong. "They burned her," she said, so that Drina didn't have to.

"Yes. No." Drina sat down and Kate could feel the trembling that came off of her, like water fluttering in a breeze. "They took her. They hurt her until she told them — I don't know. That she had brought the fever, I think. And then they — they burned her. They tried to burn her. But she had power, real power. She broke free and she ran. She was burning. She threw herself into the river and she drowned."

"Drina . . ." said Kate, but could not go on.

"So I'll help you," Drina said. "I have power and I want to help you."

Kate closed her eyes. "Help me," she said.

Late, in the warm darkness of the *vardo*, Drina and Plain Kate lay whispering. The rain tapped on the canvas roof, and Daj snored a few feet away. Taggle was stretched out between the girls, belly up, one ear under each chin, rumbling in bliss. Plain Kate told Drina about the swarm of fish, the stink of the smokehouse, the axe in the dark. About why she had traded her shadow for a handful of fishhooks.

About the man who had done it, who had pulled her shadow from her like the shell from a shrimp, she said little. In that country, people said that if you spoke of demons, demons came. Linay. Kate didn't want to say his name.

"Your shadow," whispered Drina. "But — I've seen you. I know it's always raining, but — I've seen you. Are you sure you've lost your shadow?"

"He said it would be slow." Saying it that way made it sound awful, like a slow death. She tried to back away from that. "I'm sure, anyway. I can feel it . . . like a sack with a hole in it. Spilling."

"Bleeding?" offered Taggle. "Like when you bite something small around the belly. They leak."

Kate did not feel much helped by this expert observation. "What will happen to me, Drina? Did your mother teach you — ?"

Drina was silent a while. Then she said, "When my mother died — after she died, my uncle —" Behind them, Daj snorted and shifted in her sleep. The two girls tensed, then eased as the snoring started again. Drina continued, her voice the softest of whispers.

"My uncle was a witch too. They were twins, my mother and he, and they were always together; it was like they had one heart between them. I remember, we were camped outside the walls of Lov, by the river. When my mother died, I mean. And he found her, her body, floating there against the water gate. All — all burnt and hurt, he said. They wouldn't let me see her.

"My father screamed and screamed. But my uncle got so quiet. There's something wrong, he said, he kept saying, something is wrong with her. And my father hit him. He said of course there's something wrong, she's dead! But my uncle — he didn't want her buried. And when we did bury her, he lay flat on her grave and he wouldn't eat and he wouldn't talk.

"And finally he said — she's not here. She's not resting, she's not here. Father threatened to kill him if he didn't shut up, but he wouldn't. He said: Don't bother, I'm going to kill myself. And he was a witch, you know, so it was true. Everything he said was true, one way or another."

"And — did he?" asked Plain Kate. "Did he kill himself?"

"No. He took his shadow — that's why I'm telling you this. He made a rope out of his own hair — he cut it all off and made it into a rope. And he soaked it in blood, his blood. And he waited until morning and he made a noose out of that rope, and he threw it down on top of his shadow, on top of the shadow's heart. And — I saw this, it was real — the shadow got a hole in it, like he had a hole right through him and the sun was shining through. This little piece of shadow came loose, got solid, like a bird. And he picked it up and held it in his hand.

"And then he called her, my mother. He used her name. That was — we never speak the names of the dead. But he called her and he said: 'Come and tell me where you are!'"

Drina's breath, as she echoed her uncle's cry, stirred Kate's hair. Daj shifted again, and both girls froze in silence, listening, as if it had been them who had just summoned the dead.

"She was in the shadowless country," said Plain Kate. "The land of the dead."

"But she — something — something came."

A gust of wind blew branches against the *vardo*; they scraped like fingernails. Even the cat was silent now.

"He put the shadow on her tongue," said Drina. "And she spoke. I didn't hear. He wouldn't tell me what she said."

There was a long pause. The canvas roof of the *vardo* shone faint as the dark of the moon, and that was the only light. "My uncle summoned my mother's spirit with just a piece of his own shadow," said Drina. "A shadow gives a ghost life, I think. Power. With a whole shadow — I think a strong witch could raise the dead."

"That must be why . . ." Kate trailed off.

"Why your shadow was taken. But what it means to be without a shadow . . . I do not know."

The two girls whispered together deep into the night, slept close together with Taggle between them, then got up and stirred the fires, caught the chickens, and hauled the water. And from that day on they walked side by side.

Plain Kate tried to learn the rules of magic, which were stranger and harder than the rules of living among the Roamers. In truth Drina was not a good teacher. She only half knew things herself, and remembering tore her between the joy of her mother's memory and the fear of her mother's fate.

So Kate learned only a little. *Magic is an exchange of gifts*: That was the first rule. Thus, Drina's nameless uncle had given up a piece of his shadow to give speech to the dead. And thus, Linay had had to make payment in magic for Kate's shadow. Thus, the talking cat.

"A bargain," said the cat, "at any price."

All great magic requires a great gift. But even small magics asked something, Drina said. And so a witch would put little parts of herself into a spell — hair, say, or tears.

"Blood," said Taggle. "It's always blood."

Plain Kate narrowed her eyes at him. "What do you know about magic?"

"I," he intoned, wrapping his tail over his paws and sitting up regally, "am a talking cat."

"He's right," said Drina. "Blood's the most powerful. Blood and breath. You shape the magic with breath — you sing it. That is why witches can't lie, my mother said. Power flows along your words. Lying turns that power against you. It's a real thing. It can kill you."

"So your uncle . . ." A question had been growing in Kate's mind for days, growing as her shadow thinned and twisted. "Did he die? He said he'd kill himself. Did he die, without his shadow?"

"He —" Drina paused. "He went mad. Eventually — the clan spoke death to him. They cast him out. He went alone."

"But what happened to him?"

"You don't understand," said Drina. "We spoke death to him. He died to us. His name was closed. He went alone."

It was a Roamer thing, but Plain Kate understood it better than Drina thought. Toila was coming. In Toila they would test her, and after that she might well be cast out. When they stopped next, Taggle snuggled his head up under her chin and purred while she clung to him. "Not alone," he rumbled. "Not alone."

The *vardo* inched on, farther into the wild country. One evening they camped near a charcoal burner's hut, deep in the woods. It was abandoned: The woodpiles were covered with bird droppings, the black doorway drifted with last year's leaves. Plain Kate didn't like the place, but it did mean she and Drina had little work to do — there was a well for water, and wood for burning.

Kate was almost out of cured wood for carving. She rummaged through the woodpile until her arms were smeared with black rot and her face was sticky with spiderwebs. She did not hear Drina behind her. When her shoulder was touched she jumped and knocked her head hard on a branch that stuck out from the pile. She sat down, feeling sick. Taggle sprang down and pressed his nose to hers as she leaned over and tried to get her breath.

"I'm sorry!" Drina crouched over her. "Are you hurt?"

Taggle's amber eyes shone inches from her face. "Would you like me to claw her for you?"

Kate put a hand to her head; her hair was damp, but with rain, not blood: There was no warmth. "Not hurt," she said. She fuzzled the cat between the ears. "No clawing."

"I only wanted to say — let me braid your hair." The way she said it made it sound like something dangerous. It took Plain Kate a few moments to remember the story Drina had told about her uncle carving out the heart of his own shadow: *He made a rope of his hair and soaked it in blood.* . . .

Plain Kate felt her throat tighten. "Are you sure?"

Drina took a moment in answering. She sat down beside Plain Kate in the wet moss. "I saw you, *mira*. Yesterday, when the sun broke over the river for a moment. Your shadow — it was like a river flowing away from you. Too long. Thin like a needle. And it pointed toward the river. *Toward* the sun."

Oak and beech trees brooded over them, muttering in the rain. Plain Kate looked down at her knotted hands. They looked strange: The space inside her fingers held no shadow, only more washed-out gray air. It was as if they were not real.

"We must do something," said Drina, "and it must be soon."

Plain Kate turned to look at Drina, and then beyond her, to where the charcoal-burning sheds stood like hives of shadow. "Thank you," she murmured. "Even if we can't — thank you."

"Now! None of that!" Drina stood up, shaking her skirts clean and suddenly sounding like Daj. "You're not going to die, you know!"

So Plain Kate got up, and followed Drina into the red *vardo*, where the younger girl perched on the bunk and brushed Kate's hair, and then plaited it. She was singing as she did it, something tuneless, her breath warm on Kate's scalp. Kate promised herself that no matter what happened, she wouldn't forget this: having her snarly hair brushed slowly smooth, feeling the warm fingers on her scalp and then the shifts and tugs as Drina made up the braid.

Taggle, all the while, insisted he should be next when it came to fussing over fur.

When they were done, Plain Kate had a small braid, the width of a finger, dangling over each ear. Drina tucked them up on the crown of her head and covered them with one of her own scarves: a bright bit of blue rag with a pattern of stars. She arranged it over the tips of Kate's ears and tied it at the nape of her neck. "There. Now you look like a Roamer."

"Not especially," said Taggle.

They both ignored him.

"Let it dry there," said Drina. "Keep it covered. Don't let my father see."

Then she turned to chase the cat with the comb, threatening to braid his tail. The pair of them romped off, leaving Kate standing very still under the rain-hissing canvas. She could feel her shadow lifting and twisting away.

When they were breaking the morning camp, Plain Kate went to Daj to explain that she was out of wood.

Daj looked around at the trees, the charcoal burner's woodpile. She said nothing, eloquently.

Kate winced. "Cured wood, I mean. Green wood — living wood — shrinks when it dries. If you carve green wood your work will crack."

So Daj rumbled and bumbled, and took Kate off to the men's fire, where she found Stivo hunched up over tea while the other men oiled harnesses and tack. She dragged him up by the ear.

"Take this little one into the forest," she ordered. "She needs wood."

Stivo looked around. "She's knee-deep in wood."

"Different wood," said Daj. "Show manners and mind your mother."

So Stivo got up, hoisted the camp hatchet, and slouched off, leaving Kate trotting after him.

"You don't need to come," she said, once they were away from the others. "I've looked after myself a long time."

"You go the Roamer way," he answered. "We do not go alone."

"And there are wolves," piped Drina, appearing with a pail half full of blackberries.

"Aye, a few." Stivo swung the hatchet idly, the way Drina swung her pail. "And so you'll stay in the camp, *cheya*."

"Plain Kate is going."

"She needs the wood," Stivo said. "For some reason the wood we have is not good enough."

Plain Kate thought of explaining, but stayed silent.

"Daj said I could go," said Drina.

"And I say you can't, daughter. Be off."

Drina slinked to a stop. Plain Kate hung back with her and Stivo strode on toward the woods, still swinging his axe. "*Stivo* is your father?" She had never had anything but gentleness from her own father, and found the idea of Stivo being a father unimaginable.

Drina shrugged. "Daj looks after me." But of course it was true. Behjet had told her that Stivo's wife had been burned as a witch — Stivo's wife and Drina's mother were the same person. And that made Stivo Drina's father. And Daj her . . . grandmother? Once again Plain Kate gave up on trying to sort out who among the Roamers was related to whom. It did not seem important to them. They were all family, *mira*, clan.

Stivo, ahead, had turned. "Come along, *gadje*!"

A family she was not part of. At least not in Stivo's eyes. Plain Kate gave Drina's arm a quick squeeze, then hurried after Stivo and his axe.

Around the abandoned hut, the wood was thick. Blackberry brambles hid under the skirts of the trees, growing across a forgotten wall of loose stones. Stivo was sitting on a big rock, eating blackberries.

Plain Kate looked around. "It's a bit drier, anyway,"

she offered. The thick trees were keeping off some of the drizzle.

"This rain's a curse. The horses are all chewing their feet and stinking with the thrush. Go through the whole herd, if this wet won't stop."

"I'm sorry."

"Not your fault, is it. Unless you can work the weather." Stivo got up. "Off with you then. Find your different wood."

It was dark beneath the big trees, and the brambles gave way fast to ferns. Plain Kate moved into them slowly. They rubbed around her waist, dripping and rustling. She heard something big moving behind her and shot a look over her shoulder. Stivo was following her, though not close. They went on without speaking.

Finally she found the right tree. A toppled walnut. Bolt struck, half-scorched, a year dead. It would be dense-grained and dry; it would take a knife. "This one," she said. As she said it the drizzle broke again, and suddenly the fallen tree was struck by a finger of light. Plain Kate was startled for a moment, then saw that of course the tree's fall had left a hole in the forest's ceiling, just enough for the light to slant through. It struck her too, and for a moment she could see how what was left of her shadow spun around her like ripples of water.

She stepped back out of the light and nearly knocked into Stivo. "I've noticed," he said, and her heart lurched. "I've noticed you spend a good deal of time with my daughter."

Plain Kate said nothing.

"I can smell the trouble on you, Plain Kate," he said, swinging the axe. "See that you do not bring it on my Drina. She is all I have left. Do you hear that? I will not see her lost because of some little girl they call 'witch.'"

She turned to face him. "I'm not a little girl. I am Plain Kate Carver. I have lived by my own wits for many years. I am better than any apprentice, and good as many a master. And I am not a witch."

Then she stopped. She was very aware of the blue star cloth tied at the nape of her neck, and the complex braids underneath. *Don't let my father see*, Drina had said. These were the eyes she'd been afraid of. "I am not a witch," she said, trying to sound sure.

"You had best not be," he answered. And he threw the axe, past her ear. It struck neat and deep into the split heart of the tree.

The Roamers kept walking and Plain Kate kept carving. The wild country sloped down and the trees thinned out.

The Roamers' *vardo* came back out into the river valley, where Daj said they were less than a week from Toila. The rolling hills were crested with trees, but the valleys cradled scattered farms. It was strange to see buildings after so long, and Plain Kate felt uneasy. There were so many who might see her sickly shadow.

The braids Drina had put in her hair tugged at her scalp. She could feel the river pulling at her shadow, or her shadow pulling her toward the river. It felt like waking from a nightmare and drifting to sleep again, knowing it is still there, waiting, just under sleep's thin surface — something grasping and hungry.

So she slept thinly, drowsing over her knife and making strange things while half awake. She was doing that in the twilight, leaning against a stump in someone's fallow field, when she came to herself and found Drina by her side.

"I don't want your help," Plain Kate blurted.

Drina reacted as if struck, jerking back. Plain Kate, still waking, reached after her. "No, wait, Drina — I only mean . . ." She put down her knife and scrubbed at her eyes. "Your father said —"

"My father —" Drina began, fiercely, angrily — but just then Ciri came toddling up to them. He was the young prince of the Roamers, a boy of two, the favorite of the dozen naked and cheerful children who chased chickens and snuck rides on horses in Roamers' camps. Just now he had Taggle in a headlock.

"Help," croaked the cat.

Drina shed her anger and pulled boy and cat into her lap. "Ciri, Ciri," she said, and dropped into the Roamer language, a liquid coaxing in which Plain Kate caught only the word *cat*. Ciri unfolded his elbows, and Taggle spilled out, bug-eyed.

Plain Kate picked him up and scratched his ruff. "Thank you for not killing him." By this time she knew how to flatter a cat: praise of ferocity and civility both.

Taggle preened. "He's a kitten." He arranged his dignity around him with a few carefully placed licks. "Else I would have laid such a crosshatch of scratches on him he'd have scales like a fish."

"Cat!" burbled Ciri, reaching.

Taggle allowed himself to be patted roughly and then grabbed by the ear, but flicked Ciri a yellow look. "I do have my limits."

"Talk!" chirped Ciri. "Cat talk cat."

Kate glanced at Drina, who answered, "It will be just a story. He's always telling stories. Don't worry, Plain Kate." She staggered up with Ciri in her arms. "A few more days, Plain Kate. There's a place near Toila where we always stop. We'll have our own tent there. Darkness and quiet." She swung the little boy up pig-a-back. "Come, *mira*, let's find your *dajena*." She looked round at Kate one more time. "Don't be frightened."

But Kate was frightened. *All great magic requires a great gift. . . . He made a rope of hair and soaked it in his own blood. . . .* And what Linay had said: *Blood draws things. It would be foolish to draw your own shadow to you.*

"Blood," she said.

"Sausages, I think," said Taggle, sniffing. "Get me one, would you?" But he climbed into Kate's lap and let her bury her nose in his soft fur and wiry muscle.

A few days shy of Toila, the hills spread into a broad lowland. Oak and fir gave way to willow and alder, and then to fields and gardens. Under the glares of the farmers and herders, the Roamers went carefully, the five *vardo* staying in a line like beads on a string. But the next day the mood grew merrier. "We will stop tonight with Pan Oksar," Drina explained. "He's *gadje*, but a friend to us. He keeps horses." She was almost skipping. "We'll stay with him."

There's a place near Toila where we always stop, Drina had said. This would be that place. A spell of blood and hair. "How long —" Plain Kate began.

"Long enough to let the mud set on the wheels," said Daj, from the back step of the creaking, lumbering *vardo*. "A week or so, and then it's a few more days to Toila."

"Can we —" Drina began, but Daj cut her off.

"Yes, *mira*, you two can share a bender tent, if you like."

Drina's face lit up. She gave Kate's arm a quick squeeze, and the blue star scarf that hid the spell-braids a significant glance. But then two little boys herding geese started to jeer the Roamers and toss rocks at the horses, and in the hubbub the two girls got pulled apart. They had no chance to speak before reaching the red-painted gates of Pan Oksar's farm.

To Kate, Pan Oksar's farm seemed impossibly prosperous, almost a small town. There were separate houses for animals and people, an orchard and a garden, a house just for the hens. Through the green spaces wandered horses. Round everything was a hedge of red roses tall as a building, thick as a city wall. The Roamers came through the gate singing, and the people of the household all tumbled out to meet them.

They spoke a language Kate did not know, and their dress was strange to her. "No one likes them, because their ways are different," Drina explained. "Just like the Roamers — no one likes us either. So we have to like each other."

The Roamers stopped the *vardo* just inside the hedge, with arching roses brushing the canvas roofs. And, for the first time since Plain Kate had joined them, they started pitching tents: one per married couple, one for the bachelor Behjet and the widowed Stivo, one for Daj and the smallest children — and one for the "maidens," as Behjet called them: Drina and Kate.

"What of me?" groused Daj's husband, Wen. "I don't want to sleep with all these squirming puppies!" Plain Kate remembered seeing Daj and Wen hold hands and kiss in the shadows between the men's fire and the women's, and guessed the true source of his disappointment. He was still casting glances at Daj when Behjet and Stivo took him in.

Plain Kate was not much impressed with bender tents. They were made with just a few willow saplings stripped into poles, then bent and thrust into the ground at both ends. A sheet of canvas went round the poles, and some rope secured the whole thing — though not very well. They were muggy and mud-floored. Plain Kate, who had slept for years in a drawer, would have preferred to sleep in the *vardo*. But Drina spread her arms to touch both walls, as if she'd been given a palace.

"With my mother's people, I stayed in the maidens' tent. But here there are no other maidens — everyone's married.

So they made me mind the little ones." She set about stacking a small fire in the middle of the space. "I am glad you've come, Plain Kate."

Kate found her throat tightening. She wanted to answer — *I am glad too* — but it suddenly seemed an impossibly hard thing to say. "Is this the place?" she asked. "To do the spell?"

Drina sobered — mostly. A delighted smile was still teasing around the edges of her face, like tendrils of hair curling out from under a scarf. "While we have walls, yes. So that no one stops us."

The way she said it made Kate wonder if perhaps someone should.

But of course no one did. They had stopped, Plain Kate learned, to breed the horses, a project that required both laughter and serious talk, and took everyone's attention. There was human business too: trading of news and goods, songs and stories. Pan Oksar's farm was a bustling, happy place, even in the mud and endless rain. So it was that when Drina lit the fire in the center of their tent, turning the walls golden and the little space cozy with flickering light, for the first time that Plain Kate could remember, they were quite alone, and likely to stay that way.

Drina leaned forward, nursing the newborn flames with twigs and splinters. Smoke and flares of light swirled across her dark face.

The same light rippled through Kate and she felt herself waver like water. She put a hand in Taggle's warm, solid fur. "So," said the cat. "You're cooking something?"

Plain Kate said nothing. There was an ache around her eyes because she had been holding them wide open. "I saw my mother do this," Drina explained. She seemed embarrassed, tentative. "There was a woman who had lost her memory. My mother bound it back to her with a rope of hair. She bound it with the hair and she called it back with —"

Drina stopped. A silence hung, in which the wet wood popped and sputtered.

"Blood," said Kate.

Drina nodded.

"And fire?" she asked.

"Fire," said Drina. "You gather up the spell slowly, you see," she said, and Kate could hear the ghost of Drina's mother's voice as the Roamer girl repeated something she had not herself thought through. "As a tree gathers the sun. But to loose it all at once — fire is one of the best ways."

"It really seems a pity not to cook something," said Taggle, who saw only one use for fire.

"Later." Plain Kate put a hand on his back. "Drina, are you sure —" she began, but then saw how the quickening fire was throwing Drina's and Taggle's shadows sharply against the wall of the tent. Her own shadow was spread out over the glowing canvas in writhing swirls, thin as smoke at midday. She closed her eyes and felt the light go through her like arrows.

". . . be afraid," Drina was saying, when Kate heard her again. "It's only a few drops."

Plain Kate took a deep breath. "What do we do first?"

"Cut the braids off," said Drina. "Can I use your knife?"

Kate handed her knife over and undid the scarf with the blue stars. She could not help stiffening as Drina came toward her with the knife raised, drawing back as Drina's shadow fell across her face. The braids smarted and tugged at her temples as Drina sawed at them with the knife. Finally they came free: The two cut braids were coiled up in Drina's palm like a pair of young snakes.

"Just let me —" said Drina, leaning toward her again, knife trembling in her hand. Plain Kate winced, but before she even understood what was happening, Drina had cut her on the top of her ear.

Plain Kate gasped and clamped her hand over the little wound. "Sorry, sorry!" Drina tugged Kate's hand away and put her own hand in its place. "But it's one of the best places to get blood — lots from a little wound, and you can cover the scars."

Warm blood trickled behind Kate's ear and down her neck. "It's all right," she said. She could feel the silky ropes of her own cut hair against her skin. When Drina pulled them away, the braids glistened here and there where the blood had wetted them.

Kate fingered the wound. Truly it was only a nick; she could hardly feel it. "Now what?"

Drina was shaking, but she flashed a grin. "Now this." She threw the ropes of hair into the fire.

The stink of burnt hair instantly filled the tent. The silence got tight, like the top of a drum. Taggle's fur rose into a thick ridge down his spine. And then Drina started to sing.

It was a low, mumbling, murmuring song, a song a river might sing. Plain Kate couldn't tell if it didn't have words or if she didn't know the language. It was mournful as an old memory, and it made Kate remember — suddenly and so clearly she could smell it — the moment her father had died. He had called her name, but his eyes were already seeing the shadowless country, and she didn't know — she would never know — if he was calling for her, or her mother.

Drina, singing, leaned across the fire. "Shadow, shadow, shadow . . ." went the song.

The air was thick with smoke. The tears on Plain Kate's cheeks were cold, the rest of her face was scorching. Against the tent wall, shadows whirled — Drina's thin, Taggle's dancing, and a third —

An ugly noise came from deep in Taggle's throat.

Plain Kate watched the third shadow; it pinned her eyes. It was supposed to be her shadow, but it wasn't. It was sinuous and moved like a water snake. She knew in her stomach that this was not a simple shadow, but some cold thing, some damp dead thing that should be resting. And, though their fire was the only light, she thought this shadow was not cast backward from the flame, but was drawing near to it, from outside the tent.

"Thing!" The cat yowled and spat. "Thing!"

"Drina," choked Kate. "Stop."

Drina turned and looked over her shoulder at the thing that had captured Kate's eyes. She froze. The song stopped. The shadow reached.

Then Kate dumped the kettle over the fire.

Steam and smoke flared. Both girls started coughing. And the shadow was gone.

The air in the bender tent still smelled of burnt hair.

Plain Kate was trying to coax the fire up from its pool of ash-mud, and not having much luck. Even twigs would only smolder. She picked up a branch and started carving curled wood shavings, dropping them into the chittering embers, one by one.

Taggle was pacing around the edge of the tent like a lion around the rim of its cage. "A thing," the cat hissed. "It makes me feel hungry and wet. I hate it! Thing!"

"It was not my shadow," said Kate. "It was something else."

"You don't know that," said Drina. Her voice fluttered with fear.

"But I do," said Kate. She could still feel the prickle of the thing's presence in her hair.

Rain fell through the smoke hole and hissed in the embers. The struggling fire went out again. The tent sank back into darkness.

"I —" said Drina. "I didn't think. I'm sorry."

"What didn't you think?"

"That blood —" Drina swallowed. "That blood can call

more than one thing. We — called into the darkness. We don't know what answered."

"Oh," said Kate.

They drew closer together in the dark.

"In Toila," said Drina, after a long time. "In the great market of Toila, there are charm sellers. My mother knew some of them. Some of them are really — some of them have true power. We'll — we can ask one of them, how to call and be sure it's your shadow that answers."

"No," said Kate.

"Plain Kate. We have to try."

"No."

There was a scuffling in the darkness, and after a moment, a buttery glow. Drina had found the tallow lamp in their goods box, and lit it. The little flame danced on its clay spout. Kate watched it a while. Taggle climbed into her lap and smoothed his fur — though she could still feel tiny muscles twitching down his spine.

In the safe, domestic light, the two girls sat together until their breathing evened. It seemed like hours.

"Drina," said Kate. "Drina, it's too dangerous. Even if — I don't want you to be hurt. For me."

Drina sat quietly for a moment, feeding wood curls into the lamp flame and dropping them, burning, into the damp kindling. "Do you remember," she said, "I told you my mother was a healer. And that to work a great magic, you have to give something away? That's why your magician had to give you a wish when he took your shadow."

"Drina," said Plain Kate. "What are you telling me?"

"My mother —" she said. "Don't you see? A healer must give a gift in kind to make a healing. A healer gives away her own life, piece by piece. That's what my mother did. And I want, I want to be like her. I want to help you. No matter what."

Kate watched the wood curls burn and send up their ribbons of smoke, trying to understand. "Tomorrow," said Kate at last. "Tomorrow I will ask to show my objarka to Rye Baro. In Toila we can sell them, and — find someone to ask."

Drina closed her eyes and nodded, little hummingbird-quick twitches of her head.

"But, Drina — I can't keep this secret. Someone will see. Soon, someone will see. It's better to tell before someone sees."

"Just a little longer," Drina pleaded. "After Toila."

Plain Kate nodded. "It will be better to have the silver from Toila. When we have to tell. Silver will — they might keep me anyway, if we have silver."

"Also, I can bring in very large rabbits," said Taggle. "Possibly a small deer."

"That will help," said Kate, and bundled him close, her eyes smarting with what she told herself was the smoke.

Plain Kate had meant to go to the clan the next day, but as it happened she could not. Her monthly woman's blood had come, for the first time. Face burning, she went to Daj to find out what to do.

"Oh ho!" Daj crowed like a rooster, when she understood what had happened. "We Roamers have fattened you up!"

Plain Kate had only ever heard of pigs being fattened up, for slaughter. Some of her confusion must have shown, because Daj added, "Well, you had been hungry, *mira*, when you came to us. Any fool could see it. Hunger brings the blood late. It's hard to come into your power when you're hungry. If you'd had a mother you would know that. And if you were mine, what a cake I'd make you. With berries and honey, and I might, anyway."

Kate's blush was turning from shame to pleasure, but Daj wasn't done talking. "You cannot tell the men, of course. And you must sit apart."

Daj did make the cake. But Kate was frustrated. She could not go to Rye Baro to show her objarka. She could not go to the men's fire at all, or stir the food, or fetch the water. Every time she tried to do something useful she stumbled over some new rule, and she spent long days sitting on a trestle bench, with her carving in her lap. The rose hedge dripped on her. Cream tried to eat her hair.

It was strange not to be walking, and not to be working. Plain Kate felt sullen and stupid — but the horror raised by the thing they had summoned was fading in her.

Drina brightened day by day, and was soon sitting by Plain Kate, making little bundles of feather and twig and blossom, hiding them in the folds of her skirt whenever anyone glanced their way.

"Charms," said Kate. They made her uneasy. Linay had called them foolish, and she had a feeling he might know. And she thought they could draw the wrong kind of eyes. But she did not know how to tell any of that to Drina. She settled for: "What if your father sees?"

"Faw," sniffed Drina, sounding like Taggle when he got a paw wet. "He's with the Oksar men, getting drunk and talking about the rain as if it were the end of the world. There's a sleeping sickness or something. They're all fluttered up like chickens under a hawk."

Drina plucked a red thread free from the fraying poppies embroidered on her skirt. She bit through it, then tied the bundle off with a jerk. "We need these. They will help me find the right person — someone who knows how to call a shadow. We cannot just go into the market asking. These bundles will show my gift, to those who know how to look.

"Besides," she said, "they'll add to your silver."

They stayed three more days with Pan Oksar, and then they struck the tents, harnessed the horses, knocked the mud from their wheels, and went off down the road to Toila. The first night on the road, Plain Kate went with Daj to the men's fire, to present her objarka.

Plain Kate curtsied and knelt, and offered the objarka to Rye Baro with both hands.

He took it with both hands. He raised it up.

Plain Kate had brought only one objarka to show: her best. It was an owl-eyed human face with antlers and a seducer's smile. She stayed kneeling and watched Rye Baro meet the thing's eyes. She could hear her father's voice: *The magic of carving is to tell people the truth.* What was that lush wooden mouth saying?

It was Linay's mouth, she realized abruptly. That was why it frightened her.

Rye Baro's face was impassive. No one else spoke. The inspection stretched and stretched. Daj shifted behind Kate, creaking from knee to knee. "By the Black Lady, Rye," she said. "Don't tease the child!"

Rye Baro laughed. "Well, does she not know she is good? Good!" He handed the carving to Daj. "You've a gift, Kate Carver. Your hands know things."

Daj looked at the carving. "Aye, good does not begin it. It's beautiful, *mira*. In its own horrid way, of course. There's craft in those hands."

"Too much craft," said Stivo, taking the carving. "The *gadje* don't know craft. They won't pay for it. It is good though" — and here he smiled at her, both scorn and peace offering — "little girl."

"Soon we will see what the *gadje* have a mind to pay for," Rye Baro rumbled. "We will press for Toila tomorrow. And there's that riding colt that you broke without craft, Stivo. Xeri, the one who eats. See if you can sell him before we're stuck with the feeding of him for the winter."

"Ah," said Behjet, coming to his brother Stivo's rescue. "Xeri's a good beast at heart. We'll wash him in the river and comb him till he shines. All of Toila will cover their eyes against his brightness."

They fell into talking about the horses, and Plain Kate got up quietly and went back to the red *vardo*, where Taggle was keeping her bedding warm.

And the next day they went to Toila.

seven

TOILA

Toila was bigger than Samilae, and had three markets: the market of the animals, the market of the vegetables, and the market of the steps. Which, Drina explained, did not of course sell steps, but was held on the broad steps of the tithe barn, near the river. "It's a city," she said as if *city* were another word for "wonderful." And she turned a hand-spring, just because she could. Taggle copied her: gray twist and silver flash.

"It's a city," echoed Behjet. "And in a city Roamers must be careful. Remember that, girls. Stay together."

Behjet and Stivo led the dray colt off down a cobbled alleyway, his hoofbeats thudding off the stone walls of the buildings close at either side. Kate had never seen so much stone. She and Drina seemed small in the middle of it.

"This way," said Taggle, and sauntered off with a curl in his tail. "They're selling fish cakes!"

They followed him through little nooks and twists, meeting only narrow-faced saints in niches, guarding nothing. To Kate, so long among the Roamers, the figures she had once carved looked foreign. The girls began to think they were lost. But then the alley turned and spilled through a wooden arch and into the market.

Huge and loud, the market stopped them, gaping. Just in front of them lengths of homespun in russet and ocher and indigo flapped in the wind off the river, tossing little showers of rain, chopping the view into confusing glimpses. Banks of spices. Songbirds screeching in cages. Wheels stacked in a heap. The scorched-metal smell of a smithy, the stink of a tanner. There were stalls and blankets, and barrows and people everywhere. The town's weizi stabbed upward from the center of the market, like one tree left standing in a shattered forest. Scenes of commerce were carved in its sides.

Drina was pressed close to Kate, her confidence gone. Taggle was perched between Drina's feet, with his tail straight in the air and his eyes round and shining.

"Move there!" came a voice from behind. A handcart crashed into Kate's back, crunching into her pack-basket. Plain Kate staggered and the cart spilled tin pitchers and cups clashing across cobbles. The carter glared. "What's this? A country mouse and a Roamer pickpocket? Taking the air, are we, girls? Seeing the sights? Blocking the road, at any rate." Plain Kate had stooped to gather the pitchers, but at this she straightened up. She took Drina's elbow, and they walked off like ladies.

The unpleasant carter had at least helped Drina find her tongue. "The great market of Toila," she said, "is held only thrice a summer. So it can't always be so . . . much." This seemed to comfort her. They threaded their way into the press and the noise, looking for a place to sell Plain Kate's carvings.

The girls settled on a place at the bottom of the broad steps — a prime spot neglected by the other sellers because it had recently been favored by some horse. Drina, a horse-woman in her heart, kicked the knobs of dung away with no trace of disgust. Nearby a fiddler with white hair was playing for coin. Plain Kate's heart jerked, but then the fiddler turned, and she saw his face, and it was not Linay.

"We should have brought a blanket," said Drina, startling Kate free of her focus on the fiddler. "For your charms."

"Objarka, not charms," Kate corrected. "They're not magic. I don't have a blanket, but my sleep roll is in my pack." She hated to put the clean fur down on the dung-smirched cobbles, but she did. She spaced the carved faces evenly, and when that was done, she looked up. There was no gathered crowd, but a few passersby gave glances, pursing mouths and raising eyebrows. That was enough to tell Kate, who had spent her life in a market, that her work would sell.

Plain Kate felt her mouth widen toward a smile, and to hide it she looked down at the horrible faces of the objarka arrayed before her. "It will be all right," she said softly, almost to herself.

"I told you!" Drina grinned and flipped over into a backward handspring. Taggle jumped up and rebounded off her boots. The cat flew, twisting through the air like a ribbon of silver, and landed neatly on his feet. Someone cheered. And they did it again.

Drina paused to spread out a begging scarf and kilt up her skirts, and then she and Taggle danced and flipped, bright as a pair of dragonflies. Drina was far from the only tumbler in the market, but Plain Kate would lay money that Taggle was the only and the best tumbling cat in the world. A crowd gathered. Among them, some stopped to look at the objarka. Plain Kate fell into the easy push-pull of haggling, which was like a two-man saw, and for a little while she was as happy as she had ever been.

When Drina stopped dancing, she was flushed and panting. Taggle preened in her arms. Kopeks lay on the scarf at her feet. "Look!" she said. "And you?"

"Three," Kate told her, and shyly opened her hand, letting Drina see the silver coins her three sales had garnered her.

"I knew it!" Drina beamed. "Luck will be with us here, Plain Kate. You will make your silver and I will find" — she dropped her voice and glanced around — "our answer." Still gleaming with sweat and breathing hard, she untucked her skirts and tied the scarf across her shoulder.

Kate had spent time among the Roamers now, and knew that Drina was too young to wear her scarf across her body. It was a woman's costume, the scarf and the turban. As Drina piled up her hair, she took on a power Kate could only glimpse, and didn't understand. Drina held the scarf edge out to make a pouch. "Give me the little ones; I'll stroll the crowd."

As Plain Kate gathered up some of the smaller objarka, Drina opened her belt pouch and pulled out the charms she had made: bundles of birch twigs and yarrow and herb and feathers, knotted with red thread and white horse hair. Kate looked at them. "Are you sure?"

But Drina was almost laughing with joy. "Luck is with us," she said again. So Plain Kate put the little objarka burji into Drina's sash like peas into an apron, and watched her walk away, up the broad, crowded steps.

Kate watched Drina for a while, dark and vivid among the pale damp people of Toila in their browns and beiges. In her red turban she stood out like a poppy in a wheat field. She was moving with a catlike sway Kate hadn't seen her use before, and she sang as she walked, weaving a spell of wordless notes. Taggle, elegant as a greyhound, shadowed her heels.

Drina was busy. She let young men reach into her apron, and spun them tales about the horrible little burji they drew out. And with older women she exchanged whispers and coins and pointing fingers. She was using the bundles as a passport, looking for the real witch — someone who could teach them how to call into the dark and be sure of what would answer.

But the market was crowded and noisy, and soon Kate lost sight of Drina. Without the tumbling to snare them, the eddy of people around her blanket had dissolved, but still, she had better than her share of interest. Some people merely threw glances at her or her carvings, but some slowed, and some paused, and some stopped a moment, and some stopped.

"I have not seen you here before." The man who loomed

over Plain Kate was bald, but he had long whiskers like a catfish. His dark zupan was covered with little figures cast in pewter: acorns and angels, knots and night creatures. There were hundreds of them. The man jangled faintly in the wet gusts of wind. "Not seen you, eh?" he said.

She shrugged. "I've not been here before."

"Not been," he squawked. "Not been to the famous market? The great market? The great market of Toila?"

"No."

"Not been," he said again, and Kate began to wonder if he was simple or mad. "No, not been. I would have seen you. I would have seen" — he smiled, and suddenly looked horribly sane — "such fine work."

Plain Kate said nothing.

"Bit of a witch-blade, are you, girl?"

"A carver," she said. "I'm a carver."

"Objarka, though." He raised his arms grandly, and the pewter things chittered all over his coat. "I sell objarka."

"Not as good as mine," said Kate. "But don't worry. I won't be back."

"Don't be," he said. And he turned away.

"Hmph," Kate snorted to herself. Taggle was a bad influence.

"He can't keep you from here," said the woman at the next blanket. She was selling round-weave baskets, and had a wickerworker's hands, calloused and tough as roots. "The great market is free to all. And we need better charms than what Stanislaus sells." She cast some sort of fingered curse at the departing back of the catfish man. "Objarka, ha! They're meant to draw luck, but that man couldn't draw bees with honey."

Plain Kate, looking down at the horrible faces of her big objarka, felt herself smile.

"There you are," said the woman. "You can see it yourself, surely. There's no magic in his work." She fingered her ear; the top was notched strangely, just where Drina had cut Kate. Was this a witch? "Pewter," the woman sneered. "You can't draw luck with tin. It needs a blade."

"I'm just a carver," said Kate again.

The woman looked at her appraisingly, her fingers still pinching at her ear. "As you say."

A bit later another man stopped. His zupan's front was bright and stiff with embroidery. He looked a while, then stooped and picked up the pig-snouted face. "Luck! I'm not sure I would enter my own home, if it meant passing this fellow. What do you want for him?" And he gave her eight silver without even bargaining.

"That was the master of the threadneedle guild," whispered the basket maker, when he was gone. "Now you'll sell, wait and see."

And indeed the stream of customers thickened around her, and people of all classes came to see her work, hefting the faces and running fingers over the smoothness of the carving. She sold four of her big objarka and made good silver. But then, suddenly, the crowd scattered, taking flight like a field full of starlings at no cue Kate could see. She found herself looking at a single pair of good boots and the hilt of a sword. She looked up at a man in the dress of the city watch. "We'll have no witchcraft in the market," he said.

"I don't do any."

"And your little friend?" said the watchman. For a moment she thought he meant Taggle, and her stomach lurched. She looked at the basket woman, whose eyes were wide with fear. "The lass with the pretty ways and little bundles," he said. "The Roamer girl."

Plain Kate swallowed and looked straight ahead. This gave her a good view of the watchman's sword, bumping at his hip. "Well?" he prompted.

But she could think of nothing to say.

"Have a word with her," he said more kindly. "They burned a woman here last week."

When he'd gone, Plain Kate tried to catch the basket woman's eyes. But the woman, pale, turned her head away.

Plain Kate sat trembling on her bedroll with her three masks in front of her, and didn't know what to do. She stood up and didn't see Drina anywhere. She looked and looked. Her eyes lit on every flash of red, but none of them was the red turban Drina had been wearing. She tried to shout Drina's name, and her voice caught in her throat.

People were still thick around her blanket, but now the glances were for her and not for her work, and some were hot, and some were cold. Plain Kate looked down at the objarka that had the face of a woman burning. She shifted her weight from foot to foot.

"Go find her," the basket woman said. "Hurry."

So Plain Kate snatched up her sleep roll and stuffed it, objarka and all, into her pack. She swung it up and ran into the center of the market. She found nothing but confusion. Wet cobbles skidded underfoot. Shoulders and elbows jostled her. Heads and handcarts blocked her view.

She scrambled up the steps to the platform from which the weizi rose. She'd been half expecting to see wood for burning stacked around the column, but there wasn't, only the carved figures of the weizi itself: men unloading boats, a little too big to be human, their faces too narrow, their limbs too long. From the weizi platform she could see a little way. Something was happening by one of the alleys. The eddying crowds had begun to flow in that direction. Kate saw the catfish man with the jangling coat heading that way, coaxing a priest along, a hand on the holy man's elbow.

Plain Kate leapt from the platform and fought her way through the dung and puddles. A bridge from house to house made a wooden lip above the mouth of an alley. There was a space of shadows beneath the bridge. In front of it was a wall made of human backs and shouting.

Kate heard a high screaming. The yowl of a cat.

Close by she heard the catfish man saying to the wheezing priest: ". . . the devil's bundles, holy father, with my own eyes . . ."

The devil's bundles, thought Kate. *Drina's charms*. But she could see nothing but the backs of the crowd.

Suddenly Taggle came scrambling over the heads and shoulders of the gathered men. He left a trail of blood and cursing. "Katerina!" he yowled — though in the din only she knew it was him. The cat leapt onto her packbasket, spitting, his hair stiff as a brush. "Katerina! It's —"

"Shut up!" she snapped. Drina's witchcraft charms. Her secret questions. "It's Drina. Is she alive?"

"When I left."

"What's this, then?" said the little priest, but the men were packed so tightly that they didn't — couldn't — turn.

Kate looked at them desperately. "We have to get through."

She could feel Taggle's hot breath on her neck as the cat shifted on her basket, muscles bunching. "Follow me," he said.

And before she could even think of stopping him, Taggle threw himself at the crowd.

His front claws bit into her shoulder as he leapt; his back claws grazed her ear. And then he was scrambling across the heads and shoulders of the packed people. His claws were out and his teeth were gnashing. He was huge with his hair on end, and screaming like a panther. The men — men he had already bloodied — shouted and squealed and hit and pushed against their fellows to get away from him. The wall of bodies cracked open. Plain Kate followed her cat like a soldier following his spear.

Elbows struck her. Feet tangled her. She stumbled and shoved through the hot press and the human stink. Something hard hit her temple. Another blow to her ribs. A stabbing weight on her instep. And then suddenly she was through. Panting, battered, terrified. But through. Into a little space bordered by the crowd, the walls of the alley, and a cart with a hysterical, rearing horse which blocked the way forward.

What she saw —

It was a flash of horror and blood like a moment from a dream. Plain Kate screamed even before Drina did. But screaming did not wake her.

She saw a man holding Drina by the hair. He was pulling her head back, as if to cut her throat. He had a butcher's cleaver. He was butchering Drina's ear, cutting it from the top downward. Blood everywhere. More blood than if he had cut her throat. A sick bright color. A slaughterhouse smell. Drina was screaming, screaming like a gut-speared horse. Kate was shouting. She had her little knife out and she charged at the man. Taggle ran up behind her, leapt up onto her basket, leapt past her, leapt straight at the man with the cleaver. He was gray and magnificent, an angel of vengeance. The butcher dropped Drina and shrank back. Kate caught her friend in one arm and spun around, pressing her against the wall. Drina folded down, ripped with sobs. Kate faced the crowd.

They were just eyes and teeth to her, just spit and voices. It was a moment, even, before they became people: a man with one blind eye, another whose neck was thick with the lumps and weeping wounds of scrofula. The poorest of the market.

At Kate's feet, Drina. Her scarf and shirt were torn open. And someone had chopped off her hair. Her turban was tangled around her throat. Her mouth was smashed full of blood. Blood from her flapping ear soaked half her head.

So much had happened, but no time had passed. The horse was still rearing, the carter struggling to hold him to the ground. Taggle stood between the girls and the crowd, huge and hissing. The attackers had wavered for a moment, but they were coming to themselves again, pressing forward.

The poorest of the market, Kate thought again. And knew what to do.

"Silver!" she shouted, her voice breaking. "Silver to anyone who would let us pass!" Plain Kate could see greed fight with the fearful bloodlust in the faces in front of her. Drina had pulled herself up and clung to Kate's knee. Kate hoisted her up by one armpit, and with the other hand opened her belt purse. Coins glimmered in her fist. It was more money than she'd ever had in her life. The money that was to buy her a place to belong.

"Any money made by magic belongs to the church," came the reedy voice of the priest.

"Take it, then," shouted Kate, and threw the copper and silver over the heads of the crowd. Everyone turned and scrambled. Kate and Drina bolted the other way, squeezing past the hooves of the horse and into the darkness of the alley, with Taggle at their heels, leaving a scattering of small bundles and demon faces lying in the blowing drifts of Drina's dark hair.

Drina sobbed and stumbled and Kate tugged at her. "Run," she panted. "Run!" Taggle flashed ahead. Voices bayed like hounds behind them.

Then someone grabbed Kate by the elbow and jerked her through a doorway. She was blinded by the drop of light. Her rescuer was a dim shape against the light of the door. Then the figure turned, with Drina in her arms. It was the basket woman. "Quietly a moment," she whispered. They all huddled together and listened. The chasers came close, and passed, and faded away.

Kate stepped away and banged her shin against a tub where willow wands were soaking. Half-plaited baskets nudged at her elbows. There was a thick must of herbs. "There," the woman murmured as Drina sobbed quietly. "Don't be frightened. They won't find you. They won't look, really." She gathered up Drina and pressed the corner of her turban against her disfigured, gouting ear.

Taggle was at the door suddenly. "They're gone. I let

them chase me. I led them like a sunbeam and vanished like a shadow."

At the cat's voice, the basket woman drew her breath in with a sound like a sword unsheathing. But she said nothing.

Plain Kate picked up Taggle. "We have to get out of the city."

"Aye," said the basket woman, who was tying the turban tight across Drina's ear. "Get out and don't come back." She fingered the notch in her own ear. "Marked so, little one." Drina clung to her and hid her face from Kate.

Kate stood helplessly a moment, listening to the silent street and looking at the ruin of Drina's black hair. "I'll go," she offered. "To the market of the animals. I'll get Behjet. And your father."

"Don't look at me," said Drina.

So Kate took Taggle, and she went.

eight

THE BOG CAMP

Plain Kate found Behjet and Stivo in the market of the animals and stammered out enough of the story to send Stivo running. Kate started to follow him, but Behjet seized her by the shoulder to stop her. His hands trembled a little, but he kept his movement calm as he slid a saddle onto the dray colt. They mounted together, with Behjet behind and Kate squeezed between him and the horse's pulsing neck. They rode out of Toila easily, so as to draw no eyes. But when they passed the city gates they went at a gallop.

Given his head, the horse half reared, and jolted forward. Kate grabbed at his mane until the coarse hair cut into her fingers. The horse pounded under her. The road blurred. Her basket — with Taggle in it — banged at her knee. Behind her she could feel Behjet breathing hard. His arms struck her ears and the reins whipped her hair. Still, she risked leaning out and looking backward.

"No one's following —" she shouted, her voice ripped away by the speed.

"Not yet," said Behjet. "If they get to talking — if they remember she's a Roamer girl — well. Everyone will know she didn't come to Toila alone."

The Roamers were already striking camp when they arrived. Behjet reined in Xeri, who stamped. One of Daj's daughters came fluttering up to them. "They're here. Daj is with her, in the red *vardo*. Stivo too."

"Is Drina much hurt?" Behjet asked. Kate leaned down to hear over the horse's panting.

"Her ear, and a tooth or two — but nay. Stivo's in a weeping rage."

Behjet nodded. His arms around Kate were roped with tight muscles, spattered with mud. "We'll go ahead. We must find someplace at least a little off the road." He nudged Xeri with his heels, and the horse snatched backward at Kate, snapping. "Tell Daj I'll lay a blaze."

The Roamer woman nodded. "Do you think — are they coming? Those that hurt her? Or the watch?"

But Behjet kicked the horse and they took to the road without answering.

Behjet got the ill-trained horse under control and they rode on more slowly. Every few hundred yards Behjet would pick a birch and slash a quick mark into the white bark: the blaze he promised. To stay close to the trees, they went splashing through the drainage trench at the edge of the road. They didn't speak; Kate tried to gather her breath and think.

In Samilae it had been her the witch-hunters wanted. *It is your trouble and you must not bring it upon us,* Rye Baro had said. And Stivo: *Do not bring it on my Drina.* But she had. In letting Drina try to help her, she had made her friend a target of the mob. Behjet didn't know enough to blame her, but Drina did — and Stivo would, even without knowing that he should. She should say something to Behjet, but it was hard to know what.

Taggle had worked his head out of Kate's pack-basket, just in time to get a face full of water as Xeri hit a deep spot in the ditch.

Taggle ducked down with a yowl, and Behjet chuckled. "You'd swear he could talk. That sounded like a curse. Sorry, cat." Deeper water raised another splash, soaking Kate's leggings and raising a muffled ruckus in her basket. Behjet twitched the reins and the horse's shoulders bunched and surged under her. They clambered out of the ditch and onto the road. "Bit damp, that," said Behjet. "This rain is endless."

"They . . ." Kate gathered her breath. "They won't really come after us? They weren't searching, in the town."

"Most likely not. But people get odd ideas in the twilight. Sometimes dark stories take their hearts. And that town's in trouble." Behjet guided Xeri closer to the edge of the road. An egret exploded from the ditch, and the horse reared and wheeled. He turned three tight circles before Behjet could calm him. The man leaned far forward to stroke the horse's ear and murmured. Kate could smell his sweat and feel his heat pressing into her. It was strange, being that close to another person.

Behjet eased the horse forward again. "They're talking at Pan Oksar's farm — but it's worse in that market. The harvest is failing. There will be no crop at all if this rain doesn't stop — not even hay."

The rain. The rain she'd been so grateful for, the rain that concealed the warping of her shadow. It was going to kill people.

"But," said Behjet, and let the thought hang. Plain Kate could feel the tension in his body at her back. Xeri's hooves squelched and splatted in the mud.

"But there's more than that. They say there's something

coming. Something coming down the river, down from Samilae and the high country: a kind of death. The traders are all talking about it. A fog that takes your soul. They say there's a woman in it, and music. Roamer music. They say men fall asleep and do not wake. They say boats go and do not come back. It will be the *skara rok* again. Worse. They will come after the Roamers, as they did then."

Kate was thinking hard. In Samilae, Boyar the fisher had fallen into a sleep from which he could not be awakened. And, escaping down the road from the town, she'd stumbled into a fog. And she'd heard . . . "Music," she whispered.

"Aye. A fiddle."

Linay had played a fiddle. Plain Kate's chest felt tight, a pulling ache like an old wound. Fear. Guilt. The weight of her secret. "A fiddle," she said.

"A Roamer fiddle, so they say." Behjet reined the horse into an amble. "You're squawking words back to me like a raven, Plain Kate. Did they shake you out of your wits, in that alley? Or do you know something?"

Not trusting herself to speak, Kate shook her head.

"If you do, you must tell me." With sudden decisiveness, he stopped the horse. She couldn't see his face, just his long fingers tight on the reins, the little knife in one hand. "Now you're trembling. What happened, Plain Kate? What happened to you and Drina in that market?"

Plain Kate tried to compose an answer, but found tears stinging to the surface of her eyes. She shook her head harder. Xeri stamped and struggled forward, thrashing his head. Behjet gave him rein and he took up an easy ramble. And still Kate could only shake her head.

Behjet lifted his hand — knife and all — and let it rest over hers. "It's all right, then, *mira*," he said, and she could hear his mother Daj in his voice. His kindness broke her, and she told him. A flood of details came spilling out of her like fish from a net, last caught first: The basket woman who had saved them, the arc of the silver coins over the spitting crowd, the blood on the cleaver, the rearing horse, the booted watchman, the angry tinker —

"A tinker?" Behjet interrupted, sounding urgent. "Selling charms? What did he look like?"

Plain Kate sketched for him the bald man with the catfish whiskers, selling the cheap tin objarka off his own jangling coat.

"Ah." Behjet relaxed. "I thought perhaps — well. Look here." He turned the horse almost right around, and took them up a little track that ran slantwise to the road. It curved and wound into the birch wood. Branches brushed their knees on either side and clattered on her basket. Taggle popped his head out again, and this time got a face full of pine needle. He swore in cat.

Behjet chuckled. "Sorry, Taggle!"

They rode on. The track opened and spilled into a stream-bed of rushes and willow saplings. "It doesn't go anywhere," said Kate. "It's just a deer track."

"Ah, but that's the point. Here the *vardo* may leave the road without leaving too broad a trace. And yet, it's not a path the town folk will follow, if they come looking." He swung down, then lifted her from Xeri's back. She wobbled at the suddenly steady ground, and was hardly standing before Taggle sprang into her arms. She tumbled backward into a clump of marsh marigold. Behjet smirked — but kindly. She had never before known someone who could smirk kindly. He climbed back up on the horse.

"Stay here a moment," he said, and rode off. Kate watched him go with a shaking heart, Taggle with a dis-gusted sniff.

"That," proclaimed the cat, squirming down into her lap, "was awful. The jouncing. The rearing! The mud. I have decided that we will not travel again by horse." When she didn't answer, he poked her with his damp nose, and rubbed her thumb with the corner of his mouth. "Look, I'm still damp. Fuss over me."

So she hugged the cat to her chest. "My hero," she said. "My soft damp little warrior. What are we going to do?"

Behjet was gone for a long time. The woods they had disturbed into silence filled again with birdsong and glimpsed movement, rabbits and deer. Gradually it occurred to Plain Kate that the Roamers could abandon her here, dump her off like a sack of kittens.

But finally Behjet did come back. Together they walked Xeri deeper into the woods, to where the stream widened into a clearing by the river. Behjet fished, and Kate tried to do the chores that she and Drina did together. It took longer, and was harder, drearier work alone. She was still piling firewood when the first *vardo* came nosing through the willow saplings, the horse straining to pull it through the mud.

The clearing was a miserable camp: more bog than meadow. Every step pressed tea-colored water from the grass. The wheels of the *vardo* sank halfway to the hubs. Flies swarmed and bit. The horses twitched and pulled at the sour-smelling grass. The people swatted and grumbled.

Daj and Drina did not come out of the red *vardo*. Stivo sat on its steps and sharpened his axe.

So Kate, by herself, took the buckets from their pegs

on the green *vardo* and placed them — one, two, three, four — a few paces apart along the stream. She took the big bucket from the blue *vardo* and set off toward the river. One of the women, pulling piled chicken baskets out of the bear cage, called after her: "Not alone! It's not the Roamer way —"

But Stivo interrupted her: "But she's not Roamer, is she? And she looks after herself well enough."

So Kate went alone. Full, the big bucket was iron-heavy. She and Drina usually carried it between them, their hands twined side by side on the handle, both of them leaning outward against the weight. Without Drina, Kate staggered. The bucket had to be held out far enough that it didn't bang into her knee. It made the weight more; it was like carrying her secret. She shook with it.

It was too much. Drina hurt and hating her — her silver gone — her place vanishing — her shadow twisted away. Coming into camp, she caught her foot in a rabbit hole and fell. The water spilled. The bucket tumbled under the feet of the horses; Xeri shied and struck at it, and two of the staves cracked, and when Kate picked it up she was crying.

But worse was coming. It took her all of the evening to water the chickens, fill the kettles, and tend the fires, and through it all no one spoke to her, though there was whispering.

Where the men's fire should be, the Roamers had put up a big tent, which she had only ever seen bundled and strapped beneath the biggest *vardo*. "Council tent," said Behjet, who caught her looking. "This business in Toila was bad, Plain Kate. We must decide what to do."

What to do with her, he did not say. She knew it, anyway. *I knew this*, she tried to remind herself. The test. After Toila, they were going to decide.

All the men went inside, and the women spoke only in their own language. They had forgotten that Kate was learning it. *Drina*, she heard, *gadje, Toila, market, knife, blood, witch. Blame.*

Kate settled onto the back step of the red *vardo* and tried to mend the bucket in the fading light. Inside she could hear Daj muttering and puttering, and Stivo — gruff, angry Stivo — singing a lullaby that her own father had once sung to her. She knew the tune, though he sang in the Roamer language: *"Cheya,* Drina, *mira cheya."* Daughter, dearest daughter.

The fire burning inside the council tent cast the men's shadows on yellow canvas — shadows so crisp and solid they looked like people made of shadow. Smoke billowed, dragonish, from the vent in the roof. In the women's circle, the cooking fire smoldered and sputtered, smoking in the damp. The woods pressed close and the river muttered.

Plain Kate worked and listened to Stivo sing. Drina's voice didn't come. The night closed in.

One of the women came around with a splint and lit the lanterns that hung from the back doors of the five *vardo*, which Kate had always thought made the wagons look sweet as fireflies. But tonight — the lantern washed down over her as she struggled with planing a stave for the broken bucket. And after a moment she saw the way the shadow of the step made a fluttering line on the damp grass. Nothing broke that line. Of her own shadow there was no trace.

Kate stopped. Her hands went numb, her stomach seized, her breath snatched. Gone. It was finally gone. Into the gathering dark, she hissed: "Taggle? Taggle?"

From the shifting dark shapes of the horses a smaller gray shape sauntered. The cat leapt onto the steps beside her. His shadow fell — alone — across the grass. "I found the horse," he announced. "The one that gave us such a horrible ride. I scratched his ankle."

"Ah," she said automatically. She couldn't even gather the courage to tell him, to speak the horrible thing aloud. *My shadow.* "Taggle —"

He had heard something, anyway. "Katerina?" He pricked his ears at her. His tail twitched and he sniffed at her, as if looking for the wound. "Are you hurt?"

"Taggle, my shadow —" But suddenly, inside the *vardo*, someone was shifting. The steps wobbled; the frame creaked. Daj pushed the curtain aside, and her shadow fell across Kate. *My shadow*, she thought again. But neither of them spoke. Taggle leaned his comforting warmth into Kate's side.

Feeling Daj's eyes on her, Plain Kate bent her head and tried to work. The curved length of wood was clamped between her knees. She drew the plane over the wood toward her. Pale shavings curled up like carrot peelings. "Deadly work for such little hands," said Daj at last.

"It's not hard." Though it was hard. Mending a bucket was a cooper's work, and Kate had never done it. She had to guess how the wood might swell or shrink, bend or straighten, and the stave had to be perfect. If the bucket leaked, she thought, the Roamers would surely cast her out. Still, she said again: "It's not hard."

"Well, it looks hard," said Daj. "Leave off now, kit, you've lost the light." She plucked down the lantern and peered into the *vardo*. "Not much room in here, I'm feared. Full as the king's pocket. Why don't you pitch the bender tent, have a night on your own."

Alone. At Daj's words, Plain Kate did something she had never done. She let the plane slip.

The blade skipped off some knot in the wood and sliced into her forearm. She watched it cut a strip of skin like bark. Taggle howled.

Daj almost dropped the lantern. *"Mira!"* She rushed and stumbled down the steps, yanking off scarves. "Aye! I've jinxed you!" Plain Kate's arm was seeping blood the way the bog seeped water. Daj tied the scarf around it, tight. The pink flowers were at once soaked through.

"Blood," hissed Taggle, and over him, Kate said, "Oh."

"Ah," Daj sobbed. "I'll never forgive myself." She yanked Kate up — "Come *on*, kit" — and pulled her by the wrist, staggering, toward the big tent, with the cat tangling around their feet. They burst into the yellow light and sudden silence. Faces turned to them.

There was no men's fire ceremony, no "May I pass between you?" Daj barked: "Tea!" Her husband, Wen, rose, creaking, his hands on his knees, and shuffled over with the black kettle. Daj seized it and pushed Kate onto one of the trestles. Taggle leapt up. Daj swatted him away. She ripped off the bandage-scarf. Before Plain Kate knew what was happening, hot tea was pouring over the open wound.

"Just brewed that," said Wen.

Daj thrust the kettle lid at him. "Can't you see the child's hurt?" She slapped a handful of steaming tea leaves on Plain Kate's arm.

"What happened?" Stivo was pushing through the tent doorway behind them. "Carver cut herself, did she? Little girl with a big knife?"

Plain Kate looked up at him. He was strangely colored in the yellow light, like a smoked fish. Daj looked at her looking and said, "It weren't her fault. I jostled her. And she's a better carver than you are a horseman, boy." She dropped the bloody, gaudy scarf into the teapot, and tied another scarf over the tea leaves, and another over that.

"What news of your daughter, Stivo?" Rye Baro's voice came from the other side of the fire. To Kate, it seemed as if the fire itself was speaking, as if it wanted to claim Drina.

"She'll live," said Stivo. "And it's no thanks to this one." He gestured roughly at Kate.

"What —" Plain Kate felt dull as the dark of the moon. "What did she tell you?"

The voice came from the fire again. "What should she have told, Plain Kate Carver?"

That it was my fault, Plain Kate thought. *That she was only trying to help me. That I knew it was dangerous, and I let her help me anyway. I let her go alone.*

Taggle sprang back onto the trestle beside her, sniffing at the tea-soaked scarf around Kate's arm, bleating wordlessly. His pink tongue flicked out like a bit of flame. Beside her, Wen suddenly spat out his tea. "Bah! Who brewed the bandages!"

"Plain Kate?" said the fire, in Rye Baro's voice.

"I —" she croaked.

"'Tis not the time for questioning the kit," said Daj firmly, lifting Kate to her feet. "Come along, Plain Kate. I'll clear you out a patch to sleep."

"It's full as the king's pocket," she muttered.

"No, you'll see," said Daj, leading her out into the night. "You can sleep by me, *mira*." She put an arm around Kate's shoulders and guided her back across the river meadow, through the echoing, thickening fog, as if into the land of the dead.

"Blood!"

Plain Kate struggled to wake. She was wrapped in blankets, lying on Daj's bunk in the hot *vardo*. Taggle was asleep. Drina was lying in the other bunk, her face turned to the wall, the roughly chopped hair sticking out and matted here and there with blood. Kate could see the heave of her ribs and hear the rasp and shudder of her breath. It was daylight, not too long past dawn: The gaps around the door curtain let in long slants of sun.

Kate shook her head, trying to remember what had wakened her. An angry voice, the word *blood*. That voice from outside came again. "And what does that tell you?"

"That my fool of a husband can't tell a bandage from a tea leaf." Daj's steady rasp came from just outside the doorway; she was sitting on the *vardo* steps. "'Tisn't news."

Plain Kate eased her arm free of Daj's quilts and wiggled her fingers. The new wound felt tight as dry leather, but everything moved as it was supposed to. She felt a stab of relief — and then of guilt. What kind of carver cut herself? There had been so much blood.

"He drank her blood and now he's witched." Plain Kate finally recognized Stivo's voice. There was a tremble in it that hadn't been there before — not just anger but fear. That was what had confused her. "That *gadje* child has a witch's eyes."

Taggle's eyes cracked open. "Don't like him." She shushed him and rubbed a thumb between his ears.

"Well, let's look, then." The steps creaked as Daj lumbered down them. Plain Kate heard the voices fade away. Outside a horse whinnied, uneasy.

Kate tried to pull herself together. "What's happening?"

Taggle opened one gold eye. "We're napping." He rolled over and stretched belly up in the crook of her arm. "You may scratch my throat."

"I meant — Stivo just said —" The cat was going to be no help, clearly. *My fool of a husband*, Daj had said. Wen. He'd spat out his tea last night, made some crack about the bandage — the bandage with her blood on it, in the kettle. Wen had drunk her blood. Plain Kate sat up.

Taggle spilled out of his crook and onto the *vardo* floor. He gave her a sidelong look. "Huh!" he complained.

"It's Wen," she said. "Something must be wrong with him. And Stivo thinks —" She pulled herself up and the *vardo* sloshed around her. Her arm stung. "We have to go see."

"Oh, all right." Taggle stretched and spread the fur feathers between his toes. "Afterward you may find some food for us. I smell sausages."

Plain Kate clung to the wood's edge as she crept across the meadow. She was carrying the bloodied smock she had worn the day before, and trying to look as if she wanted no more than to go to the second bucket, where the washing was done. Taggle scoffed at the quality of her sneaking, and vanished into the tussocks and reeds. Plain Kate said a little prayer for some unlucky mouse or frog.

At the stream, she bent over the smock, scrubbing at the stained arm, and watching. The Roamers, men and women alike, were huddled outside the open flaps of the council tent. Up from the riverside where the horses were picketed, a small procession was coming: four men holding the corners of a sleeping roll, and on it, Wen sprawled limp. Stivo and Behjet at the head of the blanket were like a matched pair of stallions.

In the trampled grass, they put the blanket down. Kate lifted her head, feeling danger like a deer. She could see only Wen's white hair, one gold-pierced ear, one hand life-less as a glove. Daj crouched beside him. She leaned her ear and cheek close over his mouth and waited. The crowd held its breath.

Daj rocked back on her heels. "He's breathing, any rate. Is it drink?"

"Not a drop, Mother," said Stivo. "On my life."

"It's true there's no smell of it." Daj picked up the white hand. "He's cursed cold."

"They're talking in that market," said Behjet. "Talking about a sleep —" He left the thought hanging. For Kate, who knew what he was going to say, the wait for him to say it was awful. "They're talking about a sleeping death. Come down the river from Samilae."

Someone said, "Death!" but Stivo said, "Samilae?" Kate ducked her head.

The knot of people stirred and Rye Baro edged through them, inching on his two canes. He spoke to Daj in the

Roamer language. She answered in the same, and after a moment stood up. Behjet and Stivo both started talking. And still Wen did not move.

Then Rye Baro spoke again, and Plain Kate heard him say her name. It dropped from the foreign language like a stone from the sky. She sank low over her washing and held still, pinned by its weight.

"But she's only a child," whispered Daj.

Plain Kate never heard the footsteps, but suddenly Stivo was looming over her, yanking her up by her arm. She yelped and jerked: Her wound cracked open. "Here she is," called Stivo. He dragged her toward the turning faces, to where Wen lay as if ready for the grave. She twisted, terrified, and saw her smock lift and drift downstream.

"Bloodying the water," said Stivo.

"She's *gadje*," said Behjet. "She doesn't know."

"She *should*," snapped Stivo, still clenching her arm.

"Bring her here," said Rye Baro quietly, and Stivo did. Rye Baro stood with his legs wide, leaning forward onto his canes. "Plain Kate Carver," he said, looking down at her. His leathery face was solemn and kind, like a horse's. "In the city it is different. But you are now among the Roamers. You must learn that your blood is unclean. You must wash it at the fourth bucket. The farthest downstream."

Was that all? Plain Kate, wide-eyed, nodded.

"See where Wen lies, witched."

"I see."

"What can you say about this?"

Kate drew herself straight. "That it is not my doing."

Rye Baro looked at her, long and careful. "Child," he said, "you have no shadow."

nine

THE BEAR CAGE

Rye Baro's words produced first a stun of silence, and then a chorus of shouting. Stivo wrenched Plain Kate around. She could see how his shadow spun like a cape around him, how everyone's shadow stretched in the early slant of light. "No shadow!" Stivo cried, and someone screamed.

On top of one of the *vardo* was the iron cage that had once held a dancing bear. They hauled it down and shoved Kate into it. She lurched up, banged her head on the bars, and fell sprawling. "I didn't!" she was shouting. "I didn't do anything."

Stivo was locking the cage door. He was in such a rush to back away from her that he dropped the key. Kate reached for it. Stivo put his boot over it and kicked at her hand.

Plain Kate rolled over and looked up at the gathered Roamers. The cage bars cast shadow bars all around her.

She crouched up and heard the gasp: Behind her the lines of shadow stretched straight, uninterrupted by the shadow she should have had, across the dirty straw and the white droppings of the chickens. She could almost feel them, going right through her like cold spears. The faces that looked down on her were marked with awe and fear.

"No shadow," whispered Daj. Even she looked afraid. Plain Kate crouched there, breathing hard.

"They were right." Stivo's voice was flat with wonder. "In Samilae, where they wanted to burn you. They were right. You are a witch."

"I'm not," she sobbed. "I'm not."

"It's the *gadje* burn their witches," said Rye Baro. "That's nothing to do with us."

"But it's us they burn!" Stivo exploded.

"I'm not a witch! Stivo, please." Plain Kate reached through the bars and touched his boot. "Ask Drina. Ask Drina, she knows —"

"Drina!" Stivo jumped back from her hand as if she were a snake striking, scrabbling the key up from the mud as he staggered away. "Drina! I told you not to bring your trouble on my Drina. My God, what she has already seen, without falling in with —" he sputtered. "With demons!"

Horror closed Kate's throat. She could only whisper, "I'm not."

"We are taught," said Rye Baro, his voice still thought-ful, kind, "that only the dead have no shadows. But Stivo has told us of his wife's brother, who gave up pieces of his shadow to give power to the dead. We do not know which is the case here." He cut off the rumble of voices with one raised hand. "Plain Kate Carver. What can you say about this?"

She swallowed, and sat up as straight as she could. "A witch." Her voice cracked. The crowd held its breath like one great creature. "A witch took my shadow."

"And what can you say about Wen?"

She tossed her head like a nervous horse. "I — It's not me. I don't know what's happening."

"And Drina?"

Kate's throat tightened. "She . . ." It came out as a whis-per, and even in her own ears, she could hear the guilt in it. A mutter rose from the gathered Roamers. "She was only trying to help me. I — I'm sorry." Stivo crowed with bitter triumph, and the crowd was suddenly loud. Kate wanted to say more, but was afraid to.

Again, Rye Baro lifted a hand for silence. "We do not know enough, here." He pulled at the tip of his long nose. "We must have talk about this. We will take counsel. We will see if Wen dies."

Plain Kate heard Daj breathe in hard at that. "Daj, I didn't," she pleaded. "Wen — I didn't. Ask Drina. Daj! *Mira!* Mother Daj! Ask —"

"That's enough, child," said Daj, and she turned away.

Sun. Sun after endless weeks of drizzle and mist. It felt unreal, and it made Kate feel unreal, numbed, and queasy. The bear cage grew hot. It smelled high and sour of the chicken baskets, but beneath that it still smelled like the bear: rank; and it still had some of the bear's fleas. Plain Kate scratched and pushed the stale straw to the cage edge.

Then through the straw heap came Taggle, ambling, slipping through the bars, a half-dead muskrat in his teeth. "Wrph," said Taggle, around his catch. He spat the creature out and put a paw down on its back like a young prince putting one boot on a footstool. "Did you find the sausages?"

Plain Kate snatched the cat up and whipped her head around, panicked that someone might have heard him. The muskrat tried to stagger away. "It's escaping!" the cat shouted.

"Taggle!" Kate shouted back. Then she made herself whisper, though it came out as a hiss. "Taggle, they're going to kill me."

"What? Who? And would you please stop that muskrat!"

Kate released him, and he bounded once and killed the creature with a single strike to the back of the neck. Then he turned back to her and tried to recover his nonchalance. "You were saying?"

"The Roamers. They found out about my shadow. They think I'm a witch. They — we can't let them find you here."

"Oh, nonsense. They adore me. Everyone does."

"We've both got to get away from here, Taggle."

Taggle stuck his head through the bars. The tight squeeze slicked his whiskers back. "You won't fit," he said, popping his head back in.

"I know that. We need the key."

"Well," he said. "That's simple enough. I will go and steal it."

Kate's heart dropped at the thought. "If they catch you —"

"Bah." Taggle flicked his ears. "They won't even glimpse me. I am the king of catspaws, the lord of lurking. If the key is what you need, then I will obtain it for you. Where is it?"

"Stivo," she stuttered. "Stivo hung it from his belt. Taggle, if they catch you, they'll kill you."

"They shan't catch me," he said lightly, and slipped out into the grasses.

He'd left her the muskrat, like a lover's token, like a promise of return.

Plain Kate dropped her head back against the bars. They were hard against her hair, and comfortless. The barred roof broke the sun into stripes of shade, but no shade touched her. It was like not being able to blink, like not being able to scream in a dream. She pushed up the sleeves of her smock to scratch at her flea bites and watch the long scab seep blood.

The ground beneath her seeped water, and her leggings were wet, the wool sticking to her and smelling. In the front of the cage, where the frightened Roamers had milled, the sun drew curls of steam from the churned mud. She watched it, looking at the scuffed footprints, the twin pits of Rye Baro's twin canes, which were like eyes, and the big marks of Stivo's boots. Just in front of the door she could see where he'd stepped on the key.

The shape of the key was pressed into the mud.

Plain Kate stared at it. A shape of hope.

She had, as she always did, the whittling knife her father had given her when she was three. It was tucked into a sheath stitched into her boot. If she had wood — and her mind was already choosing, something hard, ash, oak, for hard edges, strength in the lock — if she had wood, she might carve a key.

Plain Kate fingered the objarka cat on its thong around her neck — but it was too small. She started to rummage through the straw and mud, keeping her head up, watching the council tent. Voices came hard and soft, rising and falling. Outside the tent, Wen lay ashy and still on his mat, and Daj hunched beside him, her hands on her face, singing something. No one was watching the cage.

But there was no wood. Kate searched through every bit of straw. She dug her fingers into the mud in hope of roots but the only ones she found were fine as tangled hair.

Suddenly from the tent came a burst of shouting. Taggle streaked out of the front flap, running low and fast as a fox, the cage key in his mouth. Some of the Roamer men came crashing out after him. She saw Stivo with an axe in his hand.

Taggle was fast, faster than the men. He was bolting straight for her. He would make it, but then what —

Stivo threw the axe.

The flat butt of the axe head hit Taggle behind the ears. The cat tumbled tail over head and lay limp as a pelt. The axe head flew free of its handle. Stivo lifted Taggle by the back legs like a dead rabbit. He picked up the axe handle in the other hand. He strode over toward her with Taggle's head swinging.

Plain Kate was sobbing. She didn't want to cry in front of Stivo, but she couldn't stop. He dropped Taggle's body in the churned mud before the cage. "Is this your creature, witch-child?"

Taggle cracked open a yellow eye. "Her name," he drawled, thickly, "is Katerina, Star of My Heart."

Stivo leapt backward, dropping the axe handle and warding his face with crooked fingers.

"Taggle!" sobbed Kate. She reached through the bars for him. Stivo was still backing away. "Taggle!"

She fumbled and turned the cat's warm body. He was squirming a little. "Hold still," she whispered, and took him under the arms and cradled his head and eased him through the bars. She kept one hand on his heaving ribs as she pulled down the driest straw and built a bed for him. Stivo was gone. "Oh, Taggle," she said. "Taggle, I'm sorry."

He tried to look at her. His eyes crossed and he didn't move his head. "I dropped the key."

"Don't worry. Little catspaw, little lord of lurking . . ." She stroked his side and watched him get limper and longer as he drifted off to sleep.

Suddenly he opened his eyes again. "Did you save any muskrat?"

"All of it." She set it beside him.

"Mmmmm." He blinked slowly and softened again. "When I rise from my nap . . ." And then he was really asleep. She watched him breathe. She watched the council tent, where voices were louder now and she heard Stivo sounding shrill with anger or fear. No one was coming — not yet.

Plain Kate looked at Taggle sprawled out hurt and limp. Then she leaned her shoulder and arms between the bars and reached for the axe handle. Her fingers brushed it and she inched it across the mud until she could pick it up.

The axe handle was split, it turned out, and the split was tied closed with a scrap of fraying gingham. It was sloppy work and it made her angry. She could easily have fixed it for Stivo, if only he had asked. Then he might not have hated her. She wedged the handle under her foot and pulled up the split wood until it snapped. She closed her fist around the scrap of wood and took her knife from her boot.

Plain Kate carved and no one came to kill her. The men stayed in the tent. The women stayed away. Swallows swooped through the afternoon sky. Daj sang her drone over Wen, who did not even twitch. Taggle slept on, cuddling his muskrat like a child with a doll. All the while the hard wood curled away from her small blade, and no one saw.

She was so hot and flea-bitten that she was almost glad when evening came, though she could feel her time running out, the way the bread had in the *skara rok*. The key was now almost the same shape as the impression in the mud, but it would not go into the lock. She made it thinner, sliver by sliver.

With the day went the heat. Mist rose from the stream, from the river, from the wet ground itself. Kate huddled in the damp, dank straw. A fire was lit in the council tent, and the canvas glowed. Marsh light bobbed near the river, like a boat lantern. Another light came up to her through the fog and the shape of a man came behind it. It was Behjet with a tallow lamp. He was holding a blanket. He passed it through the bars. It reeked of horse. She wrapped it around herself.

"Is your cat all right?"

Kate tucked a corner of the blanket over Taggle, covering him from sight.

"He's a fine little beast," said Behjet. "But it is a strange thing, don't you see, a cat who steals keys. It makes a man think."

Kate said nothing.

"My brother says he spoke."

Still Kate said nothing.

"Stivo —" Behjet pulled at his chin. "Understand, Plain Kate. He lost his wife because she was a witch. He has nearly lost his daughter. His love has turned to anger. And his suspicion — just see. The stories from your city. The sleeping death that follows you. Your shadow. And now your cat, stealing a —"

Just then Taggle's head slid out from under the blanket. "There's bats out," he slurred, stumbling up. "Listen, they sing to me!" He fell over.

"So it's true," said Behjet.

Plain Kate looked up at him, squinting through the fog. It was almost full dark, and she could not read his face, except that the moon was round in his eyes. "Behjet, I am not a witch. And I didn't hurt Wen."

And now Behjet said nothing.

"Behjet, what will they do with me?"

He looked over his shoulder at the ghostly light of the tent. "I must return to the council."

"Please tell me," she said, but he turned and walked away.

The key was nearly done. It went into the lock and Kate could feel it catch and turn, almost turn. She had to widen her eyes to owl eyes to compare the pale wood key and the black ghost of the key in the mud.

The moon was bright but the mist blurred it. Daj chanted over her husband. The drone of it went on and on. It had become something unstoppable, like the noise of a river. Kate carved on and on and wished for something to stop up her ears.

Finally she put the key next to the key hollow and could see no differences. She set the key in the key hollow and it went in like hand to glove. Maybe this time. She lifted the key. She crouched up on her toes and looked around. She would only get one dash.

Plain Kate fingered her key.

There was someone moving in the fog.

Kate froze.

She could not see who it was, or even what. It came up from the river, and at first Kate thought it was a woman dressed in twists of hair and cloud. But as she moved one limb grew long and another short; when she turned, her torso twisted like linen being wrung out. Sometimes Kate could see through her, and sometimes she couldn't. Music came with her. She was beautiful and Kate wanted to —

Taggle staggered up and gave a horrible hissing howl. "Thing!" he spat. "Thing!" And then Kate wanted to scream.

We called into the darkness, Drina had said. *We don't know what answered.* This is what had answered. The sick shadow on the wall of the bender tent, the approaching horror. The woman-thing was drifting toward the *vardo* and the council tent. Plain Kate tried to shout for help, but couldn't. The foggy music wrapped her up like a spider-web and she couldn't even move. She watched the creature slide closer.

Then she saw Stivo, lamp in hand, going out to tend to the stamping, crying horses.

The white woman came to Stivo past the edge of the camp, where the fog swirled. He dropped the lamp and oil splashed into the grass, flaring bright. He said something, one word that Kate didn't catch, a raw shout of — fear? joy? — and threw his arms open for the creature. When he touched her his whole body twisted like a reed in water. Kate, watching, felt the impossible, horrible twist as if it was happening to her, but still she was frozen, hardly even —

Taggle yowled and bit Kate's hand.

Kate yelped, and found she could move again. "Stivo! Stivo!" she screamed.

The woman turned toward her voice. She retracted her hand, and Stivo crumpled at her feet. Eyes like pits locked on to Plain Kate.

In naked fear, Kate shouted. She banged at the bars, still caught eye to eye with the thing: skin pale and thin as an onion's, her hair white and wavering like seaweed, face knife-sharp and starving. "Help me!" Kate screamed. "Help! Let me out!"

Out of the tent and down from the *vardo*, the Roamers were coming toward her, cautious, looking around. All at once Kate found her eyes released; the white creature was fading back toward the river. Kate gasped and leaned forward against the bars, breathing hard. "Katerina . . ." warned Taggle. She looked up just in time to see Behjet, running up from the horse meadow, fall full length over Stivo's sprawled body.

Behjet pushed up to his knees, his hands on his brother, his sweet, sad face twisting in fear and grief. "Stivo!" he cried. "God! By the Black Lady, come and help us!" He lifted Stivo, pale and still in his arms. *Just like Wen*, Kate thought. *Just like Wen*.

Daj ran up to them, heavy and rolling like a bear running. She fell to her knees, and her low chant became a keening wail. "Oh, no!" she cried. "No, no!"

"Daj!" said Behjet. "What has happened?"

"God save us!" she answered. "This sleep is a killing thing. Wen is dead. My husband! My son!"

Stillness came into Behjet. He picked up Stivo's sputtering lamp. He stood slow as the tide rising. He walked over to Plain Kate.

She scooted away from the look on his face, until the bars stopped her. Taggle stood up, crooked and dazed. "No closer," he said. "I bite." Kate barely heard the gathering crowd gasp. Behjet's grief-blasted eyes caught like the white creature's had.

"Witch-child," said Behjet calmly. "This is too much." And he threw the lamp at her.

The clay lamp cracked and the tallow splashed. The cage flashed hot. The straw and the horse blanket started smoking. Plain Kate cried out and threw herself at the door, fumbling with the wooden key.

"Katerina!" yowled Taggle. His fur was already frizzled. He backed out between the bars, stumbling. "Katerina!"

"Go, Taggle, go!" But he pressed so close to the hot bars she could smell his smoking fur. Her soaked wool leggings smoldered, her light smock crawled with fire and she slapped at it. She reached through the bars, twisting her wrist backward. Her hair was full of flames. The key went into the lock. Behjet was staring but he didn't stop her. The key almost turned, then turned. She fell against the door and it swung open. She scooped up Taggle and staggered for the river. She heard Behjet start to cry, and Daj sobbing: "Enough, enough, let her go." The crowd parted around her. The water was cold, and it took her in.

ten

THE PUNT, THE POOL,
AND THE EMPTY ROAD

She rocked like a cradle. There was a *chuck, chuck* like a dove or waves on a dock. Plain Kate woke.

She was dry. She was lying on something soft. She was wrapped in quilts. There was a star of light drifting above her, and a smell like an herb garden. Taggle was a long warmth stretched at one side, his chin in her hand, his tail curled over her neck. She thought they might be in heaven.

Taggle farted.

Plain Kate coughed and sneezed. And then she was really awake.

She was not in heaven, but in a little bunk on a boat. The painted ceiling was close above her. The slap of water thudded through the wall at her ear. Taggle's tail flip-flipped over her face. She smelled his scorched fur. He squirmed around and soon his face appeared from under the blanket. "Taggle," she whispered. Her voice was rough with smoke.

He made a little meow. There weren't any words.

The golden light stirred. A rush lamp of pierced tin swung over her like the night sky. A pale face floated above it. "Fair maid of the wood," said a familiar voice. "Are you awake?"

"You," Taggle spat. Because it was Linay.

He barked with surprise and laughter. "This was your wish? A talking cat!"

Taggle's ears went back. "We don't like you."

Linay grinned. "Well, now, I don't blame you, catkins. But I can heal you, like me or not." He hung the lantern. "Can you sit, little one?" Plain Kate struggled to sit and he put his arms around her shoulders. He had a little jar in one hand; it smelled of herbs and thunder. Taggle sniffed once, squinted in disgust, and started backing up.

"What — ?" Kate tried to say, and coughed. Her throat felt like it had been filed down with a rasp.

"Shhhhh," he said. "It's only salve."

"What do you want?" she whispered.

The salve felt cool as seaweed on her burns. Linay was humming. He put the salve on her forehead and cheek-bones. The humming faded into song:

Lenore my sister: she had power
She could bring the bud to flower

Seal the wound or soothe the fever
And so she spent her life

In their fevered year they found her
Drove her mad with whips and fire
Drove her to the freezing river
And there they thought she died

But her wronged soul turned into water
Rusalka, lost ghost of the river
Vampire, siren, doomed to wander
and never find her rest

Lenore, my sister — I would save her
I would pull her up the river
Do to that town what they did to her
and so remake her life

The song was important. Kate tried to hear it and keep it, but she could not. She felt as if she might break into the air as salt breaks into water. "Drink," Linay said. There was a cup at her lips. The drink was both cool and warm.

She slept.

Kate woke again, and again the boat was rocking. She felt as if she had been asleep for days and days and days, sunk halfway in long bad dreams. The current spoke in the wood by her ear, and she could feel the surge of the boat against it and hear the plosh and clock of a pole. They were moving.

They. Linay.

She sat up. How long had she been asleep? There was dry sourness in her mouth, and the dream stretched out so long behind her. "Taggle," she whispered, and it came out croaky.

The cat was curled up in a nook by her feet, between a little cauldron and a lumpy bag: three round heaps. She didn't spot him till he lifted his head and cracked an eye open. "Oh." He yawned. "Hello."

"How long —" She rubbed at her eyes and her fingers found patches of numbed slickness on her face. "How long — where are we?"

"A boat," he said, getting up and leaning into a long stretch. His fur was scorched off on one side, but the bare patches were covered with new fuzz. "I do not care for it: There's water. But also, fish, which is nice for me." He sidled over and rubbed the corner of his mouth on her hand, marking her with his scent.

"How long — I don't remember anything. How long have I been asleep?"

Taggle shrugged with his whiskers. "It is not a matter for cats, *how long*." He tilted his chin up and looked at her — he seemed almost concerned. "I have eaten many times," he offered. "Many fish, many mice, three muskrats, two rabbits, and a small bird that was sleeping. You have had broth."

She tried to remember broth, but couldn't. There was only the long dream about burning and drowning and a woman made of fog, hungry and terribly sad. Stivo crumpling to the ground at a single touch. Daj turning away. Drina bleeding. Behjet throwing the lamp. She shook herself. *Broth.* It would have been hot. But she felt cold: In her sleep, Linay had fed her, had dressed her — her skin shuddered and her hair prickled. She got up.

The ceiling was low and hung thick with trinkets and bundles of herbs. They tangled and bumped in her hair. She stooped and inched away from the bunk and into the dim and tiny space.

Her scorched smock that had been her father's, that she had worn for years, was gone. She was wearing a linen dress, white and embroidered in white, a fine thing edged with lace. It was too big for her and the lace trailed on the floor. She hitched it up.

"I did not catch the fish," Taggle said, continuing his tale of food as he followed her. "I could, of course, but there is the matter of getting wet. He gave them to me. Though I still do not like him."

Daylight poured down from the hatch and fell in a square on the decking. The rest of the cabin was shadowy clutter. Bags and coils of ropes and strings of dried sausages hung on the wall. There was a smell of wet wood, river rot, human sweat, sausage, spices, and the musty smell of many herbs. Plain Kate looked around for her boots.

She found them slumped in the shadows. She bent to pick them up. Then she stopped. The boots were sitting beside a box, a crooked little chest of splintered planks. The lid, though, was carved and beautiful: a stag leaping.

She knew that stag. The box was made from pieces of her father's stall.

And there was something wrong about it.

All of Kate's hair stood up. The box was darker than it should have been. It looked as if it were breathing. "Taggle?" she whispered. "I'm looking for a hatchet."

"I wouldn't," said a lilting voice behind her.

Plain Kate spun around. Linay was leaning at the ladder, white in the stream of sun.

"That box is not a matter for hatchets. As you love your life, leave it alone." He smiled at her, that slow, slow smile. "Unless, of course, the hatchet is for me."

She didn't answer.

"It's good to see you up. There's no one about. Come above."

She hesitated, squinting at his brightness.

"Don't worry. It's safe enough while the day lasts." He slipped up the ladder.

Plain Kate watched him go, and threw a long look at the huddled, splintery box. Then she went to get her boots. Moving them stirred up a smell of scorched leather and smoke that made her for an instant almost sick with fear. She swallowed it and took a steadying breath. Then she pulled on the boots, checked her knife, and followed Linay through the hatch.

The punt Kate remembered from Samilae was tied up in a slow curve of the river, where the current had cut a straighter channel and left a loop of still water, shielded by a sand spit and hung with willows. Plain Kate stood up out of the hatch and breathed deep.

Big willows surrounded the river, and beyond them was a strip of wheat fields. The air smelled like bread. Beside them in the water, a gray heron was standing above its own reflection. She looked at it and it looked at her and they were still for a moment, until the heron lifted heavily on its huge wings, and was gone.

"Oooo," said Taggle, springing onto the bench at the punt's blunt end.

"He's too big for you, catkins," said Linay. He sat cross-legged on the roof of the cabin. "Could kill a pike, that beauty."

"Hmmph," said Taggle, and closed his eyes in the dappling sun.

Plain Kate stood weak-kneed on the tiny deck and had nowhere to look but at the sky, and at Linay. She looked at Linay. He was wrapping strips of white cloth around his hands, tugging them into place with his teeth. The sleeves of his zupan were hanging down his back; his arms were bare, and the bandages went to his elbows. The insides of his forearms were spotted with fresh blood.

Plain Kate knew knives: A man might cut himself there, but only on purpose.

He looked at her watching, and held up a hand as if to show the blood. She turned away.

Her face floated in the dark water. Kate saw herself and closed her eyes, her hands rising up to cover her burnt face. She felt the bubbled scars. She moved her hands away.

The water below was a pool of dark mirror, showing willow and small gusts of sky. And her face. *Plain Kate she is*, she thought. *Plain as a stick*. One side of her face was splattered with burn scar, mostly pale and slick, but thickened and bubbled where it was worst, a rectangle from ear to eyebrow. Her hair had been singed off on that side too, and was growing back only in patches, ugly as a chick just getting its feathers in.

"It's as well," said Linay gently, behind her. "Everyone will turn away from you. Fewer will see."

That she had no shadow, he meant. Once she looked past the burns she could see that being shadowless too had marked her: Her nose threw no shadow across her face; her eyes had no weight. She looked half washed away, floating in the water like a drowned ghost. She turned away. Linay was still watching her, intense, as if he were hungry.

He was bloody and wild and pale. Pale . . . He'd been pale when he took her shadow, but pale and strong. Now he looked gray, weak as she was, and wild in his weakness.

He raised a white eyebrow at her. "If you would wash, do it before darkness."

She hesitated.

"Go on. It will do you good, if your legs will hold you. I shan't peek."

Plain Kate was working her way toward the pool that was hidden from Linay's boat by the largest willow. She inched along the bottom of the V made by the steep bank and the willow's great furrowed trunk, balancing with both hands. The willow's rough bark made her feel the fragile tightness of the new scars on her hands. Her hands felt as stiff as if gloved.

"I could kill the heron," said Taggle. "If I wanted. I would lie in wait on one of the willow branches and take him from above."

"Like a panther," said Kate, who wasn't really listening. Her hands. Her hands that held her carving knife. Her skill with that knife was her whole life, the only thing she had left in the world. Her hands felt so strange.

Taggle curled his tail. "Like a panther. Ah. A panther." He sprang up on a branch and padded along by her ear.

"Taggle," she began. She wanted to ask him what would happen to her if she couldn't carve. What would happen — but she could not think of any words. And then she came clear of the willow, and found herself above the edge of a pool set like a jewel into the bank. The willow branched above and green fronds trailed like a curtain, all around.

Taggle stretched himself out on a branch over the pool. "I would wait," he announced, "like this."

Plain Kate stood looking down at the green, dappled space. Her skin was sticky and grimed as if she'd been wound up in a spiderweb for months. Her legs trembled with weakness. And her hands felt numb, bigger than they should have, and farther away.

"I will keep watch," yawned the cat, and closed his eyes.

What will I do? she had wanted to ask him. *What will I do if I cannot carve?* But it was the wrong question. *What will I do without my shadow? What will I do with no family and no people, with no place to belong? What will I do with my life in the hands of this dangerous man?* "Taggle," she began.

But the cat was so intently keeping watch that he had fallen asleep. He lay on the branch with his dangling feet dream-twitching. Kate laughed. And laughed. And found she couldn't stop laughing. It tore at her until she doubled up and her eyes streamed. And still she kept laughing, until she threw up with the horror of it.

The physical shock of the sickness calmed her. She washed. Exhausted, she slept. When she woke it was golden afternoon. Linay's boat was out of sight behind the big willows, but she could hear the river patting its flat sides. She could go back there.

Or she could leave.

Anyone who saw her would take her for a demon. She could not go among people; they would kill her. She could not live on her own; she would die.

When you are carving a narrow point, like the tail of this fish, her father had said to her, big hands over her little ones, and the carving beneath them, *this is a time of danger. The knife may slip. It may follow a grain and spoil the line. There may be a flaw deep in the wood that will snap your work in two. You will want to leave the tail thick and crude; that is safer. A master carver will be brave, and trust the wood. Things will find their shape. Kate, My Star. Lift your knife.*

Plain Kate stood up. Between her and the road was a steep slope, almost a bluff, tangled with the bent roots of the willows and clogged with nettles. She tilted her chin up. "Taggle," she said, "we're leaving."

When Kate finally reached the road she was scratched and nettle stung and shaking with exhaustion. It had only been a little climb, but her body was weak. She tried to hear her father's voice: *Be brave. Things will find their shape. Lift your knife.*

She turned her back on the way Linay had been going, and followed the road upriver. The road went with the grain of the land, cutting between the river bluffs and the strip of farmland won from the forest: fields of wheat and millet, with the wooded hills beyond. It was a narrow road, quiet. Kate walked and Taggle ambled at her heels.

As she walked, the weather changed. Butter sunshine gave way to a light like watered milk, and then to a thick fog, wet as drizzle. The fog caught and twisted the sound of crows in the wheat, hoarse as a mob of voices.

A little way into the fog they found a tree stump abandoned in the road. It was oak, big as a shed, and still harnessed to a yoke that stood empty. Plain Kate touched one of the hames: ash wood, old but well-made, its inner curve smooth as a lady's wrist. It was not the sort of thing people in a poor country left to lie in the middle of the road. Plain Kate edged around the stump — and then she saw something that made her stop. In among the biggest roots was a knot of wood, twice as big as her head. It was a burl.

Burls had twisting grains that made them hard to carve, but made them beautiful. Many a carver had made his masterpiece from just such a burl. Kate had dreamed of it — but had never been able to afford the wood. Burl wood was rare and expensive.

Plain Kate looked down at her hands, stiff and patched with scars, white and pink like the belly of an old fish. In an unknown country, with not so much as a kopek in her pocket, there were better things to carry than ten pounds of wood. And there were easier things to carve, when you weren't sure if your hands would serve you. Indeed, anything she could have chosen would be easier to carve than an oak burl.

But she took it anyway.

Plain Kate walked down the road with the oak burl under one arm. Crumbs and clots of dirt broke into the folds of her white dress. But there was no one to tut over the damage. The foggy road was beginning to grow strange with its emptiness. The fields, which should have been bustling with harvesters, were empty. The farm huts let no smoke from their chimneys. She met a cow that lowed to be milked and butted at her. Mile after mile, there was no one.

She came finally to a wheat field that was half harvested, rough-shorn as Drina's hair. It was quiet, thick with starlings that were feasting on the fallen wheat.

Plain Kate was a town girl, but she knew that wheat

shouldn't be left to lie in the fields until poppies came up through it. She walked beside the red flowers, feeling her legs begin to tremble with their weakness. Something was wrong. Something was wrong.

She kept walking. There was a brew-house sour smell of wheat rotting. A wave of starlings startled as she passed, and flew up, twisting over her head like a ribbon of smoke. Taggle craned his neck to follow the flight, but he was staying close to her side, almost like a dog. She didn't mention that, of course.

She trudged on. Her legs felt like old wineskins: her skin stiff and her muscles sloshing. She teetered a little as she walked, though she tried not to. But there was nowhere to stop. She squinted ahead. There was a place where the wheat was still standing, and beyond that, at the edge of the field, a windrow of birch. When she reached that windrow, she promised herself, she would cut a walking staff and stop to carve it. She locked her eyes on the white trees and tried to keep her feet from dragging. When she got to the windrow, she kept thinking. When she got to the windrow —

But she never reached it.

At the ragged shore between the cut and uncut wheat, there was a splash of poppies. Something dark lay in them like a log. She would sit down on that, she thought, staggering, and —

She saw that the log was a body. A half-grown lad with wheat-bright hair lay sprawled there with his scythe stuck in the ground beside him. Kate toppled to her knees.

Taggle sniffed the lad's face. "He's alive. He had fish to eat . . . but . . . Katerina. I smell the thing. The thing has done this to him."

Kate took the boy's limp hand, shook the rough-clad shoulder. The lad didn't stir, didn't even sigh in his sleep. *Like Wen*, she thought. *Like Stivo and like Wen.* She shut her eyes and tried to get up, but fell forward instead. She might have passed out. Time stopped, blankly.

When it moved again, Taggle was butting at her hand. She could feel the lump on his skull where the axe had hit him, a gnarled spot under his soft fur. "There are more of them," he hissed. His fur was on end. "The thing. More sleepers. The thing has been here."

"The white shadow." Plain Kate gagged and spit out the sourness in her mouth. "The thing that killed Wen and Stivo." She looked at the limp, sleeping lad, then yanked the scythe out of the earth, and, leaning on it, staggered to her feet. She stood panting.

Taggle was looking at the sky, a ridge of fur standing up from his spine. Plain Kate looked up too, her skin beginning to goose-bump with a slow-dawning fear. It was dimming toward evening. A fog twined off the river, snaking over the road. It would be night in an hour or two; the fog would come; the white creature would come with it. It had killed Stivo with one touch. She had no defense. "We have to go back," she said.

So they went back. Exhausted, Kate went stumbling and limping, hauling her burl, leaning on the scythe, until its smooth handle rubbed through her scars. She arrived at Linay's boat in purple twilight, both hands bloody, stooping like the angel of death.

Linay raised his eyebrows. "That was a long bath."

Taggle bit him. Kate collapsed at his feet.

eleven

A GHOST IN THE RIVER

"That cat of yours really is something of a bother." Linay was perched on the edge of the bunk; Kate saw him blurred then silhouetted as she struggled to get her eyes open. She was awake again and confused again. It took her a moment to put the boy in the poppies and the bear cage and the willow pool and the violin bow and the axe in the darkness all together, and in the right order. They swirled around Linay. They were all his fault, and there he was sitting beside her, dressing a wound on his wrist, whistling. "He's bitten nearly to the bone, look!" He held up one — scratched — finger.

It was day again, and either dawn or sunset. The light at the hatch was soft and birds were singing.

"Sit up, then, fair maid. You should be able to manage that. Though perhaps you ought not strike out on pilgrimage again." He reached for her hand and pulled her up. Her own hands were bandaged, softly and well, in clean linen.

Linay flexed his hand closed, then mimed his fingers rippling over the violin's fret. His bitten finger seemed stiff. "It will make a merry mess of my fingering." He looked at her, smiling but humorless, implacable as snow. "You're lucky I do not hurt him."

Plain Kate went cold. She could hear Taggle on the deck, yowling. And Linay sang softly, giving words to the cat's song:

> Oh bats, oh bats, oh snacks with wings —
> Come and hear how Taggle sings!
> Oh squirm, oh squeak, my wriggly bats —
> You'll make a gift for lady cats!

"I would be sorry to hurt him, Plain Kate. Truly I would."

"What do you want?" she asked.

"Blood," he said lightly. Then, as if remembering he'd said that once before, he added, "Yours this time, Kate, my girl. I've given most of what I can spare."

She was sitting in his reach, backed into the corner of the bunk. He was between her and the hatch. It was getting dark. She lifted her chin — and felt her new scars tug. "If you want blood you should have killed me in my sleep."

Taggle's yowls faded as he struck out to hunt and make kittens. Linay was still smiling. "But that's not how magic works, fair maiden. Magic is" — he spread his bony hands grandly — "an exchange of gifts. A shadow for a heart's wish, for instance."

Kate narrowed her eyes. "What do you need blood for?"

Linay looked at her. The looking seemed to go deep. "Perhaps I'll show you," he said.

They went out onto the deck. It was cool and clear, just past sunset, and the evening star was opening its eye and the crickets were getting louder. They had gone farther into the hill country, where the river split like braided hair around shouldering, wooded islands. Alee of one of these, the boat rocked at anchor.

There was a fog bank not far behind them.

"So," she said. Linay said nothing. Kate looked around. Taggle was nowhere in sight. She could hear him in the distance, singing his courting song. Bats swarmed in the pale sky, and swallows darted above the river, and she thought of him. Linay sat down on the roof of the cabin. Standing, she was as tall as he was seated on the low roof. She could see the sunburn, pink in the part of his white hair. It made him look almost human.

Looking out toward the gathering fog, he asked, "Have you ever been hungry?"

She shrugged.

"Of course you have," he muttered. "Of course."

"What do you want, Linay?" It was the first time she'd said his name. It tasted powerful.

"The dead, you know, are hungry. Those that do not rest. They are hungry all the time and cannot even eat grass." He was halfway to singing again. He seemed to stop himself. "They have mouths the size of needles' eyes and stomachs the size of mountains. It is a terrible fate."

"I know that," she said. "Everyone knows that." Though in truth the way he had said it was making her skin prickle.

He stopped talking again. His silence swelled up between them like insect song in the summer night. "My sister," he said at last, his voice little and broken. He swallowed and tried again. "My sister is one of them. One of the hungry dead."

"I saw her." Kate guessed it, knew it, all at once, and her hair stood up with the realization. "A white woman. A —"

"Rusalka," he said, lingering over the bitter taste of the word. "The ghost of a woman drowned. Of a witch wrongly driven into the river. Such creatures are called rusalka. There are not many. True witchcraft is a rare gift, and the *gadje* prefer fire when they kill us."

He said *gadje* the way Stivo had, and Kate saw that, beneath the way he wore his own witch-white skin like a mask, Linay had the narrow bones, full mouth, and uptilted eyes of a Roamer. A Roamer man, alone.

He stood up. "You have seen her before?"

She nodded.

"You will see her again." He brushed past her, and stood at the edge of the boat, looking down into the water. Plain Kate turned and looked too. There was a skim of fog wavering there: The edge of the fog bank was catching up to them. "Soon," said Linay. He unwrapped his bandaged arm; it was covered with long, deep cuts. Plain Kate stared. Suddenly there was a knife in Linay's other hand. It flashed and Kate jerked away, but the knife was gone, swept back into some hidden pocket in Linay's swirling coat.

Linay had cut himself. He held out his arm and blood ran down it and dripped off his fingertips. The night was very still, and they could hear the tiny sound of the blood drops falling into the river.

Linay sagged and sat down on the cabin's roof as if his knees had given way. "She'll come. Blood calls. She'll come."

Kate stood staring down at the fog. It had grown thicker, but the holes created by the blood drops remained, tunneling down.

Linay spoke behind her. "What will you do, Plain Kate? If she touches you, just touches you, you will fall into a gray sleep and never wake. They are calling it the 'sleeping death.' There is no way to save yourself." Still Kate would not turn. The holes in the fog were opening like a mouth. Linay said, "She is coming."

Kate said nothing.

"I can save you," he said. "I can stop her. There is a spell, with blood. If you give me blood, I can use it to stop her from killing you. I don't want her to kill you."

"You're lying."

Linay gave a heartbroken bark of a laugh. "I can't!" His voice was wild. "It would kill me, even to try. I can't lie, and I can't give her more blood, not much. I am taking her up the river, to Lov. A month that is, maybe. I don't need much blood to do it. A cup a day, perhaps. Two." Now he was wheedling. His panic frightened her.

He looked past her. His eyes locked on something. He closed them. "Decide."

Plain Kate turned around. Rising from the well of darkness was the ghost.

Plain Kate had to summon all her will to turn her back on the ghost and face Linay. She could feel the thing behind her. It was like standing by a cave mouth: The stilled breath chilled her neck. Her own breath was tight with terror. But she didn't turn around. "I want something," she said.

Linay snorted, almost a laugh. "What?"

"My shadow."

"I'm not done with it, though." He really did seem close to laughter, about to boil away in giggling, like the last bit of water in a pot. "And I might as well keep it, because you'll have no use for it in a minute. They don't wear shadows, you know, in the land of the dead. It's just not done."

Kate ignored this. "I can't live without it. So I might as well die now. We'll both die, won't we? She'll take us both."

His gaze flickered for a moment: behind her, up. "Yes."

"So," she said. At the edge of her hearing, music: A voice like a cold chimney was singing.

Linay sat still, biting the tip of his tongue, staining his white lips with blood. Then he nodded, sudden and sharp. "Not yet. I will need your shadow. In Lov. But in Lov, I will set it loose."

Plain Kate stood frozen, caught between threat and hope.

"It's a promise from a man who cannot lie," Linay said. "And it's all you'll get. Take it now if you want to live."

Something feather-touched the back of Kate's neck. She whipped around, drawing her knife. The creature was right there, close behind her as a shadow.

Kate leapt backward, stumbling. The fog bank billowed and the creature made of fog came forward. The music, the empty music, sluiced onto the deck of the boat. Kate felt it around her, in her, welling up and filling her legs. It was an emptiness that was like warmth; a heaviness that was like floating away. Sleep. "Stop!" she gasped, waving the knife. It went through the fog and left no wound. "Linay!"

"Blood," he said, sounding calm again, amused. She risked a look at him, reaching out with her eyes the way the drowning reach. He just sat, just watched. "Try the wrist."

Plain Kate tried to gather herself. Knives; she knew knives. She had nicked herself often enough to know how to draw blood. Breathing hard, she thrust the tip of her knife into her wrist, and with a flick opened a little well. Dark blood welled up. She let it run into her cupped hand.

The rusalka swept toward her — like sleep itself, the thing swept: gray, faceless, huge. The figure flickered like layers of ice, and appeared in little pieces: a long hand, a tumble of hair, one egg-blank eye. Then suddenly she had a face. It was narrow and sad and impossibly beautiful. Plain Kate fell to her knees, as if she'd seen an angel.

Kate wanted to curl up on the deck and cover her face, but she didn't. She lifted her hand, filled with blood. Nonsensically, she remembered the last time she had lifted her hand like this, for Taggle: One day when the Roamers strayed far from the river, she had poured water from a skin into her cupped hand and held it out. As Kate thought this, the rusalka dipped her head, and drank.

Kate felt something like a mouth close over the hole in her wrist. It sucked blood, or more than blood. Bones. Her own name.

Time went by.

Kate was dying. It felt like being changed into sleep and water.

Then a blur of gray came like a cannonball through the fog and thumped into her chest.

Plain Kate fell backward. Taggle was standing on her chest, crying "Katerina! Kate! Kate!" His claws prickled through her clothes. Fur stood in a ridge on his back. "Taggle . . ." She choked on his name. Groggy and sick, she pushed herself up on one elbow. The rusalka —

— the rusalka was kneeling beside Plain Kate on the deck. She was made of fog and shadow until Kate caught her eye, and then, all at once, she became human. She was young, mischievously sad, a fox in a story. Kate fell in love with her. And then she was gone.

It was like waking up from a dream. Kate sat up and Taggle fell from her chest and tangled himself around her sprawling legs, circling and high stepping, purring as a cat will do when badly hurt. "The thing!" he said. "The thing came while I was not here to challenge it!"

Plain Kate twisted round. Linay, as if he hadn't moved, was sitting cross-legged on the cabin roof. He gave a fluid, careless shrug. He picked up his fiddle. Kate got up and went below.

Plain Kate lay in the narrow bunk and listened to the skirl of Linay's fiddle, ringing wild and strange across the water. Taggle paced the edge of the bunk, up and down. His small feet pressed into her like blunted chisels. "Stop that," she said when she couldn't stand it anymore. "Lie down."

The cat sprang over her and started to walk the hand's space between her body and the boat wall instead. The third or fourth time he made the turn by her face she batted at him. "Taggle! Lie down!"

He stopped, facing away from her, his restless tail switching over her face. "I could go kill you something," he offered.

"Just sit."

He turned — stepping on her spleen — and sat. "I am sorry," he said. "I don't like it. It is a new word, *sorry*. It should not be a thing for cats."

"I suppose not."

He lay down and fit his narrow chin into her hand. "But I am sorry. Sorry I was not here to kill the thing for you."

"It's not a thing." Kate was remembering the rusalka's bright face — fear and a flicker of flame in the ghostly eyes. "She must have had a name once."

"Bah," said the cat. "She's dead now. Dead things should stay dead. Otherwise they might scratch you from the inside."

"Bah," echoed Kate. The music sighed and rippled. She rubbed her cut wrist, and then crooked her arm around Taggle's soft warmth. The nights were getting colder.

The cat rolled and shaped his spine to her side. "Sleep," he said. "I'll keep watch."

But Plain Kate lay a long time in the darkness — long after the cat had drifted to sleep — listening to the sad music, and thinking.

Linay was a witch, and a Roamer man alone. His sister was a witch, a woman both burned and drowned. How many could there be? Linay, Kate was sure, was Drina's uncle, the man who had given a piece of his shadow to summon the dead. The man who had gone mad.

twelve

FOG

The next day, Plain Kate looked for it and saw it: the hole in Linay's shadow.

He was poling the punt. The light threw his long shadow across the deck. In the center of that shadow, over his heart, was a patch that fluttered like a hurt bird. The sun broke through it, once in a while, in coins of light.

Kate watched that roiling patch. Under her, the boat surged, coasted, and slowed; surged, coasted, and slowed. The fog bank was still behind them, the watery sunrise turning the top of it pink and yellow. She was remembering the story of how he had used blood and hair to pull apart his shadow. To give a voice to the ghost of his sister.

"What was her name?" Kate asked. "Your sister. The rusalka. What was her name?"

The boat rocked a little when Linay fumbled the pole,

but his eerie-pale face stayed smooth. "She's dead," he answered at length. "We do not say the names of the dead."

"I know. Drina told me."

That drew a sudden, startled look. "Drina." He stilled himself again. "Well, well. How a life comes round. I knew as I followed you that you were with the Roamers, but I —"

"You followed me?" It was Kate's turn for shock.

"To draw your shadow. Did you think its remnants were to be sent to me by the royal messenger? The loss of a shadow, as I told you, is a slow thing. I had to be close, to catch yours as it pulled away." He shrugged. "There is only one road; there is only one river. It was not hard to follow you."

Why should she feel betrayed? But she did. His words stirred up the sticky panic of her long loss, her heavy secret, her shadow twisting away from her. She turned from him. His shadow fell past her, and hers was nowhere, gone.

"Why?" she said. "Why did you do this to me?"

She saw his shadow shrug. "I needed a shadow. Yours was the easiest to get."

Plain Kate looked down at her burnt hands, the light going right through them. She said nothing. Time passed. Then Linay was suddenly, silently, at her shoulder. She shuddered away from him, but he reached out and took her wrists. He lifted them, oblivious to her cold resistance. "These are healing well."

"Let me go." She jerked her hands fruitlessly.

"Some salve, first." He released her and produced, from the billows of his zupan, a stoppered jar. He rubbed some of the chilling, oily stuff into her scars. The mint-sharp smell washed over her. Linay's head was bent over her hands. "Lenore," he said softly. "My sister's name was Lenore. She was a healer. She taught me this. I will see you carve again."

She could think of nothing to say. Linay stayed bent over her hands, singing softly. Kate remembered what Drina had said: that all magic depended on a gift, freely given, and that healers gave some of their own life for the health of those they healed. Linay rocked as he sang, as if he were praying or exhausted. He sang himself slowly into silence. He let go of her hands but did not lift his head. His voice was low. "What does your cat call you?"

"Katerina."

"Katerina. I am sorry." Even if he had not been a witch, bound to the truth by his own power, she would have been sure that he meant it.

But that night as the fog rolled around the punt, he again summoned the rusalka. He again sat and watched as Kate filled her hand — her hand that he had just worked to heal — with her own blood. And he let the rusalka nurse on her blood until Kate found herself sliding into grayness, trying to hold on to the memory that Linay was dangerous, that he did not love her, and that she must not forgive him.

Plain Kate slept deep into the next day. When she woke, the first things she saw were cat eyes. Taggle was sitting on her chest glaring as only cats can. "You let the thing come for you again," he said. "If you die I am going to be furious with you."

Her head felt muzzy. "Where were you?"

The cat abruptly decided to groom his shoulder. "He gave me fish," came the fur-muffled voice. "I went to sleep."

"He poisoned you?"

"I will not take food from him again," Taggle intoned. "Please know that this is a great sacrifice. But clearly I must guard you, Katerina." He looked at her sidelong. "You are thinking of giving it more blood."

"I think . . ." she said, and stopped to think. The little cabin was stuffy and rocking; it made her drowsy. She lay watching the herbs and bundles above her slowly sway. "I think I have to," she said. "He will give me my shadow back at Lov. I can't live without my shadow."

"I do not trust him."

"He can't lie."

"So he says." Taggle's tail lashed. "Katerina, your shadow will do you no good if the thing kills you."

"It won't," said Linay, and Kate jumped. He had slipped down the ladder without them noticing.

Taggle did not deign to flinch, but his ears flicked back. "It will. I have made many little things bleed; I know blood. Katerina, you cannot feed the thing again. It *will* kill you."

"Well," said Linay. "There is a trick to it."

"Faf!" Taggle spat. "You are full of tricks! It is late for tricks! You weaken her; you muddle her!"

Linay ignored this. "Come ashore. I'll show you."

Kate wanted only to sleep. The heat lulled; her head pounded. But after a while she got up and climbed the ladder. She found the punt pulled up at the river's edge where some long-ago flood had left a tangled heap of dead trees. She had waited too long: Linay had gone off on one of his foraging missions and left them alone.

Sitting in the bleached and bony wood, with the sun streaming through her, Plain Kate sat and tried to carve. The knife that had once been like another hand to her now sat stiffly on top of the new scars. Her fingers had lost their sureness and strength. But still, she turned the burl wood she'd found in the road over and over under her knife, cutting away its weak-rotted places, looking for the shape in its heart. It was rough work, the only kind her hands could do.

The burl slowly took a shape like something with wings. She thought of two hands pressed wrist to wrist, with palms and fingers spread. Bound hands.

Taggle sat primly on a deadfall branch and glared at her until she gave up on carving and placated him by catching a fish. She cooked; they ate. Time passed quietly.

"When you were with the Roamers," said Linay's voice behind her, sudden and soft as a ghost, "did she come?"

Plain Kate refused to jump again. She nodded without looking at him. Yes, the rusalka had come. And the Roamers — the people who had been almost her family — had blamed Kate.

"Who?" said Linay.

Plain Kate didn't see why she ought to answer. Let him wonder. But then he said: "Not Drina . . . ?"

Drina. Her first friend, her — the word startled her as it came into her head — her sister. "No," she said. "Not Drina. Wen. Stivo."

"Ah," he said, voice flat. And he sat down across from her and speared the fish's head.

"Can they be saved?" Kate asked. "The sleepers — could I have saved them?"

Linay shrugged. "If the rusalka was roused from her half sleep, the sleepers might awaken too. I don't know and I don't much care." He flipped up the gill flap with a thumbnail and picked out the morsel of meat behind it.

"We want to see this trick of yours," said Taggle.

"Hmmm," hummed Linay. "Come closer."

Plain Kate hesitated, and shifted her foot to be sure of the knife in her boot. She did it subtly, but he saw it. "Oh, honestly." He nudged her toe with his. "I saved your life. I'm hardly about to hurt you. Hold out your hands." He mimed it, making a bowl of his own long hands and lifting it.

She looked at him narrowly. In the sun, the burn scar pulled across her scalp. She cupped and raised her hands.

"I haven't always been a stealer of shadows, you know," he said. "I was a weather worker, once — and welcome anywhere, welcome as a summer rain. And I still know the moods of wind and water." He leaned over her, fitting his own hands against the underside of hers, his long fingers lapping her wrists. "You can't expect a ghost to lick up spilled blood like a —"

"— dog," supplied Taggle. The cat had stood up and was watching them, fur on end.

"She will take blood only from a body. But what is a body? Just a bowl for life. A bowl of breath." And he blew a long breath into the cup of her hands. It was warm at first, and slowly it grew cold.

Kate eased her hands open. Inside them — taking their shape — was a bowl of ice. It was small as a bird's nest, woven like that, and shining in the sun. She lifted it into the light. Delicate feathers of frost furred its edges.

"You see," he said, smiling. "It hasn't always been ugly."

Then he stood up, fast, like a man insulted. "It's a bowl. You fill it with blood and she won't know the difference between this and a body. Thus I control her bottomless appetites. Notice that you can't do it without me." He turned his back on her and swung up the skillet as if it were a sword. "Kick out the fire and come aboard," he said. "I want some distance yet today."

But when she lifted herself over the edge of the boat he was in the hold below, and he didn't come up at once. She thought she heard him weeping.

So they went along. The country grew lower, and the weather cooler. Kate's hands healed slowly. Linay grew stronger, and Plain Kate learned why he had been weak.

Every evening she let her blood fill the bowl of ice that

lined Linay's hands. They were big hands, narrow but long-fingered. It caught up with her like sickness, the blood-letting. The first day she didn't feel different. But on the second the sun made her drowsy. On the third she found herself nodding over her carving. By the fifth a sort of heaviness came over her, and made her knife shake. She sheathed it and asked, "How far to Lov?"

Linay shrugged. The old fluidness was back in his joints; he no longer moved as if his jumping-jack strings had stiffened. "Two weeks? Three? It's not my country." He set the pole to the river bottom, pushed them ahead, and added: "But we're coming to it, *mira*. I can taste it, like ashes. Lov, at last."

His voice made her scars ache. She ducked her head and took up the wood again.

Days passed. Linay brought back from his wanderings leather leggings and a farm boy's smock, and she folded the long linen dress away, gladly. The next day he gave her a roll of hand tools: a rasp, a chisel, three kinds of gouges, an awl, and a carving knife. Kate, whose old knife was as much a part of her as her name, put the new knife away, but she used the other tools gratefully.

"No cat would do this," said Taggle. "Fight."

"I am fighting," she answered. But slowly it stopped being true.

She tried to stop herself from feeling the surge of tenderness that came to her when he worked to heal her hands: the liquid song that had once set her father's smashed fingers, the crooked sunburned part of Linay's white hair as he bent his fair head. *He is dangerous*, she told herself. *He does not love me. I do not trust him. I am only going to Lov to get back my shadow.*

He does not love me. I do not belong here.

thirteen

SHADOW

Adrift in a green barge on the tea-colored, slow-flowing Narwe, Plain Kate carved and bled.

She sat on the pole man's seat, knife in hand, drowsy in the sun. The burl wood wings were almost finished, full of long, strange twists of wood grain, less like feathers now than like long hair spread in water. They had an uneasy beauty. But the lump between the wings would not show her its face. She had cut away the rough and rotten wood and found a smooth knot, like an acorn. Was it a sharp chin and a high forehead? An owl's beak and flaring ears? Its blank curve told her nothing. She sat with her knife above it and did not know what to do. If the thing was a mirror, then her heart was blank.

She tried to summon up her father's voice: *Be brave. Trust the wood. Lift your knife.*

Kate touched the knife to the smooth curve, took a shallow stroke. The blade hit a knot and shot from her hand, skittering across the deck. Kate stood and fetched the knife. She thought about throwing the carving into the river, and maybe following it in.

Taggle was leaning out from the prow like a figurehead, his whiskers quivering close to the water. Kate glanced: Catfish stirred in the willow roots, slowly working their white mouths. Taggle was staring at them, cross-eyed with desire.

"I'm going to lie down," she told him.

"Fish, fissssshhh," he answered.

She eased down the ladder into the warm dim hold — and saw Linay.

He was kneeling beside the bunk. On top of the quilts was the box made from the ruins of her father's stall. Linay had one hand stretched above it, and blood was dripping from one fingertip, into the box.

"Don't come closer," he said.

She came closer.

From a few steps away she could see inside the box. It was empty, but it held darkness as a bowl might hold water. The clotting shadow inside seemed to bubble around the blood, like fish after bread crumbs.

She stopped coming closer.

And Linay closed the lid.

"My shadow," Kate whispered.

"All things need to eat." Linay shrugged and lifted his pricked finger to his mouth, sucking away the blood. "Tears are better than blood, but some days one just can't weep. And the shadow must be fed or it will wither to ribs and eyeholes — useless."

"Useless," she said softly, "for what? Why do you need it?"

"To raise the dead and spread the fire." He answered her as if sunk into his own dreams. Then he roused and looked daggers at her. "You're sharp, Plain Kate. Be careful, or you'll find yourself cut. If you love your life, do not open that box."

And he stalked out.

Plain Kate stood looking at the closed box. She put her hand on the carved hart and let its antlers prick the tight new skin on her palm. It was her father's carving; it was as familiar to her as her own breath. Did something stir? Behind the thin wood, as if behind the surface of a mirror, did something press its hand to hers?

Her heart gave a little lurch as if at a hero's hurt in a story. "Yes," something answered her. "Mine."

Tears, Linay had said. If she wept, would it come to her? She could almost have wept, wounded by the new hope.

The next day, when Linay went foraging in the abandoned country, Kate climbed back aboard the barge. She went below and sat on the edge of the bunk, looking at the box. Taggle climbed into her lap. "Hello," he said, then rolled over and peered up at her appealingly. "I am fond of you and present my throat for scratching."

"Taggle," said Kate. She knitted her fingers through his fur. "I . . ."

"There's this itchy spot, you see," he said. "Just over the left jawbone. Oooooo, yes, therrrrre . . ." His voice trailed away into a purr.

As you love your life, Linay had said. But she had to see. If there was any chance of getting her shadow back — "I have to try."

"Oooo, you're succeeding." Taggle's claws bared and velveted as he kneaded at the air. "You're talented, I've always said so. Ooooooo . . ."

"We're not talking about you."

The cat's inner eyelids had been sliding closed. He lifted one, lizardlike. "We're not? Why not?"

"It's my shadow, Taggle. The thing in that box is my shadow."

Taggle's eyes opened. They looked uncattishly wise. "And how long have you known that?"

"Since yesterday," she said. "You thought —"

"I thought you might have known longer, yes. I thought you might have known and yet done nothing. You have not been yourself. You have given yourself too much to that man." He tipped his head at her. "A dog, you know — her master may beat her and she will still be glad to see him. Open the door of her cage and she might still faithfully wait."

"I'm not a dog," she said hotly.

He arched his whiskers into a cat grin and rubbed his brow bone against her cheek. "I should say not." He growled with fierce joy. "Is it dangerous, this box?"

If you love your life . . .

"Yes," she answered.

"Then I will stand by you," he said.

So Kate stood up.

The box sat in its shadowy corner. She nudged it with her foot. It scraped over the deck. She'd thought it would either lean into her like an animal or stand heavy like a lead casket. But it was just a box. She picked it up and set it on the bunk. In the bunched blankets it looked bigger than it should have. It had butt joints, the simplest of joints, but even so they weren't square. Just a badly made little box.

Taggle sniffed at it, squinted, and backed away. "Bitter." He snorted to clear his sensitive nose.

Kate lifted the lid.

The box was empty, but around them, the air was slowly tightening. The emptiness began to rise in the box, sitting up on its blind haunches and sniffing at the air.

Kate's heart reached for it, and her hand followed. "Easy —" said Taggle. The shadow nosed and licked at her fingers, put its not-breath on her scarred palms. She pulled away and it whined after her.

And then it was out — her shadow.

It flowed over her — it joined her hand and foot — it rushed cold across her skin — it dove into her nose and ears. Wherever it touched her, she went numb — the kind of numbness that comes after a blow. It was between her fingers, inside her smock, inside her mouth. She spun away but it followed her, whirling around her like a dancer.

"Katerina!" Taggle spun with her, circling fast, swiping at the clinging almost-stuff.

"Tag —" Kate choked. It was in her. She felt heavier and lighter, buzzing, dizzy. But as she reeled into the light from the hatch she saw it: the Kate-shaped thing flying across the floor, across the wall, a shadow, her shadow!

Yes, said the presence, as it pushed against her. *Mine. Us.*

Kate stopped and stood panting. She lifted a hand and watched the shadow's hand-thing lift. It slid up the wall. It grew long claws. Kate stood frozen, one hand uplifted. "Is it —"

"Breaking!" Taggle shouted. One of the long shadow fingers flew off. Another. And suddenly the shadow hand came apart into whirling clots. Kate gasped, clutched at her own hand, and crashed to her knees. "Katerina!" Taggle cried.

Kate squeezed her wrist as hard as a tourniquet; her shadow was in a dozen pieces, her hand felt alien as a flock of birds. Across the floorboards, her shadow slumped as she did. She could see its edges tattering and lifting away. "The light," she gasped. "The light is breaking it!"

They don't wear them in the land of the dead, Linay's voice came back to her. The dead had no shadows. If you had no shadow, were you dead? It felt like death — a breaking apart that was well past any pain.

Something streaked down past her ear and thumped onto the deck: Taggle. He'd gone above and she hadn't even noticed. "I tried — close the hatch. Block the light," he panted. "Can't. Latched. Can't — Kate! Kate!" She had toppled sideways and lay there in pieces. Taggle seized her by the scruff of her neck and tried to drag her like a kitten, out of the light.

"The box," she managed. "Close the box."

He was gone, endlessly. And then back. "The shadow-thing won't go in," he said. She could hardly hear him; his words and the whole world was breaking into whirling birds. "What do I do?" A sudden point of pain brought her back. Taggle was biting her hand. "Kate! What do I do?"

". . . tears . . ." It was just a shadow of a thought.

"I can't!" he wauled. "I'm a cat! I can't cry! Katerina!"

And then he was gone, or she was. She was alone and broken like the moon in high branches.

And then slowly, like waking from a dream about waking from a dream, she was back. She was sprawled on the deck with no shadow beside her. On the bunk, the box was crookedly closed. Taggle was pushing at her with his nose, his fur standing out in all directions. His eyes were bright with tears. He had put her shadow back in its box.

"More," she whispered, raising a shadowless hand to touch him. "You're more than a cat."

"Bah," he said, though he was still weeping. "Who would want to be?"

She closed her eyes again. The light from the hatch was blinding, and the rock of the barge huge and sickening. She felt Taggle lean into her. "I'm sorry," he whispered, but before she could answer, she dropped into a stunned sleep.

Sun. She had been damp so long, and the sun felt so good. Waking, Plain Kate lay still and let it wash over her.

Then she remembered and flailed up. A white hand on her chest pushed her back. Linay was leaning over her, smiling. "Had another adventure, did we?"

"Let me *up*," she snapped, swatting his hand away. She pushed herself to sitting. She was not in the hold anymore, but on a mat of moss and willow branches by the campfire. She shuddered to think of him scooping her up and carrying her ashore.

Taggle was beside her, stretched limp on his side. "Taggle!" Kate was terrified for him.

"Oh, honestly," sulked Linay. "I've only sent him to sleep. He was my gift to you, Kate, when you gave me your shadow. Do you really think, after so much distance and so much darkness, I would break that exchange?" He drew a thumb between Taggle's ears. "Wake, cat."

The cat woke spitting and hissing and leapt at Linay. The magician lifted his hands and sang. The cat seemed to hit a spiderweb midair. He dropped, and pushed again toward

Linay, but couldn't reach him. Plain Kate was just glad to see that Linay already had cat scratches across his nose and neck: evidence that getting her out of the boat had not gone smoothly.

"We *really* don't like you," the cat growled.

"And I really don't blame you," Linay said, sighing. "But you must listen to me. You cannot steal your shadow back, Plain Kate. If you set it loose without my help, it will kill you. I am not sure, indeed, how you survived this time."

She wished she had Taggle's claws, to swipe him. "Leave me alone, Linay."

He sat transfixed — hurt, she thought. Then he stood. "We will rest here the day," he said, his back to her, tending the fire. "And I will bleed tonight. But tomorrow we must again travel." He walked off into the willow trees and out of sight.

Plain Kate slept, and woke feeling stronger, and warmer for Taggle's chin fitting neatly in her hand. Still, the sun was slipping away. Upriver, she could see a wall of weather: fog and cloud. A cold draft was blowing it toward them; she could smell its dampness. She sighed: more rain. "It's as if it's following us," she muttered, ruffling Taggle's fur.

"We draw it. Like a bear on a chain." Kate sat up sharply and Taggle sprang to his feet. Across the fire, Linay was sitting on a stone, skinning a rabbit. "I'm a weather witch, remember? The moods of wind and water." He thrust a sharpened stick through the rabbit like a man who knew swords. "That fog is hungry."

"You," said Kate. "You made the fog and the rain. All of it. Through the whole country."

There was horror in her voice, but Linay bowed modestly as if it had been awe. "It is no small work, I admit. I'd be ashamed to tell you the dark things I've done for such power. Your shadow is only the latest — and almost the last. I have been preparing this journey for years."

"But —" She couldn't begin to tell him what she was thinking. He'd made the fog and rain, the crops failing in the wet, the damp fear she'd seen growing like a mold in the Toila market. Even Taggle's ears were edging back as it sank in.

But then, Taggle was still a cat. "I've been *wet*," he snarled. "My paws were damp for *months*."

Linay shrugged one marionette shoulder. "The fog is the rusalka's home. She needs it as a frog needs water. It is half her skin. Even the blood-spell would not bring her without this fog." And he sang:

Foggy little oxbows
Forest pools where no one goes
Lost links of the river dreaming dreams

"Without me she'd be trapped in some lonely place where the fog never lifts. With me, she can travel. All the way to Lov."

Plain Kate pictured it. The wall of fog was creeping up the river, just faster than a man could walk. In it, the rusalka. Anyone she found, she would take — take like Stivo, take like Wen. This was the dark story they were telling in Toila. By now it was a horror. The countryside was emptying in front of it like a forest emptying in front of a fire.

And she had been helping him. Giving him blood for the drawing spell. For weeks. Kate shook — and turned sideways and was sick.

Linay raised an eyebrow and propped the impaled rabbit up over the fire.

Plain Kate felt gray and cold. Waiting for the Roamers to burn her had been no worse than this. "Why?" she said. "Why are you taking her to Lov?"

"Oh," he sang. "I have reasons. I have plans and schemes." He ripped a leg from the roasting rabbit and threw it, bloody, to Taggle — who leapt back. "Come and eat your dinner."

Plain Kate carved. She carved to keep from shaking. She carved to think.

"Are you all right, Katerina?" Taggle peered into her shattered face. When she didn't answer he shook his head — actually shook it, side to side, a human "no."

The gesture struck Kate and made her sad. It looked wrong; it looked right. It made what he was visible: not a cat, not human, something new. "Oh, Taggle," she said. What was he? What was she? What had Linay made them?

Find your shape. Lift your knife.

Plain Kate stopped thinking and carved, her knife knowing things. The gouge she'd made when her knife had slipped suggested the lower lid of an uptilting eye. She roughed it out, put in the other eye, then used the knife tip to sketch the lines of the nose and brow and mouth, and suddenly the oak burl had a face: a woman's face, narrow and strong and sad, too strange to be beautiful. With only the eyes done it seemed to look at her. And already she knew it: the rusalka's human face, the face of Linay's lost sister, Drina's mother, Lenore.

Find your shape. She was Plain Kate Carver, daughter of Piotr, the girl who knew the secrets inside the wood. The girl who was brave and lifted her knife. The girl who had told her father she would be a master by the time she was twenty.

But instead she was going to die. Because she was going to stay with Linay.

Long enough to find out how to stop him.

fourteen

BLOOD AND QUESTIONS

The next evening they anchored in a place where the fields of barley and rye came right down to the river, the grain growing among the riverside tangle of bloodtwig and basket rush. The grain — as Kate had come to dread — was unharvested, and full of feasting starlings. As the sunset lit, the birds threw themselves into the sky in tongues of dark fire that flashed back and forth across the river. Linay stood up on the roof of the hold, playing his fiddle. The skirling notes wove through the rush of wings.

Plain Kate kept her head bent over the carving, her heart beating faster as the light sank. The fog rose up around her. The fiddle grew quieter and quieter until both it and its player were lost in the thickening darkness. Plain Kate slotted her carving tools one by one into their leather roll. The tool case was a very fine thing, its felt-lined inner pockets soft with long use, its smooth-grained outside stained dark with someone's sweat. It hadn't been abandoned; the carver in Kate was sure of that. Someone had died. And then Linay had stolen it and given it to her. And she'd been grateful.

The fog was so thick now that she felt completely alone. Then Taggle came from nowhere, standing regally at her elbow, with his ears pricked and his fine head lifted. They heard Linay jump down onto the deck. He emerged from the fog and stopped in front of them. Wordless, he held out his cupped hands, ready for her blood.

Kate stood up. "I won't," she said.

"Oh, won't you? I believe we had a bargain. Your blood for your shadow."

"I gave you blood. I never said I'd keep giving it." In the rye field the birds settled into a silence that struck Kate as ominous. She drew herself up. "I want something else."

Linay folded his cupped hands together. The idea of violence was frank on his face.

"I want answers," said Kate. "To three questions."

"Three questions!" He laughed. "Do you think you're a fair maid in a tale? Shall I fetch a mirror, Little Stick, to set you straight?"

"Two questions," she bargained.

Linay stopped laughing. A thicker fog was beginning to pour over the side of the punt. "You would haggle with hell's boatman," Linay spat at her, then thinned his voice to a little girl's: "One coin or two?"

Kate tried a shrug. "Bleed yourself, if you'd rather."

"I'll help," said Taggle.

Linay ignored the cat, and spoke as if to himself. "I am going to need my strength."

The boat was full of fog now. Plain Kate felt as if they might sink into it and drown.

"*One* question," Linay said.

"One a night."

"Done. Now bleed."

So she did, letting the blood trickle into the bowl of ice in Linay's hands. In the twilight, it looked black. As the bowl filled, the fog rose and thickened and began to eddy around them and rub at them like a stray dog. In another moment the rusalka was there, thin as a rib bone but wrapped halfway around them. She leaned for the blood. There was nothing human in her face, nothing lovely — just a bottomless avidity.

Kate backed away.

Linay, though, stayed where he was, and when the rusalka knelt to drink he crouched beside her, as if he wanted to wrap an arm around her shoulders. He was singing something. Kate couldn't hear what.

She reached down and picked up Taggle. Together they

watched the rusalka and Linay kneeling together like a bride and groom. They waited.

The rusalka drank the blood from the bowl, and when she was gone, Linay folded up. He sat on the deck with his knees drawn up and his head resting on his arms.

"Linay?" said Kate. She couldn't tell whether or not he was weeping.

He fluttered a pale hand without lifting his head. "Yes, yes. Ask your question."

"Why —" she asked softly. She found, to her surprise, that she didn't want to hurt him. "Why are you taking her — Lenore — to Lov?"

"She died there." His bent head made his voice soft. "In the *skara rok*. She was tending the sick." He laughed, barely louder than the river. "By the Black Lady, they would hardly have needed to kill her — she had spent so much of herself in healing magic. But they did. They killed her. They took her for a witch, they tortured her, and they killed her. The people of Lov."

Kate sat down on the pole man's seat, not beside Linay but near. "So why? Why take her back there?"

"After —" He swallowed. "After I saw what she had become, I decided I had to save her. I studied dark magic. I went to dark places. I spoke with . . . things . . . no man should speak with. I gathered power. And I learned. I learned, among other things, that a rusalka's fate can be undone by avenging her death."

"But — people have died." *People I knew*, she thought. *Stivo. Wen. And maybe — don't let it be Drina.* "It's already done. People have already died."

Linay shrugged. "But not the people who killed her."

"Lov," she said. "The people of Lov."

"Lov," he nodded. "So at last we are going." With that he lifted his head. He was not weeping. His face was set and fierce as a blade. Plain Kate stood up and wished she had room to back away.

"Enough," he said, looking down and dashing the fragments of ice from his hands. "Go."

She went.

The carving of Lenore's face was going to be beautiful. Even in its rough form, it arrested. The nose, narrow. The mouth, rich and sad. The eyes, tilted as a fox's eyes. The hair, wild as the fog, vanishing seamlessly into those seaweed wings. All the next morning, Plain Kate worked on it, staying in the hold to avoid Linay's eyes. And though Taggle disliked the hot closed space, he stayed with her, drowsing at her feet.

Working fast and fearlessly, Kate used a chisel to free

high cheekbones and quizzical brows from the wood that had enclosed them. Lenore. Kate could see Drina's lively eyes in the carving's face. She felt a stab of loss and guilt. Drina. What had happened to Drina?

And this woman who had been her mother, with her lively eyes, with Linay's full mouth, with some alchemy of mischief and sadness that was all her own, Lenore: Was there anything left of her, inside the rusalka? Did she know what she had become? When she took her own husband, Stivo, into her gray sleeping kingdom, had she known?

At Pan Oksar's farm, Plain Kate had seen a new thing: The Oksar people, with their foreign ways, had nailed iron to trees for luck. Horseshoes and rough crosses shaped of broken plowshares and pitchfork tines. Some had been there a long time, and the trees, in their swelling growth, had edged their bark over the metal like slow lips, had grown around their injury and taken black iron into their mouths, into their hearts.

Linay had taken his sister's fate inside that way. And its weight and blackness had sent him slowly mad. No wonder his people had cast him out. He was as lost as Lenore was — more lost, because unlike her, he surely did know. He did know what he was doing.

And he was going to do it anyway. Unless she could stop him.

So, on the second night, Kate waited, slapping at mosquitoes, and Taggle came over and sat, sphinxlike, between her feet. The light grew blue and the fog caught up to them. Soon the little punt was alone in a world of it.

Linay shipped his pole and came forward, springing lightly onto the boat roof, and then down again to the deck in front of Kate. He bowed to her elaborately. "Fair maid of the wood, again the moment has come. Ask your question."

"How?" she said. "You are going to revenge Lenore's death. How?"

"Hmmm," he said. "Your interest is . . . interesting. Are you planning another little adventure? Have you given any thought to how that might turn out?"

"How?" she insisted.

"Why," he said with a little smile, "I am going to destroy the city, of course."

He was still smiling when he held out his hands for blood. All that evening he did not say another word.

"I think we should kill him," said Taggle.

Plain Kate put her head in her hands. The hold was hot, and the rocking made her queasy. "There must be," she muttered. "There must be something we can do to stop him."

"Yes," said the cat, patiently. "Killing him would stop him."

"I can't." She traced the curve of Lenore's carved cheek. "I can't."

Plain Kate stayed below as long as she could, until after the boat stopped moving, until she could smell the fog rising. When she came up the ladder she didn't see Linay at first, but when she turned he was inches away, sitting cross-legged on the hold roof, grinning like a wolf. "Well, Little Stick," he said. "Are you ready to match wits?"

Kate turned to face him. They had anchored in a mill-pond, slate-dark in the twilight and lively with swallows. The millrace chattered and the wheel turned, but the grind-stones inside were silent and the chimney was cold. Plain Kate knew what she'd find if she went inside: the miller fled, like the rest of the country, before the wall of fog and the rusalka's gray sleep. *A mill*, she thought. *This country will starve.*

"Well?" said Linay.

Kate braced herself. "How do you plan to destroy Lov?"

"Why," drawled Linay. "With your help, little one. Are you sure you want to know?"

Her scalp prickled. She could feel the rusalka somewhere close, but she was more afraid of the man in front of her. She spread her feet for balance. "How?"

"You'll die if you try to stop me," he said.

"Three times, I ask you," she said. "How."

Linay chuckled. "Oh, Plain Kate. A little hero. And I took you for the weakest in your town." He stood suddenly, gliding to his feet. Kate was trembling, but she didn't wince away. "Would you like to see?" His voice was almost amused, almost gentle. It was like Taggle when he tucked away his claws to make some unlucky thing last longer. "Shall I show you the fate of Lov?"

Fear made her skull push against the inside of her skin. Her lips were numb. Speechless, she nodded.

"Come," said Linay, and stepped over the side of the boat.

Kate cried out and reached to save him — but he did not sink. Around his feet was a sheen of white on the dark water. Ice. He was standing on ice in the warm, still evening. Linay stepped away from her, toward the mill, and the ice flowed out from him, unrolling like a carpet, like a bridge for a king. The mill wheel clattered and groaned to a stop, jammed with ice, and the stillness tightened in Kate's throat.

"She's just a ghost, you know," he said, his soft voice

eddying across the water. He stepped up onto the stone wall between the millrace and the pond and stood there as if on a stage. "Just one more of the shadowless people in this shadowy world. But add a shadow to a ghost —"

And he drew a knife across his wrist.

Blood spurted and spattered. She could hear it pattering into the black water.

As the blood fell, the rusalka rose up. It was like death happening backward, bones rising and taking on a loose skin. "Sister," Linay said, and offered the thing his hand. She took it, and stepped onto the wall beside him, dainty. She bent her head toward his bleeding wrist, but he stopped her, putting the back of his hand under her chin and raising her face to his. His whisper carried: "Forgive me." And he seized her arm and wrenched.

The rusalka twisted like a rope. Strands of her separated and coiled around one another. Her face distorted into a silent scream.

Then something ripped through Kate — cold as a hand on her neck, sudden as a dream about falling. The thing flew across the water toward Linay and Lenore, and Kate recognized it: her shadow.

Linay was chanting something. He was still twisting Lenore's arm, though she screamed. The shadow followed the ugly curves of his words, insinuating itself into the new rents of the rusalka's body, a rope braiding itself into another rope.

And suddenly, in the place of the woman-shape made of fog, there was something else. Something huge, something ugly. Linay flung up both hands. The thing screamed like a hawk and opened two wings: one white as a death cap, one clotted in shadow. The wings came together and the whole pond shuddered.

Something hit Kate's ear and shoulder and smashed to the deck by her feet. It was a swallow, dead. She could hear them falling all over the pond. The shadow-and-white wings smashed open and Kate threw herself downward to get under them. She could feel thick death moving just above her head.

Then Linay dropped his hands again. And the shadow wings closed, folded.

"She is gone for now," said Linay. He stepped down from the wall and came across the groaning ice.

Taggle sprang up on the gunwhale between Kate and the striding man. "Keep your distance!" he hissed.

"But it was her question!" Linay laughed, bitter and wild. "How will I destroy Lov? With the ghost and the shadow. It will take a spell of great power to bind your shadow to the rusalka for more than a moment. But I have worked for years to gather that power. Do not doubt that I can do it. And when I do it — do not doubt that everyone those wings touch will die. The whole city of Lov. And you, Plain Kate —"

But at that instant, Taggle snarled and sprang.

Linay caught the leaping cat with his eyes and a rhyme like a thrown spear. Taggle crashed to the deck and made a high, terrible noise. "Tag!" Kate shouted. She went to her knees beside him. The cat was shaking as if in seizure. She tried to scoop him up but Linay's hand closed on her wrist. He was back aboard the boat. He jerked her toward him. Kate felt the crush of his strong hand, even as she twisted around to get at Taggle.

"He'll live," Linay snapped.

"What did you do to him?" she gasped.

"I am still answering your question," he hissed at her, "and you will listen to me." He scooped up the dead bird from the decking. It was falling apart in his hands, crumbling like termite-rotted wood. "This is why I need a shadow. This is the fate of Lov. The city that tried to burn my sister. She will have her revenge and thus her fate will be undone. The gray wing will kill everyone in that city, from the bell ringer in the church tower to the orphan huddled in the lowest cellar. This is what I will do with your shadow."

"I won't help you," she gasped; he was breaking her wrist. "I'll kill myself."

He laughed. "Your shadow is bought and paid for, and your death will not remit that payment. You can go shadowless into the shadowless world, and your death will only be one last dark thing on my long dark road. It will hurt me but I do not care. It is all but over."

He released her. Kate staggered back. Her wrist pounded. "Go to bed," he said. "I have the blood I need."

Kate picked up Taggle and leapt into the hold, not bothering with the ladder. Her ankles jammed and she welcomed the clean pain that cleared her eyes of tears. She ran to the box that had held her shadow and wrenched the lid open. She was ready to die if she could take her shadow with her. But the box was empty, holding only splinters and air. It was gone. Her shadow was gone.

She sat on the bunk edge with Taggle limp on her lap. She waited in shaking silence, until silence fell on the deck above. Then she tied the carving of Lenore to her hip, stole Linay's socks, took the unconscious cat in her arms, and lowered herself over the side of the boat, into the river.

fifteen

THE ABANDONED COUNTRY

Stumbling down the road to Lov, Plain Kate dripped and shivered. Taggle was slumped in her arms like a little child, sleeping. He had slept through her huddled wait in the boat, slept through her wade to shore, slept through the slap and sting of alder branches as she fought her way up the bank. She tried not to be terrified for him. *He'll live*, Linay had said, and that made it true.

The night was white-blind with fog, and Kate staggered over every stone and stumbled in every puddle, but she pushed on as fast as she could.

Apart from the sleeping cat, she was almost empty-handed. The carving of Lenore banged at her hip. Her haversack held only stolen socks, a few apples, and a barley loaf. It was not much, not enough to live long. But in the abandoned country, it should be easy to find what she needed.

Except her shadow.

In Lov I'll set your shadow loose, Linay had promised her.

Set it loose, she should have asked, to do what? She could still see the swallow, limp as a glove, falling into clots of dust and feathers, broken as last year's leaves. The whole city.

And she had made it possible. Her blood. Her shadow.

The moon came out, a broken thing tangled in the birch branches. The road to Lov appeared before Kate, stretching into the distance. She walked along it until she found her eyes closing and her arm, where she held Taggle, growing stiff and numb. At last she found herself walking off the road. She eased the cat off her shoulder, muttering, "I'm sorry. I'm sorry."

"Why? What for?" said Taggle. "Did I miss something? Was there food?"

And she dropped him in her joy.

For three days and two nights, Kate and Taggle walked the road to Lov. They hurried when they could, and dozed when they had to, hiding in tangles of bloodtwig and heartsease at the edge of the road. When Kate couldn't sleep, she hunched up, shivering as if fevered, and freed

Lenore's face from the burl wood. The twisting lines of the grain flowed across the carving's features like tongues of fire. She was rushing down the road to beat Linay to Lov, but she had no idea how to stop him.

Kate carried Taggle the first day, and the second, while waves of shivering broke over him, subsided, and broke. On the third day he walked. They went as fast as they could, and following them came a line of fog and rain, solid as a wall, slow as an army.

The sleeping death had not come yet, but the flight before it had created its own devastation: The road was rutted and littered with broken wheels, abandoned boxes, the bodies of horses driven too hard whose eyes buzzed with flies. The wheat fields were trampled with the remains of hasty camps. Yet they met no one. The farmsteads they passed were empty and sometimes burned. Outside one farmstead three women dangled dead from the branch that overhung the road, signs against witchcraft slashed into their hands. Kate closed her eyes and ducked under their black feet and hurried on.

On the evening of the fourth day, the road swung away from the river and they found themselves walking in a tunnel of willows. And through them, across the river, Kate glimpsed something white. Big. Moving. It was just a glimpse but Plain Kate stopped short, squinting. On her shoulder, Taggle stirred awake. Kate put a hand up to touch him and edged forward. Her throat was tight, as if it had seen and recognized something her eyes had not.

The river bent, the tunnel ended, and Kate looked back along the bank.

On the other side of the river, something looked back at her. Just a horse, a big white cart horse. It was picketed outside a single Roamer *vardo*, red. "It's Cream," said Kate.

"Cream?" Taggle sprang down. "Cream?" He tangled himself with her feet, purring. "Cream, yes, please, how kind, what a thoughtful human . . ."

"No, the horse. It's Drina's horse, it's Cream."

"Oh." Taggle sniffed and flicked his ears. "I knew that."

Kate kept walking with Taggle beside her prancing grandly in his embarrassment. The horse Cream whinnied to them from her circle of mud, but no one stirred from the *vardo* and Kate didn't stop. The sun came down under the clouds and red light ran over the river like fire. Kate glanced back again, watching as the *vardo* got smaller. Her hands were clenched. Her pulse beat at the underside of her scars.

One *vardo*, one horse. A horse left at picket so long she'd eaten the grass down to dirt. Cream stomped and screamed to them again.

Kate stopped, turned around. "Something's wrong."

"Even if it is Cream, it might not be Drina," said Taggle. Kate tried to remember when the cat had become the voice of caution and reason. "It could be anyone."

"Stivo," she murmured.

"*He* said Stivo was dead."

And Kate remembered that it was Behjet — soft-voiced, softhearted Behjet — who, wearing Stivo's face, had set her on fire.

"I might also point out," said Taggle, "that these are the people who tried to kill us. And also that we already have a daunting quest."

"But it's not the Roamer way," said Kate, "to go alone."

And she bundled up Taggle and waded into the river.

The horse *was* Cream, with her familiar constellation of dun patches, and the *vardo* was the little red one in which Plain Kate had slept for months. In the twilight she could see the carving of the horses braided into ropes, the place on the edge of the top step where the paint had worn away. Kate's heart lurched, and she wasn't sure if it was recognition, loss, or fear. Hungry and desperate at the center of her muddy picket circle, the horse squealed and jerked her head sideways against her bridle rope. Kate edged around her, hoping for silence. The horse bellowed. But no one came out of the *vardo*. Kate crept up the steps and lifted the door flap.

A girl in a dark turban was kneeling in front of the back bunk, on which was a tumbled hump of blankets. Kate let the flap drop. It rustled. The girl turned. It was Drina. Kate had known it would be.

Drina looked at Kate with large black eyes, blank as a frightened rabbit.

Kate lifted her hand and touched the slick, bubbled scar on her own face. She said nothing.

"Oh," said Drina. She took a step forward. And then Kate could see that the heap of blankets wasn't a heap of blankets, but a man lying asleep. Drina took another step and Kate saw it was Behjet.

"Oh, it's these two," said Taggle. "I hope they have sausages."

But Kate stepped back so fast she felt her heels wobble on the edge of the step — she spun and leapt. She stood there, knee-deep in the grass, silent. Cream came over, jerking her head against the picket rope. She heard the step creak behind her.

Kate took a step forward — away from Drina — and stroked Cream's freckled nose. "You just left her tied up here?" The horse whuffled and started sniffing her hand for food. "She's been here too long. She's trapped. She, she —"

Her breath snagged, surprising her, and as clearly as if she were there, she smelled the rankness of the bear cage, the smoldering straw.

Drina lowered herself slowly down to stand with her — side by side but not touching, not looking.

"I —" said Drina, and stopped. Kate edged away so that Drina could undo Cream's lead. The horse tossed her mane and shouldered Drina aside on her way to fresh grass. "I'm sorry," Drina whispered, and patted Cream's neck. Cream stamped but didn't pause from her browsing.

"*Mira* —" Drina's voice broke as Kate's had.

"Is he dead?" she asked, without turning. "Is Behjet dead?"

Drina shook her head. "Are you really a witch, Plain Kate? Can you save him?"

"Why would I?" snapped Kate.

They both stood a while, watching the horse and listening to the night rising: bullfrogs, crickets, the birds of evening. Finally Kate turned. She saw that Drina looked thinner and smaller, and that her mouth closed crookedly, like a mis-made box. "I'm just a carver," she said. "But you have power. I saw it."

Drina swallowed as if trying to get down a stone. "I don't know how to use it."

Plain Kate remembered the spell braided into her hair,

the nick of the knife on her ear. The shadow on the wall of the bender tent. That shadow had been the rusalka. It might have killed them. Kate remembered the rush of steam into her face as she doused the fire, Drina's walnut face gray as if flashed to ashes. Drina had tried to help her, had used all she knew — which wasn't enough — and when she'd tried to find out more, the crowd had attacked her. It wasn't Drina who had set her on fire.

She remembered sleeping in the *vardo*, with Taggle in her arms and Drina's back warm against her back.

Kate was silent a moment, and then she said, "I don't know what to do. And I can't stay here. I have to get to Lov. But — I will try."

They went back into the *vardo*, where they found Behjet lying as if dead, and Taggle balanced on his chest, trying to pull sausages down from a hook on the wall.

Behjet looked as if he were only sleeping. Kate both did and did not want him to wake up, both did and did not want him to die. She crouched and picked up his hand. It was heavy and cold and a bit stiff, like a raw fish. A pulse lubbed sluggishly in the hollow of the wrist. There was a healed burn across the back of his hand, where the lamp oil had splashed when he'd tried to kill her.

Kate braced herself and shook him by the shoulder. "Behjet? Behjet, it's Plain Kate." She shook him harder. His head lolled to one side as if he'd turned to look at her. She leapt back. But the face was slack. Kate turned toward Drina.

"It's been four days," said Drina. "Daj says the body can't live if the soul gets lost. I've been trying. I've been feeding him and . . . cleaning him. I even tried to travel downriver, out of the fog. They say the sleep is in the fog. But nothing works. I cannot wake him."

"Let me try," said Taggle. He curled his whiskers toward her, smugly. "Waking is not so hard, really, if you know how."

The cat solemnly placed a paw on Behjet's elbow and another on his stomach. Kate and Drina edged together and watched. Taggle went high stepping, delicately, to perch on the man's breastbone. He lengthened his neck and touched his nose to Behjet's. He sniffed. He mewed. Then he opened his mouth and shouted, "Wake up!"

The girls jumped.

"Wake up," yowled Taggle. "Get up and feed me! Get up and scratch me! Get up and see me! Wake up!"

It was earsplitting, rattling the *vardo*. But Behjet didn't move.

Taggle lifted his nose and quirked an ear at them. "It

may be hopeless," he intoned. "WAKE UP!" he wauled. "Wake up, wake up, wake up!"

Drina was crying and giggling at once. Kate stepped forward and scooped the cat up. "That's enough, Taggle."

"He'll die," gasped Drina, wrapping her arms around her ribs. "That's how it is. The others died. My father died. And Daj's husband." Kate could hear her avoiding the names: the names of the dead. "And after you left, Magda's son — the one who grabbed Taggle, that time . . ."

Ciri. The toddling prince of the Roamer children, who'd exclaimed over the talking cat. Ciri.

Plain Kate led Drina outside and sat her on the *vardo* steps. She stacked tinder and built a fire. She fetched a pan, cut an onion free from its braid, and lifted a pair of sausages from their hook on the wall above Behjet's head. She looked down at his face.

"Good," purred Taggle when she came out with the pan and sausages. "Food, yes. I'm sure that will wake him. Food."

Kate knocked the edge of the fire down into coals and put the pan on it. "Have you eaten?" she asked Drina. "How long has it been since you've eaten?"

Drina was huddled up on the steps. She shrugged. "Since . . ."

Kate tossed the sausages onto the smoking pan and started cutting the onion. The heating cast iron smelled of Roamer cooking, smelled of being loved, of being safe, home. "I can't stay here," Kate said. "I have to go to Lov."

Drina wrapped her arms around her knees. The night was coming up fast. "I was going to go to my mother's clan. My father is dead. I have no blood tie to his clan. Daj said I could go if I wanted and Behjet was taking me. And then —" She stopped, swallowed. "Plain Kate," she said. "Can I come with you?"

Kate didn't know how to answer. *You can't. I want you to. I'm still afraid of you. You shouldn't, because I'm going to try to stop Linay and he'll probably kill me.* "Well," she said aloud. "Eat." She stabbed the sausage up on a knife and handed it to Drina.

Drina ate it without attention, and put it down half finished. Taggle helped himself and no one stopped him. Drina sat still with the firelight playing over the dark grain of her face.

"You look like your mother," said Kate abruptly. "You look like Lenore."

"You shouldn't —" Drina swallowed, her jaw clicking. "We don't say the names of the dead." Then stiffly she whispered, "How —"

And Kate, knowing it would break her friend's heart, held out the burl wood carving. Drina's hands shook as she took it. She held it by the wings and looked into the wooden eyes. "This is her. You really are a witch. This is her."

"I'm not," said Kate. "But I've seen her. I've seen your mother."

Drina's head snapped up. "She's alive?"

"No." Kate was sorry she'd started the way she had. She shifted tracks. "She had a brother. The one who went mad. Linay."

Drina shivered. "How do you know his name?"

"When I — He — After —" Kate stopped and poked at the fire. "After the Roamers burned me, Linay saved me. He pulled me out of the river. He's the one, Drina. He's the witch who stole my shadow."

Plain Kate drew herself up and started from the beginning, from the day a witch-white stranger had asked her to fashion a fiddle bow. She told her own story as if it were about someone else, and was amazed at how rich and strange it sounded, like an old tale. She told Drina about learning the rusalka's name, about trading blood for answers, about the swallow that had crumbled to ash. About what Linay planned for Lov.

"And then I saw you," she finished. "I recognized Cream — and she'd been tied up so long. . . . I thought I should come. . . . I was afraid, because you burned me. But it's not the Roamer way, to go alone."

Drina didn't answer at once. The two girls sat listening to Cream cropping grass, her tail swishing.

"They were twins," said Drina at last. "My mother and my uncle. Lenore and Linay. He was my favorite, my other father. He taught me little magics, and how to turn handsprings. He was different, after she died. After that spell, with his shadow — after he summoned her. The clan spoke death to him. He went alone. I remember watching him walk down the road."

It was full dark now. The trees were stirring and rustling. Nearby a nightjar churred, an eerie whirr that seemed to come from everywhere. Drina traced the lines of the carving's wooden face. "Plain Kate, you didn't know her, you don't understand. She would never have done this." She was crying. "What you're saying — the rusalka — it can't be true."

"We have ample evidence," said Taggle. "Scars and stuff, even."

"But my father," said Drina desperately. "He was different before she died. She loved him. How can it be that she killed him? Her own husband? And, and — Ciri!" The name burst from her. "Stivo, Wen, and Ciri! Kate, she would never have hurt Ciri. She would have died first."

"She did," said Taggle.

"Hush, Taggle." Kate patted at Drina's bunched shoulders, awkward as if patting a horse. "Drina. She doesn't have a choice. Linay, he said it was a terrible fate. That's why he's doing all this. He wants to save her."

Drina sniffed hard and swallowed. "Save her?"

"A rusalka's fate . . ." Kate tried to remember the exact words. "He said a rusalka's fate could be undone by avenging her death. That's what he wants to do. That's why he wants to kill all the people in Lov."

"Undone . . ." Drina's eyes were huge. "What does that mean? Would it . . . bring her back?"

Kate felt as if Drina had kicked her in the belly. Would Drina be on Linay's side? Lenore had been her mother. Kate had lost her father. What would she do to save him? To stop Linay, would she have to fight Drina?

But Drina fought herself. She grabbed Kate's hand and squeezed so hard that Kate's fingers ached. "We can't let him do this, Plain Kate. My mother wouldn't want — we have to stop him."

Kate laced her fingers through Drina's. She could barely see them in the dark: walnut brown and new pine pale, like a pattern of inlay. "Yes," she said. "You can come with me."

So Plain Kate and Drina went together down the road to Lov. Whatever had been between them — the lopsided friendship of Drina's merriness and Kate's cautious silences — was gone now, hacked off, burned away. But something new had grown in its place, a bond as strong as a scar. They did not speak of it, and they made the best time they could.

Riding in the *vardo* was easier than walking, though not much faster: The wall of fog trailed them, relentless. Still, Kate recovered some strength, nodding and dozing on Drina's shoulder as they sat together on the driver's seat, high above Cream's back. Neither girl was willing to ride alone beside Behjet's helpless body.

The broad road, which Kate had walked for three days, was on the other bank of the river.

On this side of the river, the way was hardly more than a track, winding through birch groves and boggy patches of basket rush and purple aster — a strangely peaceful place.

"We wanted to take the small road," Drina explained. "The great road was jammed — the whole country, and the people are angry. They . . ." She paused, looking as if she might be sick.

"I saw." Kate thought of the hanged women, their black feet brushing her shoulders as she ducked away.

"They're going to Lov," said Drina. "The *gadje* farmers in this country always hide themselves in the stone city when there's trouble. Since the time of the dragon boats, Daj says. They will all go to Lov."

And they'll die, thought Kate. *Unless we can stop Linay.*

But talk as they would, they had no idea of how to stop him. Finally on the third day, in the last of the light, the little track broke free of a wall of birch and joined a larger road that bridged the river. Snakes of fog eddied on top of the water, and the overcast had half swallowed the rising moon. Across the river, Lov squatted, cold as a toad.

They could not go the last mile — it was nearly full dark — so they turned Cream around and nosed the *vardo* back into the shelter of the trees. Branches scraped the canvas sides. They found a little rise by the river and took shelter in a grove of young birch. Drina tended to Behjet. They built a little fire.

Across the river, the city muttered to itself in the damp darkness. "It's big," said Drina. "I forgot how big it was."

Kate worked on her carving, smoothing life into wood with a leather pad wetted and dipped into sand. It was nearly finished, and she knew, she knew it was good, it was true, it was important. But whatever it was saying to her, she couldn't hear.

Cream was shouldering her way into the grove, tangling her mane in the low branches. Drina got up and set her free, then got out the softest brush and started to curry the horse's neck. Taggle climbed into Kate's lap. "You could do that for me, you know." So Kate put down her sanding pad and the speechless, useless carving and scratched her fingernails through his dense ruff.

Beside Kate the firelight crinkled on the water. It was going right through her. "My shadow," she said. "He can't make the monster without my shadow. We have to get it back."

"You tried that," the cat pointed out. "I had to act heroically in order to save you." He sat up, even though she was still petting him. "Develop a better plan."

Kate did her best to obey. The river murmured at her elbow, and the fog on it carried bursts of other voices, high laughter and thick shouts, and for a moment a snatch of eerie fiddle music. "He's here," said Kate. Drina came to sit beside her. They listened but the music didn't come again.

"I don't know how to stop him," said Kate. "I never have."

The words hung there a moment. Then Taggle said, "Why do we have to stop him?"

Drina began: "Because my mother —"

"Bah. She's dead. Her wishes are of no importance."

"Taggle." Kate put a silencing hand between his ears — and found little ridges of muscle, alert, tense.

"Give me another reason," Taggle said, flicking his ears. "Give me a *cat's* reason. Keep in mind that we do not," he harrumphed, "run into burning buildings going 'bark, bark.'"

"It's —" Kate struggled to explain. "It's a city. Thousands and thousands of people."

"Bah," said the cat again, but very softly. He was looking at his toes.

"You saved me," she reminded him. "On the boat. And Linay almost killed you. Did you have a cat's reason?"

"I'm fond of you."

"And you're more than a cat."

Kate smoothed her thumb along Taggle's eyebrow whiskers, trying to soothe him, but he lifted a paw and batted her hand away. He stood up. "There is something else we could do."

Something in his voice, the way his coat rose just slightly over his tight muscles, made Kate's scars prickle. "Taggle," she whispered. "What is it?"

"He gave me words, when he took your shadow. If we break the gift, we break the magic. Your shadow would no longer be his to use. The creature he made would come apart."

"You mean," said Drina, "you could just stop talking?"

"Oh, no," said Kate. "No."

Taggle shook his head, humanwise. "My mind is full of words. I *think* in them. It has changed who I am. That's the magic, not the talking."

"Then what — ?"

Taggle looked up at her, his amber eyes deep as the loneliness Kate had felt before he became her friend. "The traditional thing," he said slowly, "involves the river and a sack."

sixteen
THE PEACE OF LOV

"No," said Kate. "No."

"It's your wish, though," said Taggle implacably. "To save the city. All those thousands and thousands."

"It's *not*—" Kate found tears stinging her eyes. She batted them away angrily. The three of them sat staring at one another.

"Drina: If I die, Linay will lose Katerina's shadow. I am right, am I not?"

But even Kate knew he was. It was the first rule of magic: the exchange of gifts. Cream leaned over and tried to eat Drina's hair. The Roamer girl nodded to Taggle and turned and flung her arms around the horse's neck.

"There's another way to stop him," said Kate. Her voice had gone hard as oak root. "He can't do his spell if he's dead."

Drina whipped around. "Kate!"

"Yes," she said, standing up. "We have to kill him."

"He's my —" Drina began to object, and stopped. They were all standing now, facing one another, and only the horse was calm.

"I *like* this plan," said Taggle, spreading his toes. "It is much better than the other plan. This is what I think we should do. We should find him and kill him in his sleep."

Linay, who could move in a blink, who had struck Taggle down with an uplifted finger. Kate said nothing, but Taggle read her face. "It's true he's large prey," said the cat, "but you are missing the genius of my plan: the sleeping part. The finding-him part should be easy because we know where he's going."

"I can't," whispered Drina. "He taught me to swim."

"Taggle . . ." Kate hesitated — and decided. "How?"

"You can carve," he said. "Do that. Skin is softer than wood."

Kate thought of the hanged women with the hexes carved on their hands. "I am not sure I can."

"Become sure," said the cat, his eyes flashing green in the firelight. "Once you leap on a boar's back, you can't sheath your claws."

"Even if —" said Drina. "He's strong, or he was."

"He still is." Kate's wrist still ached when she thought of Linay's hands.

"Listen," said Taggle. "There's something on the road."

Through the swaying trunks of the birch trees, light danced and flared. In a moment they could see men coming up the forest track, a party of men with torches. They were all dressed the same, in dark clothes with a yellow patch on the chest, and on that was embroidered a red boat beneath crossed oars. One even carried a flag. Kate had never seen uniforms before, but she knew what they were.

In the torchlight their faces were pale. Kate saw the dark pits of eyes turn their way. The girls drew close together. Cream stamped and snorted. But the men didn't stop.

Drina was so close that Kate could feel the heat of her. "Soldiers," she whispered. "The city guard."

The cat had melted away into the darkness. In another moment he was back. "They go across the bridge. To the city."

"They're the ones —" said Drina. "They came for my mother."

They stood looking out across the river. The city stirred restlessly in its sleep, sent them snatches of sound and flares of light. "This is too big," said Drina. "We can't do this."

"Yes, we can," said Kate, who suddenly saw how. "We'll tell the guard . . ." She trailed off as the implications came to her, but braced herself and went on: "We'll go to the guard and tell them he's a witch. We'll turn him in."

Drina stood and Kate saw her start to shake as she too thought it through. "They'll burn him."

"Yes," said Kate. "I know."

They couldn't speak after that, but somehow they slept, tight together in the *vardo*, with Behjet's limp hand dangling down and resting on Kate's back. That was uncomfortable, but a comfort too: Linay had killed. In drawing the rusalka, he'd murdered half the countryside. He'd killed Behjet, or nearly: The man's skin was drawn across his skull like a drumhead, and he smelled of death. Linay had done that. He had killed the women hanging from the trees, the plowboy in the poppies, killed Stivo and Wen and little Ciri, and hundreds of others. He deserved whatever the city guard would do to him.

But he didn't, said Kate's little thoughts, *because no one did.*

And I helped him. What do I deserve?

She slept in fits and nightmares and woke just after dawn. Overnight, the weather had changed. The endless fog and drizzle had pulled itself up, and clouds crouched above them, low, green-black, rounded like the backs of river boulders: hail clouds that sent down swirls of cold air. Thin twilight slanted under them.

Lov looked bigger by daylight. Its huge walls were a muddy gray. Roofs and squat spires rose above them, tiled in slate the same color as the clouds. The whole city steamed and smoked in the chilly morning like fresh manure. Kate looked at it as she greased her feet and pulled on her socks. The road was muddy, and having enough socks that one pair would always be dry was the only way to keep your feet from rotting. She was glad she had stolen Linay's.

Linay.

Drina came out of the *vardo*. Her chopped hair stuck out in all directions; it made her look older, ravaged. Kate could see the slice in her ear; it had healed almost black with scar. Drina winced from her gaze and turned away, binding up her hair in a dark turban. Her long thin shadow stretched blue among those of the birches.

Then Taggle came back from his morning ablutions, dragging a half-dead, spitting mink. "Today," Kate told him. "Today I'm going to kill someone."

"I can live with that," drawled the cat.

They had to leave the *vardo*. There was a fee, Drina said, to take a wagon into Lov, and they couldn't pay it. Kate found her old pack-basket and filled it with what food they had, extra socks, and the blue cloth with the stars to cover her patchy hair. Drina washed Behjet and tried to feed him broth. She couldn't: He had stopped swallowing. Tears sprang up in Drina's eyes but she said nothing, just set the broth down at Behjet's hand, and went out to tend to Cream. Taggle killed the mink and cleaned his whiskers like a gentleman. And then they went.

The city of Lov stood on a hump in the marshland. The Narwe, like a great moat, guarded three sides. From behind, the city looked peaceful: reeds like brushstrokes on the square stones, a town of storks nested among them. The huge white birds stalked slowly through the dark water.

A canal came out of the river and went into the city through a metal grille. A pool at the base of the wall was jammed with small boats of all descriptions. Among them was a little green barge, painted and carved in the Roamer fashion. Taggle pointed with one paw, looking like a human trapped in the skin of a cat. "He's here."

They stood looking, silent. Then they crossed the bridge where the river road joined the great road, and rounded the flank of Lov.

The huge gate was shut. And from it, like guts from a rabbit, spilled another city, a field of tents and hovels. The road vanished into a stew of mud and worse things. Flies swarmed, slow in the morning chill.

Kate had grown used to being only with people who knew about her shadow. She felt the sidelong, prickly stares of the refugees, eyeing her burns, trying to pin down exactly what about her looked so strange. Drina tugged at her turban, tucking up the ragged ends of her hair. Taggle, though, sat up straight as he balanced on Kate's basket, proud and fine as a king.

They pushed their way into the crowd, into the shadow of the great wall. It took them an hour to go no farther than they could have thrown a stone, three hours to get anywhere near the gate.

Suddenly the cat stiffened on Kate's shoulder, and leapt. He went by her ear as yowl and claw, and landed on the back of a white-haired peddler a few paces ahead. The stooped man straightened and whirled, his white zupan and white braids flying around him, while the crowd grumbled and snickered and Kate shouted, without meaning to: "Linay!"

The magician's eyes caught hers, but only for an instant. He was busy trying to prevent the hissing, snarling cat from shredding his throat. Kate couldn't quite see what happened next, but Taggle came flying back at her like a tossed ball. She scrambled to catch him as he slid down her front and landed with a wet smack in the churned muck at her feet. Blood ran down Linay's neck and scratches covered his hands.

"Well, well." Linay bowed to them. "Fair maid of the wood. Far from home. And Drina — how you've grown."

"Mira," said Drina. "Don't do this."

"Do what?" Linay looked around him, owl-eyed as if innocent. "I seek entrance to the city."

"You want to destroy it," snapped Kate. That drew a few eyes — but only a few. The people of the abandoned country had no love in that moment for the stone city with its shut gates, and no time to listen to the ravings of a stranger.

Linay took a step toward them. Kate could smell the wild herbs on him. He spoke with a small smile. "And what are you going to do about it, Little Stick?"

"We're going to stop you."

"Are you now?" He was almost in arm's reach. The stormy light made his white face greenish. "My dear ones. I wish you could. I almost wish you could." He lifted his chin — it was Drina's chin, Kate saw, the same haughty gesture. "Come, then. Let me see you try."

Kate started to lunge at him.

Linay lifted a single finger. The air turned to glass. Kate was caught in the invisible magic, breathless, helpless — and still no one even bothered to look. Linay reached out and touched her cheek. "Good-bye, Katerina," he said. And then he turned his back on them and shouldered deeper into the shoving crowd.

"That was foolish," Kate hissed at Taggle, when he had climbed back onto her shoulder. "He might have killed you!"

"And I might have killed him," muttered the cat. "Which would have saved us some trouble. I don't think we have long. There is something in the air."

There was. Kate had grown used to the wall of fog that had trailed her all the way down the road to Lov, but now there was a wall of storm. Beyond the crowd, a cloud seemed to rise from the ground, bruise-black and solid-seeming as a mountain range. It was creeping toward them, and slowly the crowd was turning to watch it. It breathed hail-cold on their turning faces.

The cloud was driving people toward the gate like sheep to the slaughter pens. The crowd became elbows and backs, feet treading on feet and the close human stench of fear. A noise rose from it, a many-throated rumble and roar.

Through it all went Linay, threading forward like a chisel down the wood grain. Without the split he opened, Kate thought, they would not have been able to move at all. But there was something about him — a thundering, haunted power — that made people inch aside even when there was not an inch to spare. And so they were able to follow him, keeping his narrow, bleeding back in sight. And soon the gate loomed.

A clump of towers bulged from the city wall, bigger than the tithe barn at Toila, bigger than anything Kate had ever seen. In the center of the towers a tunnel gaped, with a huge gate for teeth. Behind the gate were dark-dressed city guardsmen, with the red boats on their chests like second mouths. They had pikes. Here it was: her moment. Kate stopped.

As she paused, an icy swirl of wind lifted her hair. Fat drops splattered here and there, and squalls tugged at hems and hats. The crowd moaned in fear and surged forward, smashing together. Taggle's claws skittered on her shoulder and she lost track of Drina. Kate was flung against the broad back of the man in front of her, and for a moment she could see only his sheepskin coat. And then she heard Linay shouting in a voice like a string that was about to snap: "Look!" he shouted. "Behold, the fate of Lov!"

People froze; the crush eased. Kate could move again,

and she wormed her way sideways until she could see what was happening. There was a wagon smashed against one of the gate towers. Linay was standing on top of the wreck like a stork on a stump, holding a knife, and shouting.

"I did this!" His voice was high and half singing. "I drew the rain and the sleep across the whole country. I am a witch and I curse this city." He threw his arms open. Blood was running from both wrists. "Lov: I show you horrors! Sister: Come to me!"

And from the green cloud, something came.

It was the monster he had shown her, the rusalka with a shadow, a thing made of wings and howling. It struck into the crowd.

Kate grabbed Taggle off her shoulder, folded herself up around him, and covered her head as the crowd exploded into panic and screaming. Toward the gate, away from it, in all directions, people pushed and staggered and ran. The blows of their rushing feet rained across her back and sides. Again she felt the monster's wing beats thundering overhead.

Then, sudden as they'd come, the wings folded and were gone; Kate felt them go. An eerie, moaning silence fell. It was so still that for a moment Kate could hear the sparse, cold drops of rain tocking into the mud around her. She lifted her head cautiously. The cat squirmed out from under her. Drina, turban gone and one eye swelling, crept back to her side.

The two girls were on the edge of a circle of —

They had been bodies. But they were crumbling, falling apart like rot-riddled wood. It was hard to tell even how many: a dozen? They made a ring of blackish mush, an open space between them and the gate. On the other side of it, Linay was still standing on the shattered wagon, panting and folded with effort, an ugly grin on his pallid face.

Kate was just getting to her feet when the great gate of Lov screeched open. The portcullis came up a few feet and the pikemen ducked under, slashing at the air to hold back the crowd. With them came another man in the city's colors, with a gray-shot beard and a broad red sash and a huge hat: a grand man, who looked, just then, sick with fear. "Witch!" he shouted up to Linay. "Why do you disturb the peace of Lov?"

Linay barked a disbelieving laugh. *The peace of Lov?!*

Half the crowd shouted back at him, and Linay whirled around and silenced them with a look, his eyes flashing like pearls. He turned back to the gray-faced, gray-bearded man, who said, "What's your business?"

"Death is my business," said Linay. "I'm a witch, after all. Take me off to be burned, please." He hopped neatly down — the pikemen winced — and held his hands out for lashing. The crowd roared and pushed forward again. Kate and Drina were shoved as if by a tidal wave, into the open space where the rusalka had struck. Kate staggered and fell — Taggle flew from her shoulder — she had a moment's horror about the stuff she was falling *into* — and she found herself in familiar arms.

"Linay!" she gasped. The mob was all around them.

The magician grasped her arms and hauled her up, and for an instant they were face-to-face, forearms clasped, like warriors. "Flee this city," he whispered as one of the pikemen pulled him toward the gate and the others tried to keep the crowd from killing him. Stones and mud came flying. Linay snuck Kate a smile. It was boyish, terrified, and amazed. The pikemen jerked him away.

"Linay!" Kate shouted after him.

And again, she saw his frightened eyes snatch at her, like a drowning man. She threw out a hand —

But it was too late. His smile hardened, and he was gone.

"Katerina!" Taggle and Drina were fighting their way sideways toward her as the crowd started to push again to enter the imagined safety of the city. The gate was still half raised. Linay wouldn't stoop to go under it; the guards couldn't bend him. The portcullis — it was a huge thing of iron-backed oak — screeched upward while behind it more guards lowered and braced their pikes.

Then, somewhere in the field of tents and desperate people, lightning struck. The noise of it shook the ground; its passage opened the air and cold rain poured down. The crowd screamed like one animal and surged against the gates. The girls were shoved along as if at the front of a wave. Kate hit her head on the gate and then was under it. Taggle leapt from Drina's arms and dove between the pikemen. "This way!" he shouted. They went at a staggering run, following the cat as he darted out the other end of the gate tunnel and turned sharply down a tiny alleyway.

The crowd roared on; the people of the abandoned country poured through the gates, unstoppable as a river. Kate and Drina followed Taggle. They scrambled up a water barrel and onto the roof of a shed, and from there onto a higher roof. They knocked loose slates that went skittering down the steep pitch and fell into the rushing crowd. Faces turned up toward them. The two girls lay back panting, out of sight, while Taggle peered over the gutter edge like a gargoyle.

They huddled there a long time, until the crowd thinned and only the dead were left in the gate square below.

"Well," drawled Taggle. "Now how do we stop him?"

seventeen
THE STONE CITY

"He wants to be burned," said Kate. "Oh, God, he wants to be burned. He said it would need a great spell to join the shadow and the rusalka together. A great spell — a great sacrifice. He's going to sacrifice *himself.*" The cold downpour washed over her. She remembered Linay's face, terrified and exultant. He would join the rusalka to the shadow with his own death. The winged thing would kill everything it touched. Everyone. The whole city. Kate shook. "He told me to flee."

"Hmmm," said Taggle, picking his way over the loose slates. "Fleeing is not a bad plan."

Kate ignored him. "Where will they take him?" she asked Drina. "Where did they take Lenore?"

"Katerina —" Taggle began.

"Drina, where?"

Drina looked shattered. "The courts," she whispered. "At the center of the city. But, Kate — we can't. We tried. When they took my mother, we tried. They only laughed. Our *Baro* said we were lucky they only laughed."

Below them the guards had begun to trickle back into the gate square. They were making piles of the dead: the crushed pikemen and those who had been crushed against the pikes. Kate didn't look, but she couldn't shut out the scrapes and heavy thuds. "Taggle," she said, "find us a way to the center of the city."

The cat regarded her thoughtfully, steady as two isinglass lamps. Then he turned and led them away, across the rooftops, fearless and nimble.

The downpour slowed to a cold soaking rain. The steep roofs were slippery, but they didn't dare go into the streets. Men in the dark garb of the city watch roamed in packs and harried the refugees from doorways and alleys. So Drina and Kate stuck to the roofs, inching, sliding, scraping, keeping out of sight. It was slow and exhausting. The light was sinking by the time they came to a rooftop overlooking the great square.

Across from them towered the city hall, with its pitched roof and heavy-lidded windows, and a church, its spire thick with monsters. A squat building filled the space between church and hall, its windows barred and its doors guarded. "The courts," Drina whispered. "And there —" She stopped speaking and pointed down.

On a little stage in the center of the square stood the weizi, the carved pillar that should be a town's heart. But this one was uncarved. And it was stone. That was so strange to Kate's carver's heart that she could hardly take it in. A plain pillar — no, Kate realized, it was not a pillar, it was a stake, a burning stake on a little stage, which had seen who knows how many deaths. She swallowed and for a moment wanted to just let the city fall under the rusalka's wings. That quick death was better than this city deserved.

The stone city, Linay had told her once, had a stone heart. And here it was. Nearby, the canal where Lenore had drowned slapped under the lip of the docks.

The dimming day was quiet and the lid of the sky twisted sounds. Kate wasn't quite sure whether she could hear screaming. "Linay . . ." she whispered, and gripped the gutter to steady herself. "Drina. How long do we have? Will they — will they burn him tonight?"

Drina shook her head. "They'll have a trial . . . an ordeal." She was silent so long that Kate almost asked her, almost had to think of a way to ask: *How long did they torture your mother?*

"Tomorrow," said Drina, before Kate had to find those

words. "They'll torture him tonight, make him confess. They'll burn him tomorrow. When people can watch."

Kate pushed the dripping hair out of her eyes and peered at the squat bulk of the courts, its little windows barred and squinting. "We have to get him out."

"The grand duke's army could not get him out," said Taggle.

"I don't want to watch him burn," whispered Drina.

Kate tried to stay practical, and so answered Taggle: "Maybe we can get in."

"Oh!" said Taggle brightly. "And kill him in his sleep in there!" Despite his cheerful tone, the look he threw the black building was skeptical. "There's bound to be a cellar or two, I suppose. I will look." And he jumped fearlessly from the edge of the gutter, sprang down to a ledge Kate hadn't even seen, down again to slip across a windowsill, and down again to vanish, gray, into the gray light.

The ghost of the scream came again in the chilly twilight. "I'm going to be sick," Drina choked. She backed away from the edge. Kate turned her back on the square and followed. Farther back on the roof, jammed against a taller wall, they found shelter. It wasn't much: a ruined dovecote between two huge chimneys, with a scrap of roof and a rain-wrecked honeycomb of dove boxes, white droppings thick over everything. It smelled sharply sour, like the bear cage in which the Roamers had kept the chickens, and in which Kate had been burned. The smell made her skin shudder and her mouth taste metal.

She was sure of it now, as the night fell: Somewhere nearby, Linay was screaming.

In the darkness, Kate waited for Taggle's return. She held the burl wood carving of Lenore's face in her hands, using the edge of her knife to polish a rough bit here and there. Drina dozed shivering beside her, the heavy clouds pressed close over her, and the city slept restlessly below her. Taggle was gone a long time, long enough for Kate to struggle in and out of dreams: She was bent over her cabinet box in Samilae, carving, only she had wings instead of a shadow. She was lost in a maze of stone streets and someone was screaming, and then the stones melted. She was holding Taggle's body in her arms.

She woke with Taggle's cold nose nudging hers. His fur was damp and smeared with foul mud. She stroked him and loose hairs clung to her hands.

"A dark place, full of blood smell and fear smell and grates and grilles," he reported. "It would take a rat to slip in — a skinny one. There will be no rescue."

"I dreamt . . ." Kate tipped her head back. The crumbling bricks of the chimney caught and yanked at her hair. ". . . no rescue."

Taggle eyed her. "You're planning something."

"If I go down there," she said slowly, "the guard will see that I have no shadow. They'll arrest me. And then — maybe I can get close to him."

"No," said Taggle. "No friend of mine will take on such a fate."

Kate looked down at Lenore's carved face. She remembered promising her father that she would be a full master by twenty, and she had been right: This was her masterpiece. But what was going to happen instead was that she was going to die. She said, "Someone will notice my shadow soon, Taggle. It will happen eventually."

"Not here," he said. "Not like this. You didn't see it. You can't imagine." The cat sighed and paced up and down in front of the dovecote. Finally he turned to her. "Katerina, this city is a rat's place. Let us leave the rats to the rats and go on with our adventures. What say you?"

She wanted to say yes. There was nothing to love in the walls of Lov. But there had been little to love in Toila either, and yet a stranger had saved them. And in Samilae, where an axe had come from the darkness, Niki had stayed strong and kind. "There must be a basket woman," said Kate, "or a baker."

"Well then," said the cat. "He means to kill himself in this stupid way. We must either kill him before he can, or save him from it." He shook his head, human, fretful. "I suppose one chance or the other might present itself. Personally I think we should aim for killing him."

Drina shifted in her thin sleep, and shivered. Kate watched her sleeping for a while, wishing for a scrap of blanket. The rain was so cold. Finally she asked, "Will we . . . will we all live?"

"I doubt it," drawled the cat. "We put our lives on claw tip to do this, Katerina. Tell me you are sure."

"I have to stop him, Taggle. My blood. My shadow. He used me to do this. It's my fault and I have to fix it."

Taggle sat up, slender and strong as a column, unshakable. He made no suggestions. Kate rubbed him between the ears. She could still feel the lump where Stivo's axe had hit him. He climbed into her lap, rumbling, and she huddled into the broken chimney's meager heat.

"We must get close to him," said Taggle. "Close enough to spring. If a chance comes, we must be ready."

"The stake," she said. "He'll — he'll be brought there."

So at first light they found their way down into the square, to the burning place.

The stake was a neatly built thing, and horrible in its neatness. The platform was stone and nearly as tall as they were. A flight of steps was cut into the side. A stone lip would keep the fire contained. And there would be fire: There was already a stack of split logs and branches, like a great stork's nest, around the stake. They stank of pitch and tallow. More barrels of pitch were lined up like condemned men at the platform's foot. Kate and Drina wormed their way between these and crouched down to wait.

It was a strange morning. The light was like a bruise. Cold breezes blew straight down from low clouds — clouds like a wall of boulders hanging over their heads. Above those clouds, Kate was certain, something circled. Something hungered. Something waited.

Between the curved black walls of the barrels, Kate and Drina watched the square fill. Hawkers sold pretzels and roasted nuts, tinkers peddled charms, musicians played, acrobats tumbled. But you could not buy fur or cloth, raw meat or flour, or anything that would take more than an hour to make. It was not a market: It was a carnival.

"They're saying they've caught him," reported Taggle, slinking in from the crowd. "That soon the rain will lift and life will be better. They mean to burn him at noon. Also, they are selling meat pies."

They waited. The crowd grew larger, and soon they could see little but legs, good boots, and patten shoes holding dainty slippers above the puddles. Taggle kept mentioning the meat pies. The bells in the church told the hours: Nine. Ten. Eleven. They crept out from between the barrels. Twelve.

They could hear Linay coming. The jeering in the crowd preceded him like the tide coming up the river. People around them seemed to puff up; what had been a tight crowd was suddenly a crush. Kate was jostled. Taggle sprang up on top of a barrel. Drina pressed close. They couldn't see anything.

Then, suddenly, almost in arm's reach: Linay.

His hands were tied in front of him. The gray-bearded man in the red sash, the master of the guard, was yanking him up the steps like a bear on a leash. Another guard was at his back, walking backward, sword drawn, keeping the press of people clear.

The crowd gave a roar as Linay staggered on the steps, swayed on the platform. One eye was bruised — a startling blot on his too-light face — and one side of his white hair was torn bald in patches, matted with blood. The guard master jerked him sideways. He stumbled, crashed into the stake, then grunted as the master's cudgel caught him in the ear. He stood stunned as the man cut his hands free.

No, Kate thought. *Don't make me see this.*

On the stake, a few feet up, an iron ring protruded from the stonework. Swiftly, like someone who had done it many times, the guard master lashed one of Linay's wrists to the ring.

A breathless hush settled on the crowd.

The master hefted his club again, and Kate could see it play out in her head: He would strike the throat or the back of the neck, enough to daze. He would wrench Linay around, put his back to the stake and his wrists both behind. So that the crowd could see his face, of course. While he burned. *He came to kill these people*, she thought, *and we have no business stopping him. How can we stop him?* The guard brought his club back just as Kate thought he would and swung it —

— and Linay's arm came up like a sail snapping round. The cudgel glanced off his forearm as he whirled. He struck at the man's face, fast as a snake. His hand closed over the mouth: white and wild over that neat gray beard. He leaned close. "All this time hunting witches," he hissed, "and you never thought you would find one that was dangerous?" He blew a stream of breath into the man's face.

The master reared away, clawing at his face and throat. His grand hat went flying. Kate couldn't tell what had happened until a stray beam of sun struck a gleam from the guard's face. It was ice. Linay had set a mask of ice across the nose and throat, cutting off the air. The man fell from the platform, turning an ugly purple. The crowd edged backward.

Linay grinned at them. There was nothing wavering or weak about him now. He towered and he laughed. "Come, now," he called. "Don't go! There's going to be a burning!" And he hurled something toward the mob that set them screaming. Something small and stinging hit Kate as she huddled against the barrel: ice.

The ice had hardly pricked — it hurt less than hail — but the crowd panicked. They bolted and their force, impersonal as an axe, caught Kate. She staggered, saw Taggle go flying, saw Drina go down. She dove sideways and shoved Drina behind the barrels. They clung to each other, bruised and panting, while the crowd bucked and squealed and fled.

Kate raised her head. It had happened so fast. The square was almost empty. A few people — those who had fallen beneath too many feet — were lying heaped on the cobbles, drifted at the gates. There were piggish moans in the air, and a smell of blood.

The remaining guard, the one with the sword, had held his place. He turned on Linay, and lunged. Linay, one-handed, caught the blade in his naked hand. Kate saw blood begin to slick it, and then a rime of frost. Linay locked eyes with the guard, who froze. The sword grew black with cold, and smoked — and shattered.

"Thank you," said Linay, stooping to pick up a jagged piece. "I needed a blade."

The wide-eyed man backed away.

Linay stood fixed, regarding the shard in his hand. And as the guard stumbled away past the heaped bodies, Kate, Taggle, and Drina found themselves alone at the foot of the platform.

Kate drew a deep breath, and climbed the stone steps.

And then she was standing, empty-handed, at the pillar, with no idea what to do.

"Katerina," said Linay.

eighteen

AN EXCHANGE OF GIFTS

Linay's face had a blank, soft-mouthed look, like a man in a dream. One hand was tied to the stone pillar. The other held a jagged fragment of sword blade. Blood dripped off the blade tip and dribbled over the wood at his feet, and as each drop fell, it caught fire. The little flames made spots of smoldering in the pitch-soaked wood.

"Katerina?" said Linay again. "What happens next?"

Plain Kate was shaking. "You don't want to burn, Linay."

"But I do," he insisted. "I've planned it. I've worked for it. For years." His voice was still polite, a little distant, but he was beginning to tremble. There was pitch smeared on the white skirts of his zupan, smoke eddying around his knees. He closed his eyes for a moment. "I can do this," he said. "I want to do this."

Kate edged toward him. Drina was crouched on the platform steps, Taggle in her arms. *"Mira,"* she pleaded — and then the name she was never supposed to say again: "Linay . . ."

"I wish you weren't here, though," Linay said. "Everyone here . . ."

Kate could feel it, behind the clouds, the shadow and the rusalka drawing together, lowering like a slow storm. The blood, the fire: The spell was beginning. "Everyone here is going to die," said Kate.

Linay made a noise deep in his throat, and stepped sideways, away from the fire. The tie on his wrist brought him up short. Kate reached to help him and the winged carving cut into her hip. Suddenly she knew exactly what to do. "Why?" she said.

Linay gave the heartbroken, startled laugh she'd tricked from him once or twice before. "But you know!" His eyes shifted to Drina, and he pleaded: "To save her! To save my sister!"

Kate held the carving out to him. "This is her. Your sister's face."

Linay looked thunderstruck, staring at the carving. "Lenore . . ." he said. And the thing behind the clouds seemed to answer: *yes.*

Kate set the carving on the smoking wood at Linay's knee.

"What are you doing?" said Linay. "Don't burn it!" Hot smoke made his zupan skirts swirl. The fire ticked and fluttered.

"Would she want to be saved, like this?"

"She was a witch. She understood — the exchange of gifts. The sacrifice." His eyes darted sideways to the carved face of his sister. "Pick that up."

"If you'll answer me. Would Lenore have wanted this?" Fire was rising around the carved face, pushing up from under it and arching above it with fast-beating wings.

Linay's bound wrist was jerking and jerking like a mink in a trap. He didn't seem to be aware of it, or aware that he had pulled as far away from the growing fire as the lashing allowed. "Kate," he said, his breath shuddering. And she lunged forward to cut him free.

Linay flung up a hand between them, and cowered as if from a blow. Kate found herself caught again, in his spell of glass air.

"I can do this. I can do this." Blood dripped from his cut hand, from his bound and twitching wrist, and fell burning, burning, burning. "Lenore!" he cried, and sobbed as he cried.

"She wouldn't want this!" Kate had to shout above the roar of the fire. "Linay! Let me go!"

Flames were snarling in Linay's clothes, hot yellow winds lifting his hair. Kate knew how it felt, the pain and panic. And yet still the force of his will held, and she was caught, helpless before the fire as a chestnut on the coals. Her masterpiece was turning black, flames eating through the thinnest places in the wings. "Look at her!" Kate shouted. "Look at her face and tell me she would want this!"

Above them the clouds rumbled and an ugly death stirred.

And from below, high and hysterical, came Drina's voice. "Lie to her!" Drina shouted. "Lie to her — it will kill you. It can all be over. Just lie to her!"

Linay's face — it too was turning black — suddenly calmed, suddenly hardened, and his eyes locked with Kate's. "Yes," he said. "Lenore would want this." And he folded up as if he had swallowed a sword.

The glass around Kate shattered. She plunged into the flame, clambering over the smoking wood, her knife in her hand. She sliced his wrist free, shouting, "Drina!"

Linay rolled from the fire, and Drina tugged at his arm. Blood poured from his mouth, where the lie had cut him. Kate leapt from the woodpile and crashed, rolling beside them. She saw Linay look at her, his eyes dreamy, and then they turned to the sky. "Sister . . ." he whispered.

Kate yanked her carving from the bonfire, scorching her hands. She waved it in Linay's face. "Don't!"

"Sister," Linay whispered. "Please. Help me."

And so called, out of the green-black sky, the winged thing came. Down into the trampled dead and nearly dead, the people heaped at the gates, it swooped like a striking eagle. Kate saw the double wings — fog-white and clotted shadow — saw the bodies sink into a sick, black fire.

"Take it back!" she screamed at Linay. She thrust Lenore's carved nose at his nose, though his ice-pale eyes were thawing into dull water. "Take it back. Stop it!"

The wing Kate was holding snapped, and the carving fell to the stone and broke open along hot lines. Kate crouched over it, over Linay. "Please," she said. He was dying in front of her, burned everywhere, his red mouth open. "Please stop it!"

"There's only one way to stop it," came a voice from her elbow. She turned. It was Taggle, sitting on the lip of the burning platform, solemn. "And you know what it is."

Kate looked down at the knife in her hand.

"I'm sorry," said the cat. The rusalka was coming across the square slowly, tearing at the piles of the dead. It grew bigger as it fed, filling the air above them like a ship at sail. "It has to be you who kills me," said Taggle. "I was his gift to you. You must be the one to give it back."

She felt her jaw open, her head shake itself from side to side.

"You can survive it," said Taggle. "And that is all I want. You do not need me. You can find your own place, with your strength alone." Behind him, the wings loomed. "Katerina, Star of My Heart. Be brave. Lift your knife."

Kate met his golden eyes.

She lifted her knife.

And Taggle, who was beautiful, who had never misjudged a jump in his life, leapt toward her with his forelegs out-flung. He landed clean on the blade. There was a sound like someone biting into an apple. And then he was in her arms, with the blade sticking out of his back.

Kate folded up. Taggle was curled in her arms, with the knife handle sticking out of his chest like a peg. She put her hand flat around it; it stuck out between her fingers. Blood came between them too, dark heart's blood, bubbling like a spring. Drina tried to tug her farther from the fire, and Kate batted her hands away. "Taggle," she sobbed.

The cat stirred, flinched — and smiled. Not a quirk of whiskers, but a human thing, turning up the corners of his mouth. "Katerina . . ."

The rusalka was coming toward them, its wings beating steady as a heart.

"Taggle," whispered Kate. His heartbeat slowed under her hand.

"More . . ." His voice was only breath.

"More than a cat."

"And I do not regret it." His eyes clouded. "Could you . . . this itchy bit . . ."

She scratched his favorite place, where the fur swirled above the hard nub of his jawbone. The heat from the fire lifted tears from one side of her face.

Taggle took one more breath.

The rusalka's shadow wings folded closed. Taggle's heart fluttered. The rusalka took a step forward, shrinking, and the wings sagged. Another heartbeat. Another step. The darkness trailed from the white woman's shoulders like the train of a dress. Another heartbeat, and the shadow-wing dragged itself against the cobbles.

And then it was just a shadow. And Taggle's heart was still.

Kate pulled her knife out. The cat didn't stir. No new blood came.

She put her knife — her knife, her knife — down where the fire could take it, and she thought about lying down beside it.

Beside them, Linay was breathing, eyes open, calm as a man asleep. Below them, in the square, a woman stood. Her witch-white face was stiff with horror. Her shadow jittered behind her as the pyre blazed. The woman lifted a hand against the awful light, squinting. She spread her fingers and shouted something.

The fire went out.

Drina flung herself down the steps and into the woman's arms. *"Dajena!"* she shouted, and then she was crying. *"Dajena . . ."* She buried her face in the woman's shining shoulder.

"Mira cheya," the woman muttered. "Drina. What are you doing here? Stay out of sight, I must see to this poor soul. . . ." But Drina wouldn't move from her side. So she held the sobbing girl in one arm and tilted up her chin at the stone pillar. Then she stepped forward, dainty as a deer but grim-faced, and climbed the steps, Drina stumbling along beside her.

Kate stood up.

It was surprising, how light Taggle's body was. All the substance of him seemed to have gone into Kate, into the bloody smock that stuck to her front — into her knife hand — into her body itself. Taggle was thistledown. There was nothing of him left.

And then Lenore and Kate were standing face-to-face, with Linay at their feet. He sprawled with arms and legs bent like a tossed puppet. He looked up first at Kate, then at Lenore, and then — blankly — at the clearing sky. "I feel strange," he said. "I think I'm dying."

Kate, with the little body in her arms, answered, "Good. We don't like you." But she knelt beside him and took his raw hand.

"Let me," Lenore murmured, crouching beside them. Kate felt human warmth in the brush of her arm. "Who are you, brother? Tell me your name and I can help you with the pain." Kate heard her voice slip halfway to song. "Who did this to you?"

"Oh, no," Linay sang back. "I did it to myself. Don't you see? A life for a life — how magic must be."

"Linay?" Lenore's voice broke with shock. "By the Black Lady — what have you done?"

Avenged your death, thought Kate. *Undone your fate. Traded his life for yours.* But she couldn't say any of it.

"Lenore," Linay breathed, "I love . . ." But his breath quavered and he could only blink at her. Lenore smoothed what had been his hair back from his forehead, singing. The life-tension was going out of him, like a frozen rope thawing in a puddle of water. Kate watched, with Taggle's body stiffening against hers. "He's dead," said Lenore, holding the limp body in her arms. "My brother is dead! What is happening?"

"The guard will be coming," Kate said. "Listen." It seemed to her she could hear the whole city, thousands of sounds jumbled into the pounding in her ears.

"Who are you?" Lenore stood and seized Kate's arm. Kate jerked away, twisting to keep her body bent around Taggle — but Lenore didn't let go, and Kate's arm was pulled straight and her sleeve fell back, baring the cuts of the bloodletting. The woman who had been the rusalka shivered. "I *know* you."

"*Dajena* . . ." Drina tugged at her hand. "She's my friend. Let her go."

But Lenore ignored her daughter, looking around. "I remember this. I was dead. They tried to burn me." She looked into the pyre, and down at the charred fragments of her own face. "Look." She stooped, scooping up a black-edged piece: an eye and a twist of hair, a glimpse of wing.

Drina eased the charred thing out of her hand. "*Dajena.*"

Lenore let the carving go and sleepwalked to the edge of the platform, where she stood looking down at the dark surface of the canal. "I died there. I remember it." Her face went strange. "And," she said in a voice that could have withered grass, "I remember after."

"You don't have to think about that," said Drina, "You're saved. We saved you."

Lenore shook herself and turned. "My daughter. Oh, Drina." She fingered Drina's chopped black hair. The sun was just coming out, long fingers of light piercing them, making the woman shine like a wax-cloth window. "You've grown." She took Drina by both shoulders, her eyes huge. "You are marvelous," she said. "You are brave as the sun."

And Kate held Taggle's body tighter. *Star of My Heart*. Her father had died saying that and for years she had thought he was seeing her mother, standing at the door of death. But he had looked at her, just as Lenore was looking now. He had seen her. Her father had seen her.

"Let us go," said Lenore, and swept down the stairs like a beam of light. Kate and Drina followed.

nineteen

THE NAMES OF THE DEAD

Kate walked through the streets of Lov with Taggle's body in her arms. A thin shadow was growing at her heels. The light was murky, but Lenore shone like the moon, with Drina like a shy star at her side.

The streets were still empty, though here and there they found a window being opened, or a huddle of refugees looking about, like survivors of a storm. Voices began again, slowly filling the town like birdsong in the morning. And Kate hated them all — all the thousands and thousands. They were not worth it: They were nothing beside the little weight in her arms.

Lenore paused in the open space of the gate square, where the cobbles were still stained with blood. "It cannot be so easy," she said. But the gate was open, and no one tried to stop them. They just went through.

The mud in front of the city was churned and hummocked with the half-abandoned camp. It looked as if there had been a battle. Lenore looked around. "I should not be alive," she said. But no one came to kill them. They just walked on.

In the birch grove, the red *vardo* sat where they had left it, neat as a kettle in the afternoon sun. Kate was only half aware of Drina's exclaiming and dismay: Cream was nowhere in sight. But the horse had not gone far. As they came around the *vardo*, they saw Cream's backside and swishing tail. They went farther and saw Behjet sitting on the steps.

The Roamer man was trying to shave, pulling his skin taut over his jawbone and scraping at it with the edge of a knife. The blade trembled in his hand and cast little ripples of light toward them. Cream was nuzzling at him as if he were a foal.

If the rusalka is saved, Linay had said, *then the sleepers might awake too.* But he didn't care about them, and Kate could not rouse herself to care either. Drina, though, shouted with a joy so hoarse there were no words in it. Lenore stopped. "Husband," she breathed, and paled from linen to snow.

Drina took her mother's elbow as if to guide her through blindness. "It's not —" she whispered. But before she could explain to Lenore that this was not her husband but his twin, Behjet tottered to his feet. The knife fell and sank its point in the wet earth with a sound that made Kate wince. "Am I dead? Are you my burned ones, come to take me off to hell?"

"No one is dead," said Drina, but Lenore said, "I do not know if I am dead," and Kate said, "Why did it have to be you?"

"What?" Behjet was bewildered and shivering inside the skin that hung from him as if he were indeed a walking corpse.

"Linay is dead," Kate said. "And those people in front of the gate, and the ones in the square. And Stivo and Ciri, and my father, and —" She could not speak Taggle's name. "My — my heart is dead." She picked up his knife and stood looking at it, the darkness of the mud on the blade. "Of everyone who could have lived, why did it have to be you?"

And she pushed past him, up into the golden quiet of the *vardo*.

Outside, Drina, Behjet, and Lenore murmured together like mourners standing about at a wake. Kate thought that they were telling one another pieces of their long, strange story. Then she thought of how the story ended, and she stopped caring.

She sat down on the bunk. It still smelled of Behjet's long sickness. The blanket folds were stiff with sweat-grime. Taggle was dead. It should have wiped clean the world, yet here was washing to be done. Kate took a big breath, and put his body down.

His beautiful fur was matted with blood. He would hate that. She got out one of the horse brushes. She brushed until the bristles were thick as if with rust, and his fur was perfect. She liked the grain of it, how it followed the lines of his bones and muscles. It swirled in knots over his joints, and stood in a soft ridge along his breastbone, just beside the wound that had killed him. It was strange that his fur was still so soft, while his body was stiffening.

She sat beside him, numb, forever.

She had never been the sort for ghosts, though she had seen too much of them. But she would have cut off her carving hand to glimpse one now. It wasn't fair. There should at least be a ghost.

But there was no ghost. Only Behjet, and Drina behind him, hovering at the curtain. She hadn't seen them come in.

"Plain Kate," the Roamer man said. His voice was soft as if he were gentling a horse. "I have prayed — Plain Kate —"

"Just Kate."

"What?"

"*Kate.*" She was as plain as she had ever been. And over that she was burn scarred and half bald. But Taggle had thought she was beautiful. "My name is Katerina Svetlana. Kate."

"I'm sorry," he said.

And no one said anything for a while. The canvas arch around them glowed with sun.

Then Behjet said, "Your cat. Drina has told me —"

"He was more than a cat," she said.

Another silence. "What should we do with . . ." said Drina.

Taggle's body was what she didn't say. Kate had been thinking about that. She had been thinking about nothing else. "That place where we met: the meadow by the river. He was happy there. We had sausages." She looked up. "We can bury —"

But she couldn't finish.

"I'll harness Cream," said Drina.

Inside the *vardo*, Kate took apart one of the trestle benches and put it together again as a box. She used Behjet's shaving knife, though it sat like a stranger in her hand, though she knew she was ruining its edge and somewhere deep inside, her carver's soul protested. Her knife — she had killed her friend with her knife. She had left her knife and maybe her heart there, lying in blood and fire.

But still she worked. Her hands as they cut the dovetails for the joints seemed strange to her: Darkness trailed them as they moved; their lower sides wore the darkness like a second skin. It was her shadow. Her shadow, returning.

She worked as Cream was harnessed, bits of tack rattling like muffled bells. She worked as Drina came and wrapped Taggle's body in her favorite scarf, the red one with the white birds. She worked as the *vardo* rattled over the corduroy road. She worked as the branches scraped the canvas sides like fingernails. She worked as the light failed and the *vardo* shuddered to a stop.

She finished the box. It was strong and square, and would last a long time, even in the earth. And then she waited.

After too short a time the shovel stopped. But Kate couldn't get up. She thought about Taggle's name, and how the Roamers didn't say the names of the dead. And she hadn't said his, not yet. She was afraid to. It would make it real.

Lenore lifted the curtain and paused, a pale shape in

white against the lavender evening. "If a woman," she said softly, "might enter and speak."

Kate shrugged.

Lenore came in, trailing light. Though she had asked to speak, she said nothing. After a moment she knelt in front of Kate, and bent her head to Taggle's body. A gray ear stuck out between the red loops of cloth, guard hairs arching over the intricate, delicate interior. She stood heron-still a long moment before she said: "The grave is ready."

"I know."

"I wish," Lenore said, touching the red wrappings, "I almost wish it were mine. What my brother did for me — and the memory of what I have done. They will not be easy to live with. And I feel so strange. Like a bowl that holds water on the outside; like a goblet with no stem . . ."

"What happens," Kate asked, "after you die?"

"I don't know." Lenore traced the curve of Taggle's ear. Under her long fingers it looked delicate and stiff as a cicada wing. "Death was a shut door. I beat against it — oh, so long, my skin split open. But it was blocked. I would like to think that the dead stay close." Her voice had gone wandering off. "The dead stay close. At least for a little —" And like a wing, Taggle's ear twitched.

"Fetch my daughter," gasped Lenore.

Kate stumbled backward. "Drina!" she shouted. "Drina!"

"He was right," Lenore whispered. "The dead should stay dead. And yet . . ."

Drina burst through the curtain. "Mother!" Then she froze and her face opened up as if an angel were standing in front of her.

Kate whipped around, and there was her cat. He was standing up on the bed, shaking his head and trying to paw the wrapping away from his face. The indignant howl was muffled: "Yearow!"

"Taggle!" Kate shouted. "Taggle!" She reached out but couldn't touch him, she was afraid to try in case he melted into the air. Her hands hovered. Loop by loop, Taggle wormed his way free of the red wrappings, and then he was standing there on the bunk: greyhound sleek, golden eyed, perfect, alive.

"Well!" he said. "That was an adventure!"

"Oh," said Kate. "Oh!" And she scooped him up and hugged him hard, feeling his soft fur and lanky strength. She squeezed him fiercely.

"Ooof," he said.

Drina whirled toward her mother, her face shattering. "What have you done?!"

"What I must do," said Lenore. "What I could do: one small good thing, after so much darkness." She unwrapped Drina's turban slowly, tenderly, and then retied it as a girl's headband, letting the extra length trail down Drina's back like the hair she'd lost, like wings. "It is such a gift, to see you again." She let her thumbs slide along Drina's cheekbones. "But it is a gift I cannot keep."

"No . . ." said Drina. And Kate, looking up startled, found that she could see Drina's face through Lenore's hands. "Don't. Don't go."

"What my brother did, I cannot live with. He should have known that. And he should have known that a witch cannot give life, not perfectly, not forever." Lenore looked at the cat. "Taggle."

"What?" The cat shook his head so hard his ears made a noise like birds' wings. "I'm not a murderous ghost, am I?"

"You're a gift," said the fading woman. "But not one without a cost. Kate, your shadow returns. As you gain it, so your friend will lose his voice."

"Then I don't want it! I don't want my shadow! Taggle — tell her —"

"Bah," said the cat, feigning a curled-tongued yawn. "Talking is complicated. What cat would want words?" But his golden eyes filled and shone with tears.

And Drina too was crying silently, though standing straight, looking her mother in the eye: Drina, brave as the sun. "Give us this moment," said the ghost.

And so Kate took Taggle and they went out into the long soft light of the evening. She could smell the cat: warm and clean and strong. He was alive. Alive. And yet tears were running down her face. He reached up and blotted them away with one velvet paw. "Let us not waste our time in weeping. We must be about our business. We must find you a new knife."

Kate swallowed three times before she could speak. "I know where there is one. Tomorrow."

"Tomorrow," said the cat, with a human nod. "Well. That gives us an evening free to cook things."

A last evening. A good evening. How could it be a good evening? But it was. Behjet gathered up firewood and carried water and soon they had as homey a camp as could be managed, there by the unused grave. The river ran over smooth rocks and no fog came. Behjet caught a speckled trout and roasted it with wild dill and leeks. And Kate fried three kinds of spiced sausages, with onions and garlic and the last of the dried peppers.

She saved some for Drina, who came out of the *vardo* an

hour later, alone. She paused there on the steps. It was nearly night. Stars swayed in the young birch trees. Fireflies blinked slowly over the river, wandering together in pairs.

"She's gone," said Taggle softly, to spare Drina the need of saying it.

Drina lit the lantern by the *vardo* door, and its light stroked her cheek as she nodded. "She is at peace."

"I am sorry," said Taggle, and Kate remembered when he had said it was not a thing for cats.

"There is something for you, Kate." Drina came down the steps with the lantern in her hand. Kate saw that in her hand was a small braid of white hair. "She gave me something."

"I'm done with magic," said Kate.

"A gift," said Drina, and laid her hand against the side of Kate's face, where the burn scar was thick and twisted. "A song." She bent her head, and she sang.

Kate knew the song. Linay had sung it to heal her burned hands, night after night on the haunted punt. And before that, once on a spring day in the marketplace of Samilae, Lenore had sung it for her father. Linay had sung it sad, full of minor falls. Lenore had sung it like a lullaby. Drina sang it gravely, slow and soft: a hymn.

Under Drina's hands, Kate's scars pulsed and stung. She tried to hold still. Across the fire, Taggle watched solemnly.

After a long while, Drina dropped her hands. Kate lifted hers. Her fingertips mapped the new skin. It was tight and tender, but the slick, bubbling scar was gone. "Will you be a healer?" she asked.

"Maybe," said Drina. And then, because hope will break the heart better than any sorrow, she started to cry. "It's what my mother taught me."

In the morning, they held what funeral they could, with nothing to bury but the charred fragment of Kate's carving: an eye and forehead, a bit of wing. "For Lenore," said Kate. "And Linay."

"We don't say . . ." Behjet corrected her gently, but Drina interrupted, saying it softly: "For Lenore and Linay."

And Taggle said what was the traditional blessing in that country: "May all the graves have names."

"I will carve a marker for them," said Kate. "But there is something I must do first. Linay stole me a knife once. I am going to go get it."

Behjet frowned. "That city — it might still be dangerous."

"Nonsense," said Taggle stoutly. "She is fearless. And anyway, I am going with her."

And so Kate and Taggle walked together, back toward

Lov. They started early, their shadows stretched together, cat and human, down the long road behind them. "Your voice," said Kate. "How . . . how long?"

"A —" Taggle stopped, head tilted. "I cannot make sense of time."

"It's not a matter for cats," said Kate softly.

"No."

"You will always be my friend," she said.

His tail quirked and he growled fiercely, "I should think so."

A last day. The country seemed as if a great curse had been lifted. White clouds drifted across the mirrored puddles on the road. Kate's shadow grew stronger as the sun swung up the sky.

"Do you remember that horse of Behjet's?" said Taggle. "The one who gave us such a jouncing?"

"Xeri," said Kate.

"I clawed his ankle. And the camp dog, the brown one. I rode on his back for half a mile."

"I remember."

"And the — the —" he stuttered. "That bird, big —"

"The heron."

"I could —"

"You could have killed him," said Kate. "You could have taken him from above."

"Ah," said Taggle.

"You're the king of the creatures," said Kate. "You're a panther, you're a lord."

They went in silence for a while. The road's edges were embroidered with aster and wild carrot, glowing white and purple in the sun.

"Taggle?"

"Mmmmm . . ." he mewed.

"It's nothing."

"I'm here," he said, thick-tongued. "I —"

"You will always be my friend," she said.

Evening, the bridge to Lov. Ahead of them, Kate's shadow was spread like a cape across a puddle. Taggle leapt the water in a silver arch, effortless, graceful. He turned back and quirked his whiskers: a cat's beckoning.

"Taggle?"

"K-Katerina," he stuttered. "Yessss . . ." *My voice is still here*, he meant. But it was a cat's hiss in his answer.

"Let me carry you," said Kate, and picked him up.

"Merow," he said, and butted fondly at her ear.

They came round the city. Small boats bobbed in the pool outside the water gate. White storks paced among them. And there was the green barge. Kate hoisted Taggle onto her shoulder and waded out and climbed aboard.

So much had happened to her here: The tiny piece of decking seemed too small to contain it. But the red *vardo* was small too. And the lowest drawer of her father's cabinet had been smaller still. Perhaps it was time to stop choosing small places.

Taggle poured himself out of her arms and hopped down into the hold.

She followed. That space too seemed smaller than it had, and more ordinary. The coiled ropes were looser, the wild herbs more stale. Lightning had lived there, but now it was gone.

The bunk was made up, and the box that had once held her shadow was resting in the middle of it. The stag on the box lid seemed almost alive in the swaying light. Beside it on the blanket was her white dress with its lace trimmings, the jar of salve that had healed her hands, the roll of hand tools, the knife she had refused to take. They were bundled together and tied with a red ribbon that had cost a kopek or two. Kate pictured Linay making up the bed and heading off to die. Had he been thinking of her? Had he wanted her to have the things that he'd given her, in the strange time when they had been almost friends?

She opened the box. It was no longer filled with eerie,

clotted darkness. It was just a box. There was a plain leather bag at the bottom. Remembering the weight, Kate drew open the purse strings. There was a scrap of paper, and —

The bag was full of thin, gleaming coins, mostly silver, but a few copper or — now that Kate looked — they were gold. It was a guild fee. A hundred times a guild fee. A thousand.

"Taggle," she said. "Look!"

"Ca-ca-cat," he stuttered. "K-Katerina. Cat."

She knew it was the moment, and she turned to him. The cat looked up at her with the last trace of his broken heart, and then turned to look at the gold coins with simple gold-coin eyes. He said nothing. Forever after that, he said nothing.

"Taggle . . ." said Kate. Her voice broke. "T-Taggle . . ."

On the paper, in a hand so fierce it threatened to topple and break like a wave, Linay had written:

Kate. I hope you live.

Something flashed through her, surprising her with a sting of tears. She thought it was bewilderment, anger, fear — before she recognized it: grief.

"I did," she told the paper softly. "We both did." She picked up the cat, who whirred and purred and flowed up onto her shoulder. "And we'll keep on living."

And so they did, not always without trouble, but happily, and well, and for a long time thereafter.

acknowledgments

It took me six years to write this book, and in those years have accumulated many debts.

Let me start with my fellow writers. First among these are my dear friends at the Hopeful Writer's Group: Susan Fish, Nan Forler, Kristen Mathies, Pamela Mulloy, Esther Regehr. Seeing me through between Hopeful gatherings are my online friends at the WELL: Thanks, guys. And thank you, R.J. Anderson, for reading early drafts and crying in all the right places.

And then there are the people who played midwife to this book, bringing it into the world. First is my agent, Emily van Beek of Pippin Properties. Emily, you changed my life. My editor, Arthur Levine, is a genius and a warm and wonderful human being. Thank you, Arthur — and thank you, Emily Clement, left half of Arthur's brain. And I mustn't forget my mother-in-law, Patricia Bow, who proofread this manuscript seven times.

Finally, there's my family. Thank you, Wendell Noteboom, my dad; thank you, Rosemarie O'Connor, my mom. You've been supporting me since the day care days when I demanded to have my song lyrics written down. Thank you, Vivian and Eleanor, my own lovely lively little girls, for your patience with "Mommy is writing." And thanks to my beloved husband James, fellow YA novelist, for endless idea bouncing, hand-holding, and coffee making. I could never have written this book — or any novel — without you.

This book is dedicated to my sister Wendy Ewell. Wendy drowned before she got to read the ending of this story, before she got to meet the niece she was looking forward to, before a lot of things. I could level a city out of grief. Instead I'll say: Baby sister, I miss you. This, my first novel, is for you.